In Search of Sticks

Pls econsider Reviewing

Randy Kaneen

All rights reserved. No part of this publication may be reproduced, stored in a retrieval system, or transmitted, in any form or by any means, electronic, mechanical, photocopying, recording, or otherwise, without the written prior permission of the publisher.

IN SEARCH OF STICKS

Copyright © 2013 by John Randal Kaneen

Promontory Press

www.promontorypress.com

First Edition: September 2013

Library and Archives Canada Cataloguing in Publication

Kaneen, John Randal
    In Search of Sticks

ISBN: 978-1-927559-20-8

    I. Title

Cover artwork by J.H. Morris
Cover by SpicaBookDesign
Layout by Louise Beinhauer
Printed in Canada

0 9 8 7 6 5 4 3 2 1

For my family and friends and for all those who choose to reach out.

"You must be the change you wish to see in the world."

Mahatma Gandhi

In Search of Sticks

Authors Note:

While moving through these pages some readers might want to know the details that pertain to location—longitude and latitude defined; the names of cities, villages, mountains and rivers provided. But this story is not confined to a specific geography. That which is experienced by the few is happening to multitudes and the lands in which these events have come to pass are vast.

Just as those who must endure are not limited to an area, those who choose to help are also not bound by any definition of region.

Courageous reporting, stories from reconciliation efforts and other forms of powerful narrative have made listening hearts bleed. *In Search of Sticks* is fiction but it does not mean that the lives chronicled in this novel have not been and are not being lived.

IN SEARCH OF STICKS

As time and life is understood, everything seems to be over almost before it begins. But it is within those fleeting spaces where angels breathe that all that is singularly important occurs. And so as she was born and as her mother received her did this earthly opportunity of life begin.

"The lands were generous and in the fullness of the rain and richness of the soil the sun brought forth such trees and plants and grains that the bellies of all her people did not know hunger. One neighbor, it is not remembered who, said, 'I will take that tree; it is needed to give structure to my house.' Yet another grew cold and said, 'I will cut that tree and tonight I will be warm.' There were bare patches where none had been but no one remembered or perhaps even knew to plant the small trees. As children became parents and then grandparents and were returned to their African earth, the *woods continued to retreat. At last the land had no shade and there were no leaves to give moisture to the air that would be returned as rain. The generous lands became dry and the plants and grains sickly and small."*

That is the story she was told on her second earthly day as she was carried by her mother who had gone out in search of sticks.

THE RIVER

Some watches and clocks have more than the sole purpose of supplying accurate time. They are capable of displaying additional information: lunar phase, altimeter reading, pulse rate, temperature, calendar date, and digital compass directional knowledge, to name but a few. Technology provides for the possibility of various applications, including an alarm, calculator and stopwatch. Impressively, certain designs withstand the pressures of deep sea dives, while others function perfectly in zero gravity.

But there is a World Clock that can be found on an internet website and as much as the others can amaze, this one astounds. One hour, thirty-nine minutes, and twenty-two seconds elapsed since it had been reset and in that time much happened.

Neither the journey of her life nor the releasing of her soul had been easy. Though the death was a lonely one, it was not unnoticed; the special clock recorded this painful event. There were numerous difficult deaths and each was counted. One hundred sixty-five, overcome by deep personal pain and anguish, took their own lives; for thirty-two more, existence was ended by bullets and bombs, fulfilling the objectives of both those who built them and those who used them. The earth wept. And in those same moments ninety-one succumbed to nutritional deficiencies, a gentler way of saying they starved to death. Five hundred and eighty-five contracted HIV. There were one hundred and seventy-two new malaria victims, and two people became lepers. The inconsolable weeping of the earth continued unabated.

All of this happened in less than two hours. Think of what occurs in the twenty-four of the day or the hundred and sixty-eight that form the week, and it overwhelms—so much pain, so much needless pain. Instead of an internet clock, imagine it as a watch, one that is consulted in the same way and with the same regularity as when a person wishes to know the hour and the minute within that hour. Such an instrument would not only heighten our awareness of these crises but also serve as a constant reminder of our failure to address them.

In Search of Sticks

The details in this timepiece tell of the great problem and the immensity is such that it speaks of no possible single solution, except, of course, if a savior is discovered. People pray for this. Both the hopeful and the desperate tirelessly search for the appearance. Would he or she be found among the elite and privileged or with those who live the common life? Would there be a discovery at all? And if there was, would this savior even know about, or appreciate, his or her destiny?

৵৵৵

In the bright morning, the sun sparkled off the lines of cars much like it does a great river. The east-west connectors became fully gorged streams. It has been said by many that life is a journey and for James A. Terrance most often the voyage took him eighteen point seven miles in, and accounting for the loop necessitated by one-way streets, nineteen point four miles to return. This was a five, sometimes six time a week occurrence. Familiar signs announced the closeness of his exit. James no longer consciously read them. He maneuvered his vehicle into the right lane and, as he had done almost since the remembrance of time, left the river. There were, of course, the occasions when one road or another was being repaired, thus necessitating travel along a different route. He hated detours, cursing whenever he was forced to deal with one.

Little did James know that soon his life would become a detour—all normal patterns abandoned.

Parking was reserved and therefore a simple matter. Out of the car, past the granite fountain, into the building and then the elevator, push the button. Number twenty-two. Such was the routine.

Susan, the dark-haired congenial receptionist, was greeted by those who passed with the conventional yet ineffectual "Good morning, Susan." Some added important sounding phrases such as, "Hold all my calls." Most strode by, intent on consuming that special coffee held in the non-dominant hand.

James A. Terrance was not like the rest. Certainly he was professionally accomplished and reasonably talented but this was no Heinz 57® type of guy. Today he was a sidewinder fresh out of the American West or Canadian Prairie. At other times he chose different characters. He might be an industrious immigrant from India, a Jewish rabbi, an Irish priest, an Australian from the outback, even a Buddhist monk. His repertoire was extensive, unrehearsed, and natural. He had no idea how he was able to assume the roles. It was a gift, perhaps one of convenience. While busy being someone else, he didn't have to be himself or spend time discovering who that might be. To date the strategy had been successful; James still had no idea who he was.

Every day he brought to work the expected qualities associated with middle management:

insightfulness, occasional ingeniousness and an industrious quality that verged on the personally destructive. But on some days, he was James A. Terrance with a difference. This was one of those days.

"Well, Suzy," he drawled, bringing his left hand up to pull down an invisible cowboy hat. "She's been a long trail and a hard ride. I've been spittin' and squintin' outta this here weather-beaten sorry excuse for a mug right into the unforgiving, blazin' sun. I'm saddle sore and weary as a cowpoke finishin' up on a too-quick, too-long, too-dusty cattle drive. But if I'm not bein' overly forward ma'am, I ain't done in so much as to not see that there's somethin' troublin' you."

Susan responded, telling a tale of small woes. James listened and heard and wished her "fairer weather on the trails ahead." When the coffee guy came around, a complimentary "tin-boiled wash water brew, set to curl the spirit of anyone who dared to down it" was delivered compliments of "cowpoke James." It tasted pretty much like a cappuccino.

James was in the water business. Manufacturers from many places had developed devices specifically set to regulate the amount of water flowing to homes, farms and commercial enterprises. The increasing level of demand for this finite resource resulted in the need to utilize high-tech efficiencies. But there were no one-size-fits-all answers. Each issue required a distinctive solution. Therein lay part of

James' responsibilities. He was an office-bound engineer. Rarely did he see the site in question as he worked from details provided by field workers such as Richard.

"So tell me about this place Richard. Is the house located on a hill overlooking the valley? What kind of dog was in the yard? Did you get to smell the home-cooked bread that was being baked for the farm hands and see them come in for their big noontime meal?" James gazed wistfully out at nothing.

"I don't know, James. I went, I got the data that I was told to get, and I came back. Nothing more," Richard responded with considerable impatience. He had been through these conversations before. "You've got the specs. Three water sources with defined capacities: two wells and specific river water access rights. There are seven sections of farmland, most are flat and they need irrigating. You have the list of desired crops and harvest times. That's it. I don't know from Adam about houses, dogs and the smell of too much food being cooked at once. Maybe next time I'll include that in my report." He should have avoided the use of sarcasm; it did nothing to elevate his perceived status.

James A. Terrance worked out the possibilities and while doing so saw the small children playing with the hardworking affectionate Border Collie. He walked up the long graveled driveway that had been neatly defined by white fencing and then sat down at one of the tables in the shade of a great leafy tree.

He mopped his perspiring brow. There, with the rest of the hands, he ate chicken, potatoes, homemade bread and huckleberry pie. His detailed analysis was completed and submitted by mid-afternoon.

James left the office forty minutes before the mass exodus. Even so, the streets were fairly crowded and the commute slow going until the last ten or twelve miles when it opened up. Then, like the others, he drove about 20 percent faster than the posted limit. Air conditioning protected him from the oppressive summer heat made worse by the compromised city atmosphere. He had turned the radio on but wasn't particularly listening. Thirty minutes later he disarmed the security system and entered his upper-middle-class home. Melanie, his long standing but not long suffering wife and mother of their three adult children had not yet arrived. James used the remote and summoned some of his favorite music. Uncorking a bottle of midrange Californian red he poured himself a healthy amount and began dinner preparations.

Whatever James did, it was with a sense of carefulness and completeness. Usually, though not always, his actions were without the obvious signs of urgency that are associated with many. This is not to say that James was tension free. From time to time the annoyances of life would predictably surface, and when this happened the occasional reaction was disproportionate to the event. James was a great guy but he was no saint. The Chicken

Caesar came together well and he was just completing the table presentation when Melanie walked in.

Melanie, or as James like to call her "Mel", carried her middle-aged one-hundred- and-forty-pound frame with an assuredness that had defined her whole life. As a young child she was certain she would win her grade six public speaking contest and in the ninth grade she knew she would beat out Harold for the All-Around Student award. In her graduation year, it was clear to her that she would be the valedictorian. She was confident, and, as it turned out, accurate. Things generally evolved as she envisioned. After university she joined a major airline company knowing she would become a star employee and in fact the only thing that came between her and the regional vice-presidency was her unexpected love for James and her subsequent commitment to have children and be active in raising them. Still, she became the assistant to the manager, a position of responsibility commanding both a good salary and benefits. As might be expected, all three of their children, two boys and a girl, were also rapidly becoming accomplished. Now young adults, their destinies unfolded in different locations. Accolades accompanied their host of individual endeavors. Melanie read books for entertainment and she did not like surprises. She was, however, affectionate.

"Hey there lover boy," Melanie flowed through the room, pecked James on the cheek and picked up the goblet of wine which moments before had been readied for her.

"How was your day?" both asked simultaneously. Melanie answered first, speaking matter-of-factly of certain frustrations surrounding systems management. James provided similar information but there were spaces between his sentences.

Their lives were, as the expression goes, 'on track' and they were progressing quite well by the standards that one was accustomed to measuring a life by.

But evenings for James had become something of a great space. In the overstuffed chair and in the comfort of air conditioning or central heating he sat for hours without any obvious occupation. Unlike Melanie, he usually did not take his work home with him. Novels held only a certain appeal. Not that he didn't read, but books, for him, were not a major force. Television with its set formula of offering temporary relief from life, a life which to this point James had not demonstrated any aversion toward, offered no escape, as none was required. Of course there was the internet but that had its limits. Not even sports with its overly mobile players held anything more than momentary appeal. It had obviously become a business, nothing much for the common man and his common family to identify with. Not that James was common, but that was his background and such was his perception.

So almost every evening James was left with his own thoughts, a circumstance both wondrous and dangerous. His regular ritual of reading the newspaper absorbed him for only a very short period. Rather than becoming involved in the details, he usually applied scanning techniques to the various scripts. However, on one particular night an article caught his attention and he read it and re-read it and did so yet again, *"Relative Incomes of Different Countries."* This was not the usual all-hype, few-details style of reporting that had become commonplace in recent times. For most, this would appear to be a pretty dry piece of journalism but not for James. It simply listed the average family incomes in different countries. The extent of the differences amazed him. It shouldn't have. He had always thought he understood the concept of wealth and the inevitability of accompanying inequities. Still, he read it a fourth time. He knew these were significant statistics that demanded comprehension. What did they truly mean?

The evening sun combined with various particulate pollutions to form a sky of pinks and purples, but James did not see this. He did not know that the night had progressed to deep black and only when Melanie tenderly stroked the side of his face was he aroused from his state, whereupon he went to bed.

There are those who in the presence of physical pain or personal loss can find sleep only in the smallest of fragments. Others, overly occupied with events in their daily lives, fall victim to the anxieties of future expectations and know nothing of peace. And there are some, a tiny percentage of the Earth's population, whose awareness of the throbbing impending sense of crisis in this world leads them into the uneasy rest of desperate angels. James found very little sleep that night. In the morning, as per his routine, he joined the river. He was not yet aware that his life would never be the same.

Randy Kaneen

HOPE

She had not been named for the first three seasons. It was thought this would be easier for if the child passed, the great pain that comes with remembrance might be lessened. It would be said, "The fifth one died and the third became very sick and could not take food, and the one who came after the year of no rain did not breathe at all." This would be, in some indescribable way, better than if one said the name and remembered all that goes with a name. She was carried by her mother who, with her husband and the rest of the living family, walked to the field. On that warm sunny spring day, they named her in their language what in ours is known as "Hope."

SHIRAZ

"Hey, nice shirt, Phil," James commented while passing by the office door of Phillip Morrow, his colleague and friend. Almost the same age, both possessed similar creative and intellectual gifts. Their relationship had developed during lunch breaks where they often found themselves eating together in one of the numerous venues available at street level. There, as per the routine, the two of them emptied their morning highlights over the fake granite tabletop and sifted through them this way and that, in an effort to discover meaning where none was readily evident.

Phil, standing up from behind his desk, gestured outwardly with both arms, "You like? The tailor I told you about, you know, the one on Main and Forty-Third, by Mulligan's."

James quipped, "'Dressing for power': I think they invented that phrase just for you."

Phil smiled his quick smile. "You do what you gotta do in this life. As I see it, you got three options: some are the part, some dress the part and some are the part because they dress the part. You decide where I fit in. For sure I can't."

James refused to rise to the obvious bait. He knew Phil didn't get to the heights of middle management without certain strengths. Phil dressed well. Money, sometimes large denominations, changed hands, and the clothes looked good. That was just Phil. There was no need for further analysis.

Phil's office also reflected his tastes. He had taken the generously spaced rectangular shape and transformed its interior into the representation of current times. Stainless steel was in vogue and the side tables and desk, with their cold, shiny, bright legs and tops of tempered glass, conformed beautifully. Polished gleaming lamps contributed to the crisp ambience. Chairs were leather and dyed in soft earth tones. A few items told another story. The large soapstone image of an Inuit mother and child had been purchased in his misspent youth as he explored the Canadian North in search of himself. The handmade carpet of rich reds and blues was bought in Eurasia on another self-discovery mission, that one following his failed marriage.

Phil slipped easily around his desk and moved to James, "Your mom forget to check you before you left home again?" He fixed the collar and adjusted James' perpetually poorly knotted tie. James smiled and turned to leave, but Phil, picking up on something indefinable, put out the big question, "You okay, James?"

"Yeah, yeah, no issues here." James responded in the dismissive way utilized by some who have had too many bravado lessons.

"You sure?" Phil continued his line of inquiry.

"Like I said, no problemo. Not a lot of sleep last night, that's all."

Still unconvinced, Phil returned to his desk. James was free to go but didn't. For a few seconds there was silence before he spoke. "Phil, you ever wonder about things?"

"About things?" Phil looked up.

"Yeah, you know, things." He gestured around the room at the obvious efforts at opulence. "It's a stupid adolescent question but do you ever think— why me? How come this?" Once more his arm moved outward, this time in a broad sweeping motion.

Phil studied James in a serious way, searching for what lay behind the mask. "You got cancer or something?"

"No, no, nothing like that." The response was immediate. "I'm fine, the family's fine, that's just the point. We're okay, but others are not nearly as fortunate. There are some people who live very difficult lives. You ever wonder about that?"

"Well, then, in answer to your question James, no." Seeing that his friend was still intently locked on and waiting, he expanded, "I just go with it."

At lunch they ate together at a popular noodle shop. Conversation revolved around Australian Shiraz.

ANGEL SWEEPS

    After the soil was turned, the furrows drawn and the seeds sown, such beautiful rain came and for weeks it fell in quiet ways, slowly yet assuredly misting the fields, soaking the earth which embraced the water as it had done so in distant memory. The sun, the hot sun, became the good sun and brought a kind warmth, and the grains appeared as a field of small green grasses. The air held the foreign sounds of laughter and examined them curiously and wondrously, not wanting to let them go. Old men and old women in Hope's village told jokes, and families sat in front of their dwellings, and together they smiled at the world. At times, in the next months, the rains came at night—not in torrents but in angel sweeps, brushing the grains and caressing the earth. The green turned to yellow and then the world was gold.

IT HAPPENS

By the time work was done, evening had set in. The first twenty minutes of the return trip took its usual course but out of nowhere, *Bam! Thump!* James maneuvered his car to the side of the road. Flat tire! A string of vulgarities passed through his lips. He was driving along in his recently leased vehicle, minding his own business, but an inconsiderate bozo had let a short section of rebar fall off the back of a truck. It was possible that the offending piece had been on the road for some time, perhaps even hours, and people had been successfully navigating around it, or the steel could have fallen off thirty seconds earlier. He didn't know and one could only speculate. Irrespective of conclusion, the result remained the same. His right front wheel hit the metal, and there you have it.

So James was by the side of the highway. He wasn't hurt. No worries there. Absolutely no other damage to the car. No concerns in that respect. Even his tan pants and light cotton shirt were in no danger of getting greasy; he was, after all, a paid-up member of the Automobile Association. He had his cell phone. Someone would drive up in a service vehicle and change the tire for him. Still, as traffic whizzed by, he cursed his luck in a most profane and loud fashion though there was absolutely no one there to listen.

In thirty-five minutes, he was supposed to meet Melanie at Café Fanfara where the cuisine was to die for. He had been looking forward to this all day, but now he would have to call her and then cancel the reservation. That evening they'd be settling for a restaurant where one can get in just by waiting in line. To make matters worse, some schmuck and his date would walk in off the street into this most desirable café. Not having planned a thing, they would ask for a table and get the one set for Melanie and him. So he stood at the side of the road and he cursed and while doing this, kicked at the wheel. After some time passed he took out his phone and began to deal with this luck.

Actually, the food he ate that evening was rather tasty and the surroundings were pleasing. He would have enjoyed both the meal and the ambience if he had the ability to do so. Even the wine did not loosen him. James could only fixate on his favorite restaurant and the fact that some other couple must be enjoying his table.

The next day he told his friend all about it, no detail spared. "Shit happens," was Phil's consoling summation.

A SIMPLE THING

Just as dawn arrived, so too did they. There are many well-known sites where God resides and against which much is measured; Chartres, Mecca, Jerusalem, Varanasi, and Mahabodhi, to name a few. But there are thousands upon thousands of other locations where the Creator also takes up residence and where people acknowledge the greater plan, their place within it, and to give thanks for this.

So they arrived at the place where, for centuries, people had come on this very day, at this very time, for this very purpose. The ceremony was not complicated. In songs and offerings and prayers, that which should be said and which people wanted to say was said. Giving thanks can be such a simple thing. They returned with light hearts and much laughter.

"I am feeling the happy child in my body," spoke one.

Another, an older woman, seeing the stretched cloth move said, "And see it kick! It wants to get out into this beautiful world." She put her hand on the young woman's stomach and with this touch remembered and smiled.

A handful of children ran past, chasing each other while pushing something with a stick. They had discovered a small rock that resembled a wheel and had fashioned some kind of game around this fact. Their faces were full as children's faces should be. There was no visible evidence of the memories, of the times past with little food where people with sunken eyes sat and looked without focus because that was what their energy allowed for. Nature had not always been as nurturing.

With smiles and the singing of songs they hurried back to their village. There, the celebrations took on new forms. Food, drink, music, and dancing were everywhere. And just when one might think people would tire and return to their beds, new energy arrived, and there was more music and dancing and more food and drink. It continued in this pattern for the day, that night, and most of the following day. After all, there would be food, not just for tomorrow but for next week and next year. And if people were careful and did not overly celebrate the occasions of their families and their faith, the abundance would last beyond that. What was done that the heavens should smile in such a wonderful way?

THE TRUTH

Time passed and the patterns of work and home life remained constant. Predictability had come to visit James and had decided to stay. But one night, while once again sitting in his overstuffed chair and looking out, it happened. To be clear, this event was not accompanied by a blinding flash of light. Nothing overtly marked the occasion. There was no epicurean event. It simply occurred.

James, having successfully completed his university level statistics courses and having applied "averaging" in the daily demands of his work, discovered he actually knew nothing about what "average" meant—at least not when people are involved. People are not water-flow figures.

In determining the consistency of a water source, one might add up all of the rainfall for the last ten, twenty, or even fifty years. Simple division would reveal the average yearly precipitation. There may not have been even one year when that precise amount of water actually fell, but it's of little consequence, particularly if the sampling of years is large.

However, people were different. The now months-old newspaper article surfaced to haunt him. It's true, he thought, the annual income of certain countries' citizens constitutes a shocking commentary on the disproportionate access the populous has to what one might consider to be a reasonable lifestyle—an acceptable opportunity for happiness. But in many poor countries the earnings of a handful of wealthy individuals, normally comprised of the despots and their entourage, can as much as equal the total income of vast numbers of the remainder of its citizens.

If these rich people were included in the averaging then things might be even worse than he had believed. James had questions. How bad could it be, and did he really want to know?

Extrapolating from raw facts became a dominant pastime for James, the pursuit, of which, resulted in surprising discoveries at very different levels.

NORMAL

The day presented itself in the normal range. "Normal," when used as a descriptor of life is a complex word, its meaning consumed in rituals, beliefs, and opportunities, all of which can and do vary in extreme ways. "Normal" requires its own set of examples. This was a normal day.

Hope woke shortly after sunrise, but like most thirteen-year-olds, she did not get up. She languished in her bed, firmly placed halfway between dreams and reality, waiting for the dictum and knowing the inevitability of this. As per usual, her father had already left to the field, so the directions came from her mother.

"Rise up, you sleepyhead. Did you not hear the rooster crow? Did you not feel your many brothers scramble over you as they rose to greet this day? The younger ones have been out running and I will need your help to tame their wild spirits."

The message was stern, but Hope's mother said these words in a kind way, all the time laughing and smiling within. A woman of thirty-plus years, the eight births, including three stillborn, had taken their toll. She now moved in the deliberate ways associated with Western women and men almost twice her age. Still she was fortunate; five of her children lived.

Hope's two older siblings, both brothers, worked with their father. When she stepped outside, the persistent easterly winds, already dry and warm, enveloped her and told their familiar story. "We have come from great distances, across lands which a thousand years ago were forests but are now sands; we crossed the defoliated earth of more recent times and we fear that someday these places too will be deserts. Where once we carried moisture and gave life, we now take. We unmercifully steal from the soils that are clutching on to the last of the small winter rains. We seize from the drying ditches that are used by farmers in their desperate efforts to irrigate parched lands. And bit by bit as we work in partnership with the hot sun and swirl around the men and women and children, we diminish dreams."

Hope leaned against the outside front wall of her home, listening to the corrugated metal roof move with the uneven rushes of air. She understood these winds. She chewed on cold flatbread which had been readied the night before, and she stared down the dusty road past the row of small homes and looked beyond. Hope's day had begun.

"I'm going to get the water now," she called inside to her mother who was putting away the last of the sleeping materials and readying the two rooms for daily life. Three chairs and the table had been taken from their places against

the walls and put back into the middle of the larger of the spaces. Pots and all things needed for the cooking and eating of the evening meal were placed in easy reach and a rough loom was brought out for use in the quieter moments. Later in the day, Hope's mother would, with her younger children, make her way to the field and join her husband where together they would toil under the hot sun.

Hope picked up the large steel cans and started the long walk. Years before Hope's remembrance, it had been shorter, not three minutes from the village; but these waters became foul and many got dysentery and some died. A new source was located, only this, of course, was not as close. After the passing of time, the pattern of sickness revisited and other waters from even farther away needed to be accessed. Now the walk was nearly forty-five minutes, and the return much slower. Hope met her friend Grace, a girl close to her age who lived seven houses from her.

"Did you get a good nights' sleep?" Grace asked.

"Yes, for once no brother or sister rolled on me, and their bladders and bowels held strong." Hope laughed as they kicked small stones on their walk.

"Have you seen Mistair with her orange cloth?" Grace eagerly inquired. "I have not ever set my eyes on such a colour—and to have enough for a full dress. It is amazing!"

"She is close to the marrying time," Hope replied. Mistair had played with them in the past but was almost four years older. No longer at school, her responsibilities within the home had changed considerably. For one serious moment both Hope and her friend walked together in silence. They looked straight ahead.

"And you, I'm sure you slept last night and I'll bet I know what you were dreaming about." Hope's good-natured tease brought giggles from both girls. A certain boy had, with some frequency, found himself near Grace's home. Each struggled for conversation: enquiries around health, observations on the weather, the state of farming, bits of gossip, reports from the panhandler about things on the outside world, that sort of thing.

It was during one of these awkward exchanges when Grace learned of the boy's oldest brother who apparently did not like farming at all and who got kicked last year by the cow. His arm had been broken. This, by itself, was nothing of note but the person who did the mending of bones was away that week and would be for the next few. His father, who had some experience, did this for his son. Unfortunately something went wrong and the arm healed in a crooked manner, so much so it resembled the curve of a plough's head. Now he carried the image of his despised occupation wherever he went, as if this was the God's way of taunting him. The two laughed at the thought of this boy, soon to be a man, who despite his aversion to farming would be cursed with carrying a plough for the rest of his life.

On the return trip, the girls walked with some of the others, who, in their struggles to carry the now full containers, resorted to song in order to keep their minds off their aching arms. They did not stop to brush the flies away for if they did they would have had to pause after every second step. So they sweated and sang as the flies walked freely over their bodies.

In Search of Sticks

We are the songs of birds
Just before the crickets assume the music.
In our hearts we paint the skies
As we would like them.

We walk with the rhythm of our blood,
One foot and then another.
As with the gift from the Ultimate,
Each breath a testimony to the beauty of our mortality.

We carry the water,
And we carry life.
Even in our youthful years,
We serve.

We are the songs of birds
Just before the crickets assume the music.
In our hearts we paint the skies
As we would wish them.

This was one of their walking songs. By the time they reached the village, many others had been sung.

MARK 1:40

As all living things, James was subject to the realities of time. The new wrinkles, the graying and receding hairline, the increasing aches and pains and simple malaise and general deterioration spoke of its feared powers. His reflection in the mirror now visibly held the ghosts of his father and grandfathers.

Scientifically, time's effects are incremental. Mankind, however, has a predilection to view things in stages, each defined with its own range of possibilities. Mention the teenage years and a series of images enters the mind, the same for the twenties, thirties, and so forth.

James had started to reach into decade number six and all that goes with it. Often this is thought of as a winding down time where there can be a consolidation of material goods and a lessening of the intensity that tends to define one's life. A sense of philosophy replaces the drive for doing. In a way, this is viewed as the last vital stage before the entrance into twilight with its long walks, extensive gardening periods, protracted coffee times and holiday tours at off-season prices.

For a few, these are the most desperate of years—a time for one final effort to make a lasting mark and frame the events of the world in ways which might lead to personal meaning. James was beginning to be consumed with his internal search: "Mr. James A. Terrance, who is this guy?"

"Kricky, the barbie starts in half an hour and you're not dressed. I guess you've been flat out like a lizard drinking, all this time." He was being Australian. It fit with the details of Melanie's invitation. Her company's annual barbeque theme this year was "Life in the Down Under—the land of Oz."

Melanie could easily match the lingo. "Rack off, you bastard," she replied affectionately. "I'm ready when I'm ready."

"Well, I'll be stuffed," he retorted, adding, "Hey, no worries, mate." Grinning on the in and the outside, he picked up the remote and proceeded to surf the channels.

Click, on came the TV. Click, a sitcom, click, game show, click, sports, click, different sports, click, news, tech stocks are on the road to a slow recovery, the upper hand is being gained over a newly mutated disease, another bombing—more innocent victims sacrificed in the name of some glorious cause, click, cooking, click, reality show, click, renovating, click, Hollywood gossip, click, click, click, STOP!

There for all to see was the hurt soul of silent suffering. It presented itself in the form of a young girl. A translator told her story. Shunned by family, stoned by neighbors, she retreated. The cameras contributed to the uncomfortable narrative—almost no fingers and large parts of her feet were missing. Her walk, which in truth was on the stumps of legs, was excruciatingly painful to watch and for some of those moments, James looked away. She continued to speak and the translation flowed but it was as if James didn't need a translator. He seemed to understand her every word. He marveled at the grace in her voice and was drawn to the strength, to the kindness which filled her eyes and commanded focus away from the severe scars and wounds. This was leprosy and she was a leper.

The contents of the show could be summarized in good-and bad-news ways.

Effective pharmaceutical drugs do exist and when administered the progression of the disease is halted and people are cured. The daily cost for this medication is less than the price of a cup of coffee and most patients positively respond with a six-month regime. One fewer latte a day for half a year and a human soul can be spared great pain. Normally this might be considered pretty good news, but James remembered the article in the paper. He understood the awful news: though appearing reasonable, these medical costs constituted far more than the annual income of the entire family. So for many, the resultant chapters of isolation, deterioration, and painful death had already been written. It is a script that has been experienced throughout the millennia. Real peace had been elusive for James and this knowledge contributed to his unsettled sense of self. The infomercial ended. He turned the television off.

Melanie appeared, gracious and as attractive as always. James got up and encircled her, "Will you allow me this one waltz, Matilda?" He danced her around the room, humming the unofficial Australian national anthem. Laughing and enjoying each other's company, they slid into their recently acquired jade-colored vehicle. If the advertisements were to be believed, this was more than transportation; they were at the controls of a vision of possibilities. After forty-five minutes, they arrived at a large, white home complete with expansive park-like grounds. The uniformly green lawn had been manicured and selected plants provided a pleasing relief of shade and color.

Melanie rang the bell and the thick, carved door almost immediately swung open. "Melanie! James! Come in!" An enthusiastic man also dressed in summer attire did the inviting. He continued with the same vitality, but there wasn't even a hint of Australian in his voice; perhaps it had disappeared after the first dozen or so greetings. "Where on earth did you get the shirt, James? And the bushman hat—now that's a find! Melanie, do you let him go out in public like this?" The words came with ease, energy, and speed. He laughed, gave James a quick jab on the shoulder, and enveloped Melanie in a short hug. He was tall, fifteen years their junior and the regional manager of the company Melanie worked for. His name was Craig.

"G'day, mate," James piped in. "Think I'll go out back and get me a coldie. I'm as dry as a dead dingo's donger." His accent was almost perfect. It was indeed a gift.

"Melanie, I didn't know you married an Aussie," Craig teased.

Laughingly Melanie replied, "Neither did I, but something tells me I'm going to find out exactly what that would be like." They proceeded to do the expected; they moved, they mingled, they talked.

"G'day, James, How ya' doin' mate?"

James was approached by a man he saw two, maybe three times a year: at the annual barbeque, the Christmas party, and if he couldn't find a way out, the odd retirement due. Spencer did the greeting. As with most everyone there, James didn't know a great deal about him. Melanie wasn't one to bring the gossip home, and James isn't the prying type; no dossier existed. However, given the number of years he attended these events, he had come to realize Spencer was a bona fide sports nut. Not that you could tell by looking at him. His double chin actively sought to add a third, and his well-rounded, average size frame reflected those soft facial features.

James gave out an Australian phrase, followed by a second. "Bugger me dead if it isn't Spence. Pardon me for saying so but you look like a stunned mullet. Do you want me to nick off?"

Spencer looked at him with a blank, searching expression, not having the foggiest notion how to respond. The one "g'day" was all that he could muster. Like most who imitate life, the superficiality soon became apparent. They spent some time discussing the boys of summer. Baseball is a wonderful equalizer. You can always talk about baseball.

"Hey, ya' wanker!" James stopped, turned to the left and found a tall, willowy blond Scotch-taped to an even taller, blonder man. His big, white toothy grin was offset by a deeply tanned bronze face. She, quite simply, was gorgeous.

James seemed pleased to have been found. "G'day, luv. You're looking pretty swank and you, ...well, I can see you're as fit as a marlee bull." They were husband and wife, Bryan and Sylvia.

As with previous encounters, James' engaging efforts to be colorfully Australian were met with amused smiles and North American responses. Even in these events where it was commonplace to move from one social arrangement to the next, Bryan and Sylvia stayed together. Was it Sylvia's shyness, Bryan's insecurity, or their love for each other?

"What have you got James?" Bryan pointed to the glass.

"Well, it's not the blood of Christ, mate. Something Hungarian. Good value for its price point, a nice full body. Thought I'd give it a go." James responded, holding up the red wine.

"Ah, an adventurer," offered Sylvia.

"Who would have believed that about good old, safe James," added Bryan.

"Who really knows where one's capacity begins and where it ends?" Sylvia wisely noted.

James listened, appreciating the essential truth of the observation. Although not a wine aficionado, he did possess considerable knowledge about the subject. It is widely understood no one should drink too much at an office party. One can pay for an indiscretion, and the effects of alcohol reduce the carefulness that governs a working life. James drank only a glass or two, as he generally did the driving and the laws and social expectations had tightened up in this respect. But talking about wine doesn't require one to be over indulgent.

Bryan, Sylvia, and James, relieved to have found a level of conversation to pursue, did so in detail. All facets were covered: the making, the tasting, and the drinking. The discussion finished with a hearty "Good on ya', mates," and the three parted company.

Gord, Paul, Tom, and Beth were next. Politics was the guaranteed topic; government policies, the effects on themselves, their families, and their aspirations. Rarely did these conversations venture forth to include the world stage. This group could get a bit heated. James came in, but not tentatively. He tried for humor while still pursuing the Aussie theme. "Gordie, you're sounding as cross as a frog in a sock. And Beth, why you seem as mad as a cut snake." The interchange stopped for a moment. "Oh, hi, James," they acknowledged and got right back to arguing. Some might try to call this debating, but that would not be accurate.

Numerous guests discussed business. He could choose from several groups who were immersed in the topic of high finance. Stock tips, the dos and don'ts, fortunes made and lost, many intent on explaining to anyone who would listen about their ingenious strategies. In some years everyone boasted while describing slick moves. This year, however, everything was comparatively quiet. The relative silence told its own story. The economy had cycled down and the geniuses of yesterday seemed the fools of today. Still, there was a little bravado, some efforts to look forward. Small victories were shared and exaggeration abounded.

This time James didn't even bother with the Australian lingo. He had it all saved up, but outside of the sea of khaki clothing which dominated the fashion sense, no one seemed to be into it. So the group missed out on hearing phrases such as "flick it on," "he hasn't got a brass razoo," "that's the dinki di," and "getting a fair suck of the sav." Should he have said any of these things, they would just stare at him as if he had "a few roos loose in the top paddock." Too bad; there were plenty more where those came from. One thing became evident: none of these people had the ability to assume another's character beyond the delivery of a single line.

The party turned out to be first-rate. James circulated clockwise. He crisscrossed, meandered, and then escaped to the perimeter. Melanie still chatted and moved her way easily through the crowd. Having finished the initial foray, James stood sipping his wine and eating some delicious appies. The smells and pervasive smoke of the barbeque contributed to the ambiance. Later, Melanie and he gratefully accepted seared steaks, complete with baked potatoes, sour cream, chives, and a green salad whose dominant leaf was dandelion. They wolfed everything down.

Melanie advanced into the crowd for round two. James stayed back, choosing his own company. This was deemed acceptable. At this point, many of the spouses of the employees seemed similarly inclined. For Melanie, the whole dance started again. She circulated counterclockwise, finally weaving in an apparently aimless fashion, though nothing was unplanned about it. The sun gave up its warmth and people began to filter away. James and Melanie thanked their gracious host and joined the latter part of the exodus.

Once home, Melanie readied herself for bed. But not James, he found his big overstuffed chair. For him, returning late from a meeting or evening function required an unwinding time. Without this, the insomnia god would not only visit, it would take up residence. James sat and the images of the day started to appear: the people, the food, the efforts at being Australian. In this room of soft light, his thoughts began to move unpredictably; long walks, first loves, battles lost and won, a story he heard while attending church as a child. In adult life James had made no alliance with any formal religion, yet some of the early impressions remained. He got up and pulled the bible from the top right corner of the shelf. It is a book which is in many households, but its presence does not necessarily speak to familiarity. James, upon rediscovery, read silently at first and then audibly, his voice echoing in the semidarkness.

"And there came a leper to him, beseeching him and kneeling down to him and saying unto him, If thou wilt, thou canst make me clean.

"And Jesus, moved with compassion, put forth his hand, and touched him, and saith unto him, I will; be thou clean.

"And as soon as he had spoken, immediately the leprosy departed from him, and he was cleaned."

Before going to bed James wrote a check. Tomorrow it would be slipped into an envelope, and sent off and someone would be "made clean."

In the morning, an undefined sense overwhelmed James. He and Melanie had a passionate joining which spoke of their love, their commitment, and their thankfulness that their two souls had found one another.

NO FAVORITES

The normal day continued. There wasn't a school in the village; in fact none existed in any of the surrounding communities. A decade ago things had been different; a small building, now someone's home, had been the school. The government decided, in order to save money and because there were not many teachers anyway, one would not be located in every village. Rather a single school was to be constructed on a site mutually convenient to many, which meant it was convenient to none.

The land this was eventually built on belonged to a government official who sold it at a "fair price." Certain economies had been implemented that weren't projected. Benches appeared instead of desks, and even years later, the textbooks had not arrived. No one knew why. The government insisted the school had been fully funded. What could one do?

In Search of Sticks

The contractor came in with his laborers who did not live in the village or the surrounding villages. The school had been built in this way and if one wished to attend, one took the long walk.

This process of construction was alien to Hope and her people. In Hope's life, there had been need and there had been help and those who received were not always receivers and those who provided did not always give. One day her father ran out and stopped a beating before it became something worse. At another time he stumbled, breaking both an arm and a leg. The men of the village worked his plot of land as the mending took its course. Every person who returned in the lateness of the evening because it had been his time to work the field walked with a lighter gait. Within the village, each house, each granary, each shed bore the marks of many. Nothing was a singular effort. The simple-minded man was welcomed into the different houses.

And there was death. In sorrow and sympathy, the pain became a shared pain and in some indefinable way this, too, became help. Grandmothers helped mothers and mothers helped daughters and grandfathers helped fathers and fathers helped sons. Older siblings helped younger siblings. So they walked to a school where, for them, there was no spirit as there had been no giving. On this leaving occasion, seventeen took the journey. Sometimes more left, other times not as many.

"Where is Jewel today?" Hope asked a younger boy.
"She is at home with our oldest sister."

His response was somewhat vague and so Hope pursued the course of questioning. "I didn't know she was here; I thought she had left to the city."

The young boy's reply was not immediate, and they continued to walk with an intent pace typical of people trying to get somewhere. "She came back very ill with only the weight of three or four birds."

Hope was quiet. This was something she understood too well. More children were without parents and the numbers of sisters and brothers also diminished. People who had been away for a while were returning only for the dying. Jewel would not be going to school today, and if the pattern was similar, she would be absent for a long time.

"Did you think of yesterday's lesson?" the young boy asked, moving away from his hurt.

Hope certainly had thought of yesterday. Of course: who wouldn't have? Such a story. It had the marks of a fairy tale or a legend where imagination frames the truth in ways that it eventually gains a "once upon a time" feel. For the next piece of the journey, they both walked in the silence of remembrance, struggling for meaning.

"Over here in this part of the round Earth is a large country called America and to its north another giant named Canada." The teacher held up a globe. "There are groups of smaller ones in western Europe and the one known as Australia lies near the bottom of the world. In these places and in more I have not mentioned life is different. I will tell you about their lives, and they neither are those of kings or queens or their sons or daughters nor are they the lives of others with much wealth. Electricity is all day, not for the

small hour in the morning and the few in the evening but for the entire day ... and if one had need or wish for it, also for the whole night. This is not for one room or two rooms. It is for all the places in their houses."

He paused, soaking in the radiance of his students. "And what houses! They have many rooms and these are not the palaces. A separate room is for cooking and eating and yet another for feasting when friends or relatives visit and one is for sitting and talking. An extra is built just for playing. In most of these houses, there is a room only for the parents, and one for each child to sleep in and to be in with their thoughts."

At this point it was too much for the class to take, and the air filled with laughter. "This cannot be true, dear teacher," said one who spoke with levity. "Why are you spinning such a tale around our ignorance?"

"My earnest students, I assure you I am serious." The silent pause of disbelief shouted their incredulity. "Most honestly I speak the truth. I have been to a city and seen some of what I talk of, but not to the extent of that which I described. I looked at pictures and read books and met people who know even more of this." He stopped briefly while the class absorbed his statement, then with excitement he continued. "Each of you understands what it is like to be at this school. Well, in those places all the students have their own books so they can study and learn. There is much paper and no slate and they do not need to copy from the board half the long day. Some even have a kind of thin book which is able to bring to them the pictures and words about almost anything that is happening or has happened in the world.

This looks like a form of magic but it is not. There is no jostling on benches while trying to find the space to write as each student has a table and chair to use.

About illness, also much can be said. If you are sick, there are hospitals to get proper medicines and people who die from some diseases one gets here often do not die from the same things there. Those who are disfigured from diseases here do not become ugly at all. Very few of the babies die, and most of the small children live. People who are with this world for a full fifty cycles are not even thought of as old." The teacher stopped for a moment, intently inspected the wide eyes of his audience and reflected, "There must be less sadness in the families."

A young girl sitting in the middle of a crowded bench suddenly sprang up and shouted, "Master teacher, surely you are playing games with us or you are mad! Should you not sit and drink some tea?"

"No, no, dear one. I am perfectly fine and there is more I could tell you and I will. But I fear you heard too much for one day already. We should do the arithmetic now and next our country's geography, after which time some may practice the formation of their letters."

Still steeped in these thoughts, the young boy and Hope, along with the others, arrived at school. The teacher did not speak of this and when asked to add to the story said, "At a time of my choosing there will be more words but it must be remembered that this kind of knowing is different from learning about numbers and memorizing the names of the mountains and the stars. Some knowledge comes with the uneasiness of other questions." He was a wonderful teacher. He had captured his pupils with his understanding and fairness and his willingness to come each school day. Despite the fact the class size could at times swell to sixty or more, discipline was not much of a problem and he rarely used his stick.

At midday, the students sat outside eating the foods brought from their homes. These were not the generous amounts common in the Western world, but nonetheless they were sufficient. The last harvest had been reasonable and the vegetables and fruits of the time made welcome contributions. There were, of course, the memories. Sometimes meals had been quite different; the variety was first to suffer. There were no vegetables and then no fruit and the portions of food made from the grains became much smaller. Finally the sustenance was not enough to fuel the long walk. In such times people stayed home and conserved life; a few struggled to the fields only to view the hopelessness which enveloped them and had brought to them a pain beyond tears.

But on this day, Hope sat chewing and watching while others played soccer in the clearing. A plastic bottle had become a substitute for the ball. Real footballs were a prized commodity. On the occasions when one did appear, the young men kicked it until it didn't hold air any longer. At that time, the children would fill it with straw, sew up the tears and proceed to literally kick the stuffing out of it. Today no such ball existed, so the green bottle, filled with sticks and grass, became the crude tool for the game. The fact this didn't roll in any predictable manner presented certain challenges but the players seemed perfectly willing to operate within these restrictions.

Hope paid little attention to the competition unfolding before her. Rather, her time was spent in quiet reflection. Such was her nature. The linking of seemingly disassociated ideas had become a preoccupation in Hope's life. Yesterday's lesson was still being assimilated and she tried to bind this new information to her own understandings, ones that had naturally evolved from the structure of her life's experiences.

Hours later, in the final heat of the thick afternoon air, Hope had returned to help with the meal and to check the energies of her younger brothers. Following the serving and the eating and cleaning, Hope sat with the rough loom and continued to weave a most beautiful scene of hills and crisp houses and contented people. The colors were bright. Golds and blues and magentas dominated. Once every two months, a man came by in an old truck and offered currency and goods in exchange for these weavings. Then they went to the city where it was said visitors from far away purchased them.

A week after this "normal" day had passed Hope ventured forth, this time while finishing the last strands of purple: "Do you ever think about the people who buy these? Not the man in the truck, but those who stop at the shops and say, 'This is a wonderful village, I will pay for this and take it back to my house and hang it in one of the many rooms. On a wall of my choosing I will welcome this happy scene.'"

Hope's mother stopped her preparations for the night and spoke; "I have heard you talk of these homes and I do not think they can be real."

Hope's response was quick and emphatic. "Oh, but they are mother; they are all of what I told you about and much more. Since I last talked of this, I have learned of other things.

In Search of Sticks

There is no need to carry the water as it flows freely into some of the rooms. Most of these people own automobiles, sometimes two or three, and they take trips to far away places for no other reason but to see them. Some even visit our country, though not many come near to us."

And her mother responded with continued disbelief. "Such talk, how can this be precious child of mine? How would the Earth allow this?"

"Whatever do you mean, mother?" Hope spoke, moving her threads to gold, starting to create a field of waving grain.

"God does not have favorites."

That night Hope sat outside in the darkness. The electricity had been off for some time and only small lights from candles and oil lamps came from a few of the houses. Mixed with the great ink sky, the clear stars offered their beauty and humbling perspective.

SOLILOQUIES

The chain of time is a thin necklace, the links for which are all but invisible. Yesterdays and tomorrows came and vanished. Seasons passed.

"There is much, so, so much," James said. The emphasis was on the elongated single syllable word '*so*' on the second instance. That and the sweeping of the right hand underscored his intensity. He continued. "The needs are everywhere, across the ocean and across the street. You only have to listen to the news or read the papers to realize this. The crisis, if not increasing, is certainly increasingly obvious." James paused. He sat in the kitchen with Melanie, gazed around the room while looking at nothing in particular. Perhaps he had been distracted by the patio door blinds that were dancing with the movement of the air.

The winter had been harsh. The snows reluctantly retreated, and the rains which replaced them were decidedly cold. This was the first spring day where a certain combination of smells and warmth provided promise of better times to come. In an effort to chase out stale air, the front and back doors had been opened and the incoming rush of freshness shocked the interior of the house and challenged the senses of those within. James persisted with his speech.

"Since what we know about this world crisis can't be pleasing to anyone with even the vaguest sense of moral construct, one might think we would do something positive to at least improve the situation." He audibly inhaled and once again looked about. "The logic is simple."

James cradled his coffee; the warmth emanated from the mug, seeped into his palms and comforted him. It was Saturday. He and Melanie were easing into the weekend creating their to-do lists, when the conversation strayed. This would not have been a surprise. The subject had become a preoccupation for James and his talk time often took a detour into the descriptions of human condition.

"It's difficult for us to disregard. Images are everywhere: on the TV, in magazines and newspapers, reported on the radio, yet ignore them we do. Are we so hardened this means nothing? Are we so self-absorbed, so insular, that we are not touched by any of this? Maybe people think this is a Hollywood movie and everyone is waiting for the happy ending. Or is the problem so immense we as a human race have just given up? I don't know the answer, but this I do understand: five bucks dropped into the Salvation Army bucket or the silver in the beggars bowl only serves to ease our conscience. The tiny act helps us submerge, for at least a short period, the sense of guilt which can accompany a person's affluence and good fortune. I get that. But I also get this: it isn't enough. At best this action offers a temporary refuge, at worst, hollow hope. I wonder about the measurements of generosity." James arm extended outward, more in a searching rather than a challenging style.

"I've been wondering about this a lot. We— not just the 'we' in the western Christian context, but the 'we' in the major world religions—we all, in a way, have adopted a notion that includes the existence of a good-deed book. At the end of one's life, there's a form of accountability." James stopped to sip his coffee and to further frame his thoughts.

Melanie sat waiting, not expectantly but knowingly. More would come. This was the pattern of late and being part of this conversation did not require an exchange.

"You die, and the omnipotent Being sits beyond the skies with a calculator and does the math, simple addition and subtraction. The idea is some kind of scale exists. Points accumulate when good deeds are done while harmful actions result in demerits. You can quickly get into negative territory. Violent crimes will, in an instant, wipe out an entire lifetime of gains." He exhaled and slowly refilled his lungs.

"A sliding scale and a day of reckoning. Under normal conditions we might become a bit anxious. Let's face it: this could be somewhat subjective. But we're not talking about human beings; the almighty judge is at work here." He took another deep breath, more to give Melanie the time to catch up to what he was saying than for any personal need to pause. "This may be overly simplistic, but that's the essence of it. At the end of the day, most of us think there's a judgment time. How the process unfolds goes a long way in deciding whether you come back as a grasshopper or a monk. Do you get the keys to heaven, or do you have penance to do before you're allowed to make the grand entrance? Could it be you are now the owner of a one-way ticket to hell?"

James again drank from the coffee which had become lukewarm. "I'm wondering if that isn't it, or at least not all of it. What if it ends up being as much about that which you didn't do as well as the things you acted upon? What if those who are fortunate enough to have the means to be generous are also measured on their ability to recognize positive opportunities—to demonstrate a willingness to act on a grander scale—to be liberal with generosity in ways which take one well beyond the charity dinner and the beggars' bowl?"

James stopped and focused on his wife. "Should this prove to be the case then at the end of the game many of us who think we've basically been okay and can collect our reward will be in for one hell of a surprise." Despite the seriousness of the topic he chuckled at his last observation. The pun had been unintended. "Breaking away from the chains of apathy may be the only way to ensure spiritual salvation."

Melanie provided the singular focus for his speech. While James was in the process of reconstructing his personal moral logic, she had become his convenient audience. These thoughts and phrases had been percolating inside James' head for awhile and his cerebral sense had begun to take on a cohesive form. The monologue was gaining polish.

Although James did not end this soliloquy by posing a question, the need for some kind of affirmation was implied.

"I have the same sense of things dear and the truth is millions, hundreds of millions, share your sentiments if not the exact conclusions." Melanie confirmed his observations, just as she had done on other occasions. She looked towards her husband as a spouse of many decades does: not at him but rather into him.

The cross breeze that moved though the house continued its assault and the ever-moving sun began to shine through a corner of the window and spread its brilliance into the room. Shadows appeared. She saw the unsettledness which invaded his spirit. The controlled assuredness that had always belonged to Melanie and had brought with it a sense of calm and orderliness to her life had truthfully never been a part of James' being. Unlike most, she had not been fooled by his measured manner. Something within James was continually twisting.

As the passing of time brings a philosophy of understanding and resignation to many, she remained hopeful for peace for her husband and, in selfish ways, an extension of the quiet for herself. Sitting beside each other on the deck chairs in the calmness of the afternoon: was this too much to ask for?

She walked over to the sink and dumped the remains of her cold coffee directly into the drain so the dark liquid wouldn't tinge the stainless steel which had been left gleaming the day before by the cleaning lady. After pouring a second cup, she sat down. Her right hand pulled at her left sleeve as she spoke. "I get it James, you get it, a lot of people get it. This is not news." She used an emphatic tone which might be interpreted as impatience but could just as easily have been revealing a hidden fear.

Melanie took a long silent breath and when she resumed her words became quiet and gentle. "Here's the thing James, my lovely James, my intelligent James, my James with the soft soul, my strong James, my ever-vulnerable James." She leaned over and touched his face and with one finger gently traced a forty-five degree line which had become a permanent etching on the right side of his forehead. "I don't like to see you this way. This problem is so immense there is no chance of anyone really comprehending it. This is a monster that can eat you up. It can destroy you. I feel this. Now, more than ever before, there's worry in you. You have fewer smiles, and I can't remember when the last time was where you truly laughed. I'm asking you, James, to be careful." Melanie looked across the room and then sideways. Finally focusing on her coffee, she picked up the cup and took a gulp. This outpouring was out of character for her, and after having said that which needed to be said she didn't know what to do next. James rescued her.

"I know, Mel. I sense this too, and like you say, I've got to be careful with this. I understand I've lost a bit of my outward zest, and I'll work on getting it back ... but you need to believe there's one thing I'll never lose and that's my love for you. I may not say this often enough, but not a day goes by when I'm not grateful for our times together."

The sun which was working its way through the kitchen found the table and flooded onto Melanie's face, revealing her moist and glistening eyes. Melanie was not prone to cry. To strong people, tears are a betrayal.

"I made the grocery list. I'll go shopping," she pushed out the words.

"Good," James replied. "I was thinking of working on the sundeck, and the first thing I'll do is scrub off the winter scum. Then I'll scrape at the stairs, so when the wood dries out it'll be ready to paint."

They spent the rest of the day busying themselves within their own lives, Melanie following her list, and James preparing for spring.

RUMORS

The rumors had been circulating for a full season. They could be heard at the watering hole and were echoed by the farmers as they went to and returned from their fields. People spoke with one another in the shady spots as mothers and the aged watched over the young children playing in the dusty streets. Conversations took place on the long walks to the bazaars and the schools, and words were exchanged in the evening places where some did their gambling and drinking. The talk was everywhere.

It happened on an afternoon which had thus far been ordinary, where the regularity of the routines was uninterrupted, and the weather displayed the sun and cloud variances common to the season.

In a person's life, there is a blending of days and months that happens. As time passes many have trouble distinguishing between the years. There is inevitability in this. Even the most intense efforts to commit each detail of an experience to memory appear to be doomed. It would seem almost the whole of one's remembrance, and therefore of one's being, becomes a flow of feeling rather than a chronological directory of specific experiences. Who can truly say they remember the exact flower or the precise angle of the chin? But who can say that they don't remember?

The day seemed destined to be a part of the blending but then five very new, very big cars appeared. These stopped at the village office where the most important people, those positioned either by blood or other reasons, had assembled. They were the arbitrators, the decision makers, and they dressed in their finest clothes. Everyone stayed in the building for what, to an outside observer, might be viewed as an eternity. Protocol and its reliance on process ensure an elongated time frame.

The visitors left and got back to their cars. Many curious villagers, who had gravitated to this spot, looked down and sideways and scurried this way and that in comical efforts to appear busy with the routines of the day. This the adults did but the children, despite being directed to stay away, gathered in groups and stared intently as the automobiles passed. The chauffeurs drove slowly, perhaps out of concern for the safety of the citizens or possibly in an effort to keep the dust from seeping into the pores of the cars, thereby causing a measure of discomfort for their passengers.

Afterward, nothing was said. Important people do not easily pass information. Still, a careful observer would have detected a lightness in their walks and a shimmering in their eyes as they once again retreated to the office. Of course, at home, those who had attended the discussion talked with their families at the meals, and naturally certain questions were asked. Even though answers were vague, there were replies nonetheless. And through observations and the skeleton of succinct response the rumors started. This visit would prove to be the focus of conversation for many months.

The first visible signs of the actual content of the meeting came when the building materials arrived. These were stacked on property on the outskirts of the village. There they stayed for several days. It had yet to be decided which of the sons and brothers and nephews of the town's decision makers would be involved in the construction and who, apart from the multitude of supervisors, would benefit from the monies left behind by the men in the big cars. In the meantime the materials sat. During this period, virtually every villager walked by and wondered and speculated. Thievery was not common and when the work did proceed, nothing was missing from that which had been left.

Sounds made by hammers and saws filled the air. Sometimes much shouting accompanied the activity. There was one set of plans but several interpretations. Within a couple of weeks, the living quarters had been finished, or at least completed to the degree possible given certain of the items said to be a part of the delivery had mysteriously not arrived. Still the villagers were adept at improvising and in the final analysis things had worked out relatively well.

Shortly thereafter a truck drove up with more material and, once again, a decision-making process was affected. A second building took form, followed by a third. In total they built a small house, a community room and a medical clinic. Another wait began.

HEADWATERS

Fire is a strange phenomenon. Housed within its essence are the polar possibilities of giving and destroying. Humankind's primeval desires for warmth and light are satiated under its glow. In these generous moments, those who are benefactors stand to be transcended by its presence. Can anyone say, when staring into the brightness of the fireplace on a cold winter's night, or sitting by the campfire in the dusk and developing darkness, that they have not experienced some degree of meditative spirituality?

Fire is necessary and can be good. But beware of fire. It has devoured forests and left only charred remains. Animals fled before it in terror and their homes and those of the people who lived with the trees or by its perimeter have been destroyed by fire. In the tranquility of an evening it has, without warning, taken a house and the dreams of those within and swallowed them whole.

It is said a fire burns inside each soul. It then becomes a question of type. Is it controlled and nurturing, or has it gained a menacing presence, intent on consuming everything in its path and in the process ensuring its own destruction? Will it build possibilities, or destroy them?

James looked at his friend in a serious way, one that resulted in the appearance of two vertical creases above the nose. He took a deep breath. "I'm burning up on the inside, Phil."

"You know James ... that's life. I hate to put this crassly but just be glad you're on the winning team," Phil spoke. It was lunchtime. "My friend, you keep pushing this. You and I have been around the block more than a few times. We work together, we eat together, and sometimes, sadly, we rely on one another for entertainment." He did a full stop, looked right at James and then continued. "I'm saying this as a friend, let it go!" He repeated, this time leaving spaces between each of the words. "Let it go. It's getting in your way."

"I know you think that but as we both know we're not the new guys anymore and no disrespect for you and your talents, or I guess mine, for that matter, but any thoughts of upward mobility we once had are long gone. The next generation is already here. Work is not part of the equation, the kids are out the door, and the house is bought and paid for. So Phil, what exactly is it getting in the way of?"

They were sitting around a sidewalk table. It had become the vogue in North America to eat like the Europeans; perhaps not in length of time, but at least in location. Busy outside venues, especially those with good sun angles proved to be the most popular. Some customers had coffees and people watched, while others who had ordered meals relinquished their observer status and concentrated on the food before them. Irrespective of preoccupation, they all sucked in the fumes from passing vehicles and absorbed the din of the comings and goings. Outdoor speakers, round, tiny affairs set into the overhangs, did their best to counteract the industrial effects. But the pop Muzak was mostly drowned out by the street noise and in the final analysis it only served to heighten the frenetic feeling. Despite this, or perhaps because of it, on warm sunny days outdoor tables were the first to be taken.

Phil chose not to respond to the uneasy question James had posed. Rather, he shifted in his chair and while doing so managed to move the topic to different ground. After they beat up the local politicians—"Can any sane person make sense of the new parking policy?"—Phil picked up his newspaper. This was not a rude action intended to snub a friend but rather one which could only be achieved because of their relationship. In a way they had become those two old guys on the park bench, bathing in the soft sun of the early morning, feeding the pigeons, talking a bit, reading the paper, and spending blocks of time staring outwardly in silence. Without apparent signal but right on cue they leave, glad of each other's company and looking forward to tomorrow. And so Phil began to read, whereupon James slipped a pen from his shirt pocket, took a napkin and started to compose. He still twisted.

"Dear Editor." Stopping, he crossed out the "dear" and applying his sorry excuse for penmanship, chicken-scratched over the top and wrote "To the." For a while he sat. What next? He focused on the cars idling in the traffic, waiting for the light to change. He checked out the people in the distance crossing the streets. His aging eyes were no longer able to differentiate between individuals, but he still understood the movement of the herd. He examined the store windows; he looked at Phil; he stared at his feet. Nothing. The pen did not magically contribute wisdom.

James' natural inclination was to be forthright, but through his work he had come to understand this approach can be misinterpreted. It is often viewed with suspicion and is not easily embraced. Direct people put forward ideas that are not couched in diplomatic, sensitive language. In big block letters at the top of the napkin he wrote, "I am not impressed." After a few seconds, he followed up with more words. The flow had begun. He was in the river.

Randy Kaneen

To the
~~Dear~~ Editor
 'I AM NOT IMPRESSED! I own my house; count me among the comfortable yet I am not impressed by this material circumstance. How can I positively view a system which allows for my prosperity while so many others on this earth struggle for basic necessities? I am not unemployed and not ill, but should I get sick and require medical attention, this is available. Count me among the lucky ones. Still, how can I be impressed with practices and procedures which allow for my singular fortune against a world background of poverty and suffering? History confirms economic stratification has been around since the earliest structures of civilization, but the extent and depth of the nightmare has never been as obvious as it is today. Don't take my word for this. Read the papers, watch the news, check out the net, all will be confirmed. The gap between those who have and others who do not continues to widen. The extent of the need is amazing; the details astound. If we should stay the course, I have but two questions. Will we as a society implode or explode? Can something be done to change this direction or is our fate already sealed?
Yours truly,
James A Terrance

 He folded the napkin and put it into his shirt pocket. James' believed if you are going to say something important, it is better to be succinct. This allows for fewer interpretations, or, more to the point, a reduced likelihood of misinterpretation; hence the brevity of the note.

Phil placed each section of his newspaper in its proper sequence and with the traditional check of the watch and the usual "Is it that time already?" exclamation, they returned to work.

In the afternoon, James could be seen re-reading that which he had penned. It is one thing to write a business report, quite another to see a man's inner moral thought process on paper. "Who is this person who wrote such words?" he asked himself. "Is he a good man, a true man? Is he a man of action or simply one of vision?" As of yet James didn't know.

After he finished dinner and cleared the dishes, James disappeared up the stairs to the computer room. The scratched and nearly illegible words took on a crisp form. The correspondence was folded, slipped into an envelope, stamped, sealed, and placed in the inner vest pocket of his sports jacket, the one he was especially fond of and wore to work more often than he should have. The next morning he dropped the letter in with the office outgoing mail.

In the time that followed, his routines were slightly altered. Each day, prior to entering the expressway, he stopped to buy the edition of the same newspaper which would later be delivered to his house. Then in the privacy of his car he located the letters to the editor page and scanned the headings. All were the creations of the editorial department: "A Win, Win," "The Loyalist Rewarded,"

"The Teacher, Every Politicians Target," "Everybody's an Expert," "Park This," "Dog Days for Dog Owners". Day five arrived and there it was: "How Much is Enough?" He read it. Not a single typing error and his name had been printed for all to see: James A. Terrance.

So it was out there. Perhaps more to the point, *he* was out there. A sense of expectation came and this surrounded him. Feelings of release, exhilaration, and anticipation were clouded in a form of anxious worry. For him this was a bold statement, a flash of color on the canvass of life. But what about the rest of the world?

After ordering and consuming his lunch, Phil moved to the reading of the newspaper. No words were spoken. At work and in the house, not a syllable was uttered. James waited for anything; a sound, an affirmation, an acknowledgment. Nothing transpired. Within the void, he felt betrayed and lonely and depressed and puzzled and directionless. He slept poorly.

The next day he found himself unable to maintain his silence. Placing the article right in front of Phil he demanded, "Read this! It was in yesterday's editorial section. Every lunch time you read the paper. So why didn't you read this?"

Phil, taken aback by the tone, focused on what was before him. "Letters to the editor. Letters to the editor," he repeated. "What can I say? Honestly James, they're my last resort. When I'm waiting for a haircut and the magazines on the table are over six months old, I search for a newspaper, and if I'm lucky enough to find the current edition and after I've read everything I want to and I'm still waiting, then out of pure desperation, maybe, just maybe, I'll check out the letters to the editor. No disrespect, James, but for me it's mostly full of people popping off, desperate for an audience. Why bother with that?" Phil then set himself to reading the letter. After a long pause he looked up and in a half laughing manner joked, "The secret's out. James Terrance, James A. Terrance, has a social conscience. Well, who knew?"

James became defensive and countered quickly and forcefully. "And just what, might I ask, do you mean by that?"

Phil, not knowing how to respond, retreated. "Not a thing, James, not a thing." Seeing his friend needed something, he reached to find some words. "Nice letter, right to the point. Makes a person think."

James accepted his friend's efforts. "You really believe that?"

"Yeah " said Phil. "I wouldn't say it if I didn't mean it."

They followed normal routines. Phil read while James sat staring into space, thinking, and wondering. So much at stake. Were there others concerned about the extent of the suffering? What of his own salvation?

SKIPPING SONGS

    In the intense heat of the summer days a quietness took hold of the village. Those who were not working or otherwise occupied retreated to their favorite spots where the combination of shade and slight breeze made these times more tolerable. Between houses or by a bush sometimes a few friends could be seen conversing in whispers much as soldiers might do in their overwhelming urge to tell their stories but still remain vigilant against alerting adversaries of their whereabouts. To the villagers, it was as if the noonday sun had become this enemy who was intent on searching them out and torturing them in its relentless brilliance, baking their bodies so they resembled the texture and color of the dry, splitting soil. Within the hushed environment things could be heard: the slight sounds of neighbors talking; the buzzing of searching flies; the corrugated roofs and grasses shifting with the air; an occasional baby's cry; and, in recent times, desperate soft voices emanating from far too many of the homes.

Any person walking into one of these places would enter into darkness. The cloths used to cover the few window openings were drawn closed as the decision had been made to try to keep whatever coolness remained in. Light was unavoidably sacrificed. Though there were two people in the home of Hope's cousin, only one knew for certain it was dark.

In the vast regions of the world where people live, flowers also grow. These are not necessarily the flowers of deliberately constructed gardens whose plantings are carefully considered. No one predetermined the sufficiency of moisture or the suitability of sun and shade. No one assessed the vitality of the soils. No one weighed out the factors around competing plants. No one planned the aesthetic importance. And no one had assumed or been assigned the responsibility to ensure the gardens' continued robustness. Still, these flowers grow.

Sometimes this is expected; the climate is lush and the gifts to the earth so generous that color is everywhere, and at all times. But there are other locations where things are not as easy: the high mountains, the northern tundra and the parched deserts. Yet even in these places flowers grow and when they bloom it is a massive celebration. There is not one living soul who, once having witnessed this, has not been awed. They are amazed, not just at the beauty before them, but by the fact this happens at all.

The unconscious awareness is that these flowers serve as a testimony to life itself. There is struggle and there is a blossoming. A name for this exists in Hope's language, but in *ours there is no true translation. Here, when someone is named after a flower, one sees the image of the flower but not the perseverance required for it to live. That is the equation. In Hope's world the entire life context is understood within the word.*

It is true roses grow in the most English of gardens and prosper when nurtured and pruned. They are loved for their fragrance and prized for their beauty. But the wild roses also thrive and do so both in the black earth and in the soils that hold many stones. A delicacy and majesty bursts forth from each of their flowers. She is called Rose, but think not of her as the English rose but as someone emanating from a wild variety. When she is referred to, know her in her totality.

Hope, stroking the forehead of her ill cousin and her friend, did so with the greatest of gentleness. Her words were even softer and the music and love within each of their syllables beckoned for remembrance. Rose, unable to see or talk and now struggling as much with her mind as with her body was, with Hope's help, once again able to find the memories of her life.

She had been a happy girl, forever smiling and laughing. And she was kind, unusually so. Her mother and father had been known to talk about this, not boastfully to the neighbors and relatives, but to each other. When they spoke there was pride in their voices. In the small spaces of their home sometimes Rose overheard them. She did not do this deliberately; it would just happen.

"While you were on the lands today I saw Rose, the little bit of a thing that she is, going to an older boy who lives down the road and who was crying because he was without

friends. The others he tried to play with teased him as he is not thinking clearly. This is the way he was born and it is the way he will always be. It is what has been given to him. The teasing boys and girls ran away and left him all alone, alone and with his tears. Then Rose, our own dear Rose, walked over and dried the waters from his cheeks. Together they made up a game of sticks and straws and played this the whole afternoon long." And the hardened strong father and the toughened stoic mother wiped the corners of their eyes, momentarily overcome by the great gift of this child.

Hope cooled Rose's forehead with a damp cloth, all the while talking, when for no apparent reason, she sang the skipping songs. These had been taught to her by her cousin. Rose, though a full seven years older than Hope, had taken the time to teach her how to skip. She was generous in every way, and this included an unselfish generosity with the greatest gift of all: time. This was not done in a deliberate fashion, with a conscious sense of bestowment. Rather it happened in the wisest of ways where there are no clear distinctions between the giving and the receiving, between the giver and the receiver. The two acts become, in fact, one. When Hope sang the songs and Rose heard them, both of them became bound in singular memory.

Fetch the water in the morning sun
Look after your brother, he has the runs
Sweep the floor and wash those feet
Your father's in the field and he wants to eat.

"I cannot skip, I have the grace of a cow," spoke Hope. Whereas Rose replied, "Hope, how could you say that? For

me you are a butterfly landing on the tiniest of petals. Now I will turn the rope and you can try once again." Under the warmth of the sun and with Rose's encouragement Hope felt she should not give up and within each of her failures Rose found a small victory and presented this to Hope. After many tries and much laughter and talking time Hope jumped to the exact rhythm of the turning rope, not once or twice or ten times but well beyond that.

He is handsome and she is pretty
She is a girl going to the city
They come from the east; they come from the west
How many boyfriends will pass her test?
One, two, three, four ...

As Hope chanted these silly verses, Rose made small rocking motions with her prone, curled-up body. This and the twitching of her eyelids which remained shut served as the only outward signs of remembrance. Hope's tears silently flowed. She could not offer other words and held Rose's hand in the stifling afternoon heat.

But the talking and the songs had a lingering magic. Rose saw more vividly than she had in recent times and this excited her. She reviewed images and whole scenes in a frantic, desperate search for meaning.

Marriage and all that goes with such a union featured significantly in her memories. There was the day itself, a wondrous occasion where the colors of everything became brighter, clearer, and more alive. She had been exquisitely presented in a lovingly fashioned, rose-pink flowing dress. Her husband was so handsome and happy; his smiles radiated toward her. Such energy, such optimism! For them this was a feeling and a time for the whole world to enjoy, and briefly, it seemed everyone did.

The more and the longer the sons and daughters lived, the more fatigued the soils became. The village had grown in size, not overly, but noticeably. Elders spoke of places which did not exist in early memory and of whole rows of homes that had been constructed in one's lifetime. Perhaps the land understood the nature of this growth most of all. Pressures to produce had increased and because of this the earth had less time to rest. Over-cultivation and over-grazing became common practice, and predictably production decreased.

Rose's husband was the fourth-oldest male. The weakened family's lands, which were not able to provide enough, would never be his. Rumors of opportunity combined with the zeal of youthful adventure and together they overtook these two. With anticipation for themselves and a resulting sadness for all who knew them, they decided to escape the poverty and pursue their dreams in a city, far away.

Rising just before the sun, Rose and her husband took what they thought could be carried and went outside only to be surprised by several dozen people, those who had the hardest time letting go. Hope was there as were her mother and father and brothers and sisters. Rose's entire family had assembled.

"Here is some money so you may take the bus to the market town. This will save you walking time and start you fresh on your journey to the city." Rose's father presented this with great flourish to his son-in-law but all the while he looked at Rose. And Rose's mother offered foods which had *been lovingly made and carefully wrapped and these she gave directly to her daughter. "Stay well, my child; may the heavens smile upon you." And she touched the side of the face she had always loved, desperately attempting to fix the image into her mind. She tried not to do too much remembering, and she tried not to cry. She was not successful.*

Brothers and sisters and aunts and uncles and cousins and friends came up offering their good wishes. Then they all sat together and ate a breakfast even a king would relish. When the market bus did arrive and it was time to board, Hope was the last to give Rose a hug.

THE SALT SEA

James didn't recognize the number on the call display; nevertheless, he chose to pick up the phone.

"James, …er, James A. Terrance please."

Unable to identify the voice, James applied auditory forensics to the high-pitched tones. No match was discovered. It must be sales, he concluded.

"If you're selling something, I'm not interested. Our household practice is to avoid doing business over the phone." He reserved this line for all telemarketers.

The voice on the other end moved to an even higher elevation and acquired an anxious sense. "No, no, you don't understand. I'm not selling anything.

It's not like that. I read your letter and since the newspaper also included your middle initial, you're easy to find in the phone book. I just wanted to talk to you, that's all."

It is interesting how silence can have its own set of meanings. With the absence of sound waves one might conclude no auditory communication is possible, but this is not the case. There are many types of silence, each having a distinct form of quiet. There's awestruck silence, another in grief and one in stillness when souls communicate. There is the silence of terror, of sheer boredom and of intense concentration. The kind James emitted was of the puzzled variety. Finally he spoke. "Pardon me¿"

"The letter, the one you wrote to the newspaper several weeks ago. I read it. I was wondering if we might meet, talk over coffee. You do drink coffee ...¿"

James' response was quick and could be accurately described as aggressively defensive. But the reaction was just a clever disguise, one intended to mask his delight that his letter had been read. He wanted to keep his emotions in check and guard against excessive personal exposure in case this was a crank call or he was speaking to a somewhat deranged individual. "Even if I do, I'm not likely to be drinking with you. No offense, but I'm not meeting with anyone I don't know and I have no idea who you are." While talking he followed his cordless and cell phone routine—"the walk." It was more like a pace than a walk, a wolf's pace; to be more precise, a caged wolf's pace. He moved from room to room, stopped for the briefest of moments and resumed the prowl. At last he took refuge in the kitchen. "I wrote a letter, that's it. Beginning, middle, and end of story."

The high-pitched caller jumped in. "Let me get right to the point, James. I know what you are saying and I think you'll fit in with our group, the Society for Human Justice. Thought you might want to look into this."

Excitement built in James—the letter had been read! Still, he wasn't about to let his guard down, but by including a question in his response he left a small opening. "I'm sorry, maybe you didn't understand me. I'm not in the habit of talking to strangers and just who are you anyway?" James' published declaration was accompanied with the sense that should have gone with the opening of Pandora's Box—a fear of uncharted paths.

"William Sanchez, sir, at your service."

"Well, William, begging your pardon, but I never heard of you and I have no idea who the Society for Human Justice is. So please tell me, why should I go any further with this conversation?" James used his flat business tone, another deliberate effort to suppress emotion.

"Because, as we both know, much hangs in the balance."

James swallowed hard. Someone else was aware of the precarious situation those on this Earth found themselves in. For a moment the universe stopped. Physicists speculate about the possibility, science fiction enthusiasts dream of it. Time and space become deflected energies. No longer operating as parallel continuums they momentarily intersect. Subsequently, everything and everyone is locked in a state of suspension. That is how it was for James. After the Earth realigned itself, the two made a determination. James would soon be meeting Mr. William Sanchez.

He envisioned this differently. People can say they are without expectations; however, reality challenges the existence of this notion. The sense exists universally, and does so both in negative and in positive forms. It is often experienced in more subtle ways for givers than receivers but it exists nonetheless. Phrases such as "I wasn't prepared for the way this turned out" or "It was exactly as I imagined" evidence the reality of this notion. While weighing the past, one looks to the future and out of this process, expectations are formed. They are not to be glorified or avoided; rather, they are to be accepted as part of the human construct. James was hard-pressed to reconcile his pre-packaged set of images with the people—and person—before him.

"James Terrance I presume." The skinny fingers and hand that seemed detached from the long decidedly non-athletic arm met the hand of James. William Sanchez was a tall man who had an extremely thin neck. It was devoid of chicken skin, one of the telltale signs of advancing age. The crown of his head held only little wispy hairs and the front had receded considerably. Male pattern baldness had visited William, and it would seem by the overall countenance it had done so early.

"William, nice to meet you." They shook hands.

James moved his attention from William to this place and to those around him. He sped through the situation, making mental notes as he went. It was an open room in an older building in a nondescript part of the city. Before him stood a confusion of different looking chairs, approximately thirty in total, and these had been placed into four rows. A folding table and three more chairs sat at the front. As for the people, they were an eclectic lot, to say the least—some complete with body piercings and tattoos, others casually clothed and middle aged. A number were geriatric. The gender mix seemed even.

Without warning, a woman wearing a well-worn grey track suit shouted, "Take your seats everyone! Take your seats please!" Despite the lack of presidential appearance, no objections surfaced and with relative efficiency they all complied. Chatter quickly abated and the meeting began. The lady in grey assumed the role of chair.

"At this point, we only have a few things on the agenda. We'll talk about the march to Government House this weekend, follow this up with regular items then listen to a little something Jenny put together. So we might as well get right to it."

Robert's Rules of Order were nowhere in evidence. No one kept a speakers list. They discussed an upcoming protest, when to meet, the route to take, which groups would be represented, and how many to expect. One of the members persisted in asking question after question. James found him annoying. He could discover no aesthetic value in this young mans giant nose ring; it resembled one which might have protruded from a bull's nostrils.

During the orders of business a number of small things came up and when they did James drifted away and entered his lonely space. This was not an unknown occurrence and in recent weeks its frequency had increased. He sat watching but not seeing. People spoke but he didn't hear. James enunciated soundlessly under his breath: "There is no time" and with that, the waves began to wash over him—the waves of things undone, the waves of regret, those of repentance. "No time, none at all. Is it too late?" And then the great waves of pain presented themselves. Thundering upon him, they came one after the other and from different directions so he couldn't brace before the next one arrived. They were the waves of the sufferings of the world. The massive hurt of starvation came and nearly swallowed him, those of disease and particularly needless disease shook the foundation of his spirit. The waves of violence were in blood red form and as they pounded the beach they became a frenzy of screams. These were followed by the greatest waves of agony: those bringing the pain of no hope and no hope for future hope. The salt sea revealed itself for what it truly is, an ocean of liquid sorrow.

"James, you all right?"

The nudge in the ribs brought him back to the meeting. He found himself sitting in his chair with evenly spaced tears moving down his cheeks. "Yeah, yeah William, hay fever. Get it this time of year. Never fails." James offered this recovery, and pulled a tissue from his pocket to soak up the waters.

"We're in for a treat now," William said, looking toward the front and smiling.

"A treat?"

"Jenny's name was drawn for the talk tonight. Hold on tight: fire and brimstone is headin' our way." In his reply, William became quite animated. All limbs moved and his head bobbed from side to side.

A slender woman stood up, hair flying everywhere. Her long flowing dress was reminiscent of those worn by sixties flower children, a large silver ring pierced her bottom lip, and three smaller ones penetrated the left eyebrow. The entire exposed right arm was heavily tattooed. She was young. "Perhaps mid-twenties," thought James.

"First of all, I want to thank everyone for coming and for staying. I've written a short piece." She waved a crumpled sheet in the air. "I would like to share this with you. I call it 'They Came.'" She took a sip of water and using a voice that easily projected and dominated the room, she began. "I stood on the sidewalk at the corner of 45th and Main when they made their appearance. They were predominately male but were also represented by a number of the female species. Most wore grey or black. Those who didn't had chosen blue, not a light cheery sky blue, but a rather dark blue, the kind that almost qualifies for black. Nothing came off the rack." This was a practiced story; not once did she refer to the paper she held.

"When they passed me, they didn't look left or right. Why would they? You see, I was invisible, or at least I was to them. I thought, 'Hey, I can follow. No need to be surreptitious in my movements, no need to sneak around, hiding behind this and that corner.' For all practical purposes I did not have a physical presence. I walked half a dozen paces behind.

"In the course of observation it became apparent I was not alone in this newly discovered form, or should I say, lack thereof. The qualities associated with my invisibility were shared by others. Then again, maybe I wasn't invisible. Perhaps these blandly dressed people had an affliction causing them significant visual impairment. In which case it made their movements quite remarkable as they negotiated heavily trafficked streets and moved fluidly down crowded sidewalks." She paused at this point, looked out and somehow connected with each audience member.

She continued. "They passed someone sitting on the sidewalk. He had come to a full stop in his life, sat down on the damp cement and taken one shoe off and addressed his toes. And he wasn't doing this in any quiet manner. We're talking biblical southern Baptist preaching here.

"'Have you abandoned me?' He bellowed.

"'Has the burden been too much?'

"'What has become of the times?'

"'Are we left to wait in the silence of our prayers?'

"'Tell me!' He looked up from his toes and focused on the passing parade of people. 'Can you tell me?' he pointed as some walked by. 'You or you?' Looking down he returned his attention to his right foot." Jenny inhaled deeply.

"The walkers continued without acknowledgement. Visual challenges must have been mixed with auditory issues. They arrived at their destination, a favorite coffee shop where they proceeded to order lattes, mistos, and double caramel macchiatos—nothing decaffeinated. I discovered that, despite their movement, they had simply temporarily relocated their world. The nature of conversations revealed as much. These were business people and the talk was all about their work. At that moment I came to understand their eyes were not blind but rather selectively shut. This and the hearing impairment required no medical solution. I left, and when I did I took something. It was the question." She stopped, drank from the glass of water, searched the audience, and in the process, once more locked onto anyone whose attention might have even partially strayed.

"How can we get people to understand? How can we get them to open their ears and eyes? Where is the lesson plan to help them comprehend the most important issues? Those addressing universal need. Those of harmony and balance. Those of equity and peace."

She pointed outward. "This weekend we will march with our placards and cheer as the speeches are being made and be glad of each others company. But when we leave with our hearts full of awareness, will we have convinced anyone to lend a hand in the change process? Or will we, out of pure desperation, once again go home and dream of a messiah hoping he or she will make an appearance in order to right the wrongs?" She dropped her hands and lowered her gaze.

The audience responded with loud applause and whistles. James, no longer seeing the piercings or body art, clapped with enthusiasm. The fact his ideas had been framed by someone else left him feeling reassured and excited.

James, needing to be alone with his thoughts, gave his thanks, spent appropriate polite time with William and the others around him, then excused himself. He drove home, timing the lights perfectly.

A CRUEL PHOENIX

As Hope gently held her hand, Rose continued to retrieve fragments of her life.

The distance between the market town and the city is defined differently depending on whether one rides or walks. As the weather and seasons vary, these also influence the time it takes to traverse the geography.

If it rains hard, which is seldom, the soil, which has a clay consistency, becomes greasy and builds up layer upon layer on the bottoms of one's sandals. Walking is uneven and traction almost nil. No amount of scraping will counteract this. Within a few steps, the effects of the layering process are noticeable and after fifty–or certainly no more than a hundred paces–the stopping and cleaning routine needs to be repeated. Finally, in frustration the shoes are taken off. Bare feet prove to be superior in such times. As slow as this is, progress is at least guaranteed. The same can not be said for the drivers and passengers of the vehicles, as they slip and skid their way forward. Often they find themselves off the road entirely.

When it is sunny, and in particular in the hottest months, walking happens in the early and late hours, but is avoided at midday. Automobile traffic is similarly limited. Whenever a vehicle negotiates the road, an impenetrable cloud bursts from the ground. The incredible silt-like dust chokes the radiators and affects their ability to cool the engines. To avoid overheating, or at least reduce the likelihood of this, many choose to drive in the times that are slightly cooler.

No matter which variables are present, it was a very long way to the city. In ideal conditions it requires almost a full day by car, seven or more by foot. Rose and her husband, having arrived at the market town on this hot day, found the southern road and began the walk. The long journey had begun.

In one's lifetime words can sometimes fail. What is seen or experienced is without expression. There are no synonyms as there is no initial vocabulary.

They had arrived in the city and, by necessity, walked just beyond. What stretched before Rose knew no language. It can be photographed or painted, but not explained. It can be graphed, cross-referenced and analyzed, but not understood. It can be lived, day by day, hour by hour, moment by moment, but not be truly known. It will, however, be remembered.

Submerging memories is an interesting notion; some would say a theoretical condition. It seems conscious and unconscious forgetting has limitations. Just when something is thought to be buried and obliterated, a cruel phoenix appears and the skeletal remains rise once more. Rose shuddered with these memories of her time in the city and of that which she encountered. She trembled uncontrollably, and Hope, not letting go of her hand, reached with the other and caressed her and stroked the sweat-drenched forehead and ran her fingers through the tangled hair. Swallowing the sobs that were within and wanting to erupt, this wonderful cousin soothed Rose with gentle, even, reassuring words. Exhausted from battling the deep and hopeless pain, and quieted by such touch and voice, Rose fell asleep.

Hope, now sitting in this dark room, listened to the uneven troubled breathing. To escape the anguish which lay before her, she attempted to focus on something else, anything else. She settled on the three recently built buildings on the outskirts of town. "What" and "why" questions drove her speculation as she waited for Rose's mother to return from the market.

THE CARIBOU

The images that come while one sleeps are not as disjointed or as bereft of meaning as what they may appear to be. Much published material concerns itself with interpretation. After arriving home from his meeting with the Society for Human Justice and following his routine of sitting in the overstuffed chair, James went to bed. Sleep came quickly, as did the dream.

The first of the snows presented themselves as soft gentle flakes. These danced with the winds before settling in indiscernible ways on the ground. All of the caribou were, as usual, grazing, preoccupied with their own preservation. Most took no notice of this change in the weather.

In Search of Sticks

The gifts which they had received were enormous and necessary. Their hairs were hollow and compartmentalized. This trapped the air, keeping it still. That and the sheer number layered one on top of the other were important for survival. Without them, freezing to death would be more than a possibility; it would be the likelihood.

There is cold and extreme cold. This was neither. With the swirls of air, two or three flakes collided on the tip of the nose of one of the caribou and he looked to the sky, not in a startled fashion, but in a knowing way. "It has been awhile since we last met, I have been expecting you." There was resignation in the words.

The reply was sage and factual: "As it is told in legend it was you who chose to enter this Earth from the distant galaxy, to travel across the blackness between the stars, and live under our one moon and one sun. I have been here always, and though I could apologize for my existence, this is what I am. You, who are used to long journeys, must now prepare for another." With that, winter's presence was gone. The whiteness disappeared as swiftly as it had announced itself.

From that day forward, a restlessness began to take hold. Others felt it as well, and together they drifted south while still eating the last gifts of the grasses on the expansive tundra. The movement was accompanied by an attraction which defies scientific explanation. They were met by more caribou in the east and the west and those who ranged further north had quickened their pace and caught up. As of yet, no definable urgency in their movement was apparent. Still, what was once ten thousand had increased almost tenfold.

"Ah, my friend, I find you in a different place but not so very different. Out of respect I have extended your sanctuary, but now I can no longer deny my essence. As you know, this is what I am." With that the snows fell, and the winds blew, and a coldness came which foretold of the difficulties ahead.

An amazing journey began—a walk of incredible length and indescribable proportion. The flat lands were intersected by streams that had been fed by the final melting of last year's snows and the begrudging release of the glaciers. Though cold, these waters were relatively small and easily forded. The muskeg spaces required diversions in the pathway, forcing moves in distances and directions which seemed counter to the animals' desires. Many journeys are never straightforward. All the while the wolves stared from the distance. The mountains, tall and barren, formed formidable barriers, but still the caribou carried on. Now instead of being scores wide, they sometimes marched in single file, moving on lands and in ways as their ancestors had for thousands upon thousands of years.

He also walked.

Just as had happened over the eons, the bulls locked in fierce battle to determine the rights of propagation. The strongest and most resolute prevailed, thereby guaranteeing the strength of the genetic structure. Bloodied though not bowed he joined the ranks of the victorious.

They conquered the mountains but the journey down also required care. At last, they found the trees. The wolves, who had never left them, continued their watch—only this time they ventured closer. Would someone stumble? Would a weak one fall behind? The snows kept building and blackness descended, embracing the nights and defying the days.

Finding himself belly up in the soft snow, his curved hooves adeptly located the nutrient rich, age old lichens hidden below. These he ate. Sometimes the night temperatures reached more than fifty degrees below zero and the special qualities of each hair and of his small ears became increasingly important. The wolves remained vigilant, waiting for one to stray or stumble. Already there were blood red spots that had been covered by new layers of white.

Finally the darkness lost its grip, and with the lengthening of each day came an increasing restlessness. The snow now only reached to the knee. He looked up and was visited once more. "I am going, but I will leave you the melting snows and the gorged rivers and the soft ice. As difficult as the journey was to arrive, the return will require even greater strength, awareness, and more determination. By the time your young are born, you will be weak and the wolves emboldened. Those who survive will eat the grasses of the tundra, but the mosquitoes and flies will present new challenges. The only quiet you will find is when the wind blows. My first frosts will reduce this misery but also reawaken your memories reminding you of the times ahead."

James woke up covered in sweat. Stumbling out of bed, he went straight to the kitchen and drank a tall glass of ice-cold water. He did not immediately return. Instead he chose to sit in the semidarkness of his living room and in the shadows began to consider this dream. "An endless journey of incredible hardship mixed liberally with the cycle of false promise," he whispered. "An epic struggle of survival. But what does it mean?"

SIXTY-THREE

The three buildings had stood empty for many months. This was especially pleasing to the rodents who had exercised great caution while taking up residence, but no longer found it necessary to operate covertly. They abandoned their nocturnal disposition and could be seen moving this way and that at any time of the day or night. Two full seasons had passed. Emotional tension of anticipation is not something which can be sustained indefinitely and those in the village began to focus on things of more immediate consequence. Speculative gossip found new directions. On an unusually cool and cloudy day all that changed.

"Careful, careful!" directed the man with the colorfully patterned royal blue shirt. "Take it into the first room. Then we'll get it out of its crate."

Three full trucks had come, and the men who had been drivers and passengers collectively engaged in unloading the cargo. The man obviously in charge was quite small, but he more than compensated for his lack of physical stature with a loud and commanding voice. Between orders, he could be seen consulting a notebook. Sometimes this would be studied for long periods before he pointed to something and barked out another direction. "Take those to the back room! See the mattresses covered by the blue tarp? Pick them up one at a time, not two at a time, and bring them to the building! Set them up on the wooden beds." His hands and arms were active, several gestures accompanying each command.

This process went on until early evening, at which time everything had been unloaded, more or less unpacked, and placed in a spot thought to be suitable. The last act was to padlock the front doors of the various buildings. Several of the windows were just openings: that is, no window had been placed in them. Mysteriously they had never been dropped off. The ludicrousness of the efforts to screw in latches and put on locks was apparent to everyone. Still, directions needed to be followed.

By the time the workers got into their trucks and left, a huge crowd had assembled. It had been building the entire day and eventually constituted the majority of the villagers. These watchers and waiters reluctantly filtered back to their houses. Speculative conversation flowed in the homes, at the fields, and on the streets. As before, it dominated. The rodents, seeing the changes and perhaps sensing others, once again moved cautiously.

Only days later, the people arrived. The most important of the seven appeared to be a tall, sandy blond-haired woman. A strident gait revealed her sense of confident purpose. Whether moving from room to room or heading out to deal with her dysentery, the pace did not change. Her degrees and internship behind her, she had taken leave from an established practice to make the trip.

Some who come are driven by profound beliefs which focus on the need to provide relief and, at the same time, offer a particular form of internal salvation. Groups of these people are unevenly distributed throughout the lands. Hope and her villagers had heard talk of them. Dr. Sylvia McGregor's presence was neither scripted by a formal spiritual map nor motivated by material gain. Unlike Rose's journey, this pilgrimage did not result from desperate poverty. Sylvia had signed up with an aid agency. She intended to offer her services and skills for free.

Among the group were a husband and wife, recent graduates who held agricultural and education degrees respectively. They were young and focused. Despite being thoroughly briefed before the departure, their eyes told a mixed story–not just the expected tale of anticipation but one where anxiety is laced with an indefinable fear. The truth is, irrespective of preparations made, no one is able to predict how one will react when the uncensored story of humankind unfolds.

Within a week, the operation had limped to the starting line and the translator let the villagers and others in the surrounding villages know of the services which would soon be available. When the time came for the clinic to open a queue began to form in the late blackness of the night. By dawn, hundreds had arrived. There was no jostling, no pushing, and no efforts to better one's position. Each story of suffering was respected.

The line itself resembled a strange organism, a giant diverse entity composed of the most ancient and the newest of lives. There were those who talked and those who were stoic within their problems. Some had come independently while others relied on the caring of a friend or relative for their current and continued presence.

When Dr. Sylvia McGregor rounded the corner and she and her two helpers saw the length and make up of what was before them, they stopped in their tracks. For a full minute they stared out disbelievingly while the first piece of the pulsating line became instantly quiet and stared back.

There was no discernible way to efficiently differentiate between the conditions and establish a scale of need. Dr. Sylvia McGregor assessed the situation and, having understood the impossibility of assigning positions based on personal misery, took charge. In the order of their appearance each patient was provided a number thus eliminating any sense of arbitrariness. People beyond numeral seventy were advised to come back the next morning and baring obvious emergencies, assume their place. Despite the best efforts of the translator to persuade them to go and return another day, it proved to be a slow and reluctant dissipation. For those who held numbers forty through seventy, there was no success with the stated strategy which involved leaving and then returning in the early afternoon. Hope clutched the small white scrap of paper. Number sixty-three.

In Search of Sticks

The lands surrounding the building site and beyond had been nearly completely cleared. Almost nothing was left to offer shade. Some stooped by a few of the small bushes which had been spared. But the scores of people who formed the head of the line did not even benefit from this possibility of relief. They stood or crouched in the open while being assaulted by the summer sun. This they did without complaint, waiting for their time to arrive.

"What is it that troubles you?" Dr. Sylvia McGregor looked at Hope and used a language that had no immediate meaning to her. The male translator asked the same thing in a dialect familiar to Hope.

Quietly, timidly, almost fearfully, Hope began to speak. Though her voice was soft, the words were clear. "I am very sorry to be a bother to you. I am not here for myself but for a cousin, a wonderful person who today is without strength, who breathes in shallow ways and whose eyes now know only shadows. I came to you to discover if there are any mercies which might fall to such a soul who has always shown the deepest of loves and kindnesses to those around her, including this cousin who stands before you. I wish to ask what can be done to ease the burden of one who has touched the earth in such tender ways."

The translator, who had spent the day patiently listening to stories and quickly and directly summarizing each affliction for the doctor—"this one has a sore elbow, this one acquired a persistent rash, this one is troubled with dysentery,"—knew no way to shorten the story. So it was told word for word and feeling by feeling, just as it was related by this girl who had waited nearly all the hot day not for herself but for another. The same person who now stood before them, releasing silent crystal tears.

Dr. Sylvia McGregor did what she had been advised never to do. "I fear I can be of no use. Still, if you wait until I see those who are left, I will walk with you and visit your wonderful cousin."

Hope could not draw out the words to give thanks but blessed both the doctor and the translator, who then gently moved her to an outside spot where she could wait and later be found.

By the nature of who they are, the care and concern of doctors runs deep. But in the breaking which is almost always around them, they must be the source of strength. This is just what it is. Dr. Sylvia McGregor listened to the troubled breathing in the soft glow of the paraffin lamp and spoke kind words and stroked the tight skin and while doing this nearly drowned in the waters that flowed within. It was as feared. Medicines which would have benefited had not been available for Rose, and the lateness of the disease screamed out its inevitability. So this kind doctor gently moved her fingers across Rose's forehead and addressed her spirit using the most compassionate words any language ever had. Though Rose understood nothing, she knew their meaning and in her trembling and pain she once again began to retrieve her past.

In these memories, she found herself in a walking time, still moving toward the city. She was with her husband, and a tall, thin, older man who spoke.

"No, you do not go to the city—not with that which you have in your hands and on your backs. If you choose this

path, you will surely be beaten by the men who are told to keep the order. They are paid to do this and as it is understood this also includes making certain you and I and others who carry our world with us do not stay. They will hit you, but not in the ways that stop the going. They will not break your legs or cease the beating of the heart, nor will they cut you so much that with the losing of blood you will weaken and not be able to leave or even understand the need for leaving. They do not wish your body to be a burden to them, as they cannot let this lie on the clean street and by the busy shops. The stinking, decomposing corpse would become a home for a multitude of flies and diseases. So in the hitting they will bruise you and perhaps break an arm or a jaw, and sometimes demand you give them what little you own. This they would do to keep the order, to maintain the safety." Rose and the husband of Rose stared at him with incredulous eyes that showed no understanding. The language was not the problem; they knew all the words.

"It is much better you walk with me. I will take you to the place which is not of the city but near enough so if you are one of the ones who are smiled upon and get the work, you can arrive to it. Then you will travel in the blackness of the morning and return under the moon and the stars. There is no living in the city unless you have much money or work for a family who is rich and wants you to take care of their home and their children and wipe their noses and asses all the seasons long."

The man who did this talking walked with Rose and her husband on the dusty roadway. This is how it happens when the walking speed of one is quicker or slower than that of another. In the case of the passing or of the being passed, there are small words and smiles and the nodding of heads. Sometimes conversations take place and the separate paces become one. It was in this way the tall and thin man came to say these things. His strange gait spoke of a previous injury that had healed but left its memory. He was somewhat slow, and Rose and her husband had done the catching up.

The two looked at him as someone does who is trying to make sense of something which makes no sense. The things they had heard had not been in their experiences. What does one do when there is no relationship between the words and the knowing? In Rose's life, if one happened to go to another village, even the third or the fourth nearest—and this didn't happen often, but when it did and a traveler returned with the stories and the descriptions of the countryside and its people, there were never words of unwelcome.

Undeniably there are the memories of those who returned from the city, of the few who came back for the last of the times. Little was ever said of this. One does not speak of great pain; one endures it. Certain pains are beyond description. Even in Rose's language, which is rich in feeling, there are no words. What Rose knew, she learned through the eyes and not the voice.

They walked under the one sky, moving ever forward, ever nearer. In one of the hungry times, they sat and unwrapped their bundles. A small amount of food was chosen and they chewed in silence. A car drove by, so full of people and their things that the bottom nearly scraped the road. The fine red clay dust absolutely swallowed the three travelers. Still they remained, unmoving, squatting by the roadside, looking outward in a kind of silent vigil. Another vehicle passed, this time a truck. It held only one driver and traveled quickly. Speed, combined with the largeness of the wheels, created even greater amounts of red dust. Again no effort was made to escape.

Rose and her husband had experienced this before. At first they moved back and shook themselves, brushing the redness off of each other, but they soon understood the futility of this. Now the only outward signs of irritation were the squinting of the eyes and the movement of a hand covering up the mouth and the nose, and this was just done in the worst of the moments. They were fatigued and remained sitting well after they had finished eating.

During these times, other walkers came by, sometimes singularly, sometimes in twos or threes, seldom in larger groups. While passing, some acknowledged their presence. "It is a good day: the sun is not too hot and not so many cars stir up the road."

"Yes this is a fine day," Rose and her husband agreed.

Others simply walked forward, resigned, intent and weary, one foot placed in front of the other. They looked neither left nor right. It was not clear if these people even saw the three sitters. Maybe they did and their aching did not allow for any speaking. Perhaps all remaining energy needed to be reserved for the journey ahead. Like a moth to the flame they continued.

"How is it you know of this city? How have you come to learn of the corners and walls as if it was your house? Did you do the living there?" Rose's husband asked this of the tall and the thin man.

"I did."

"Is it that you left and do now return?"

"It is."

For a long while, all three walked in the quiet of the blistering hot day. A small sense of safety comes from being with a person who has some of the knowing. Between Rose and her husband, an unspoken decision had been made to slow their pace in order to travel with this man who had an awkwardness in his walking. They were moving to the unknown, and an indefinable anxiousness had firmly taken hold within. Staying together eased some of the tightness. After a considerable distance, Rose's husband continued the conversation as if no time had elapsed.

"Permit me to ask, but do not feel the need to provide the reply. It may be my question is too bold."

The traveler who was spoken to continued to look towards the horizon. Hearing neither permission nor objection, Rose's husband considered the silence and proceeded: "Why is it you went away and then go back?"

The tall and the thin man shifted his eyes and while still maintaining his pace began to inspect the ground before him. He walked some more and just when it might be thought there would be no response, one was forthcoming. "I took a friend to his home. He had the need for the going but could not do this alone." He spoke this softly, and though there wasn't any volume, a resonance accompanied each of the words. "No place exists in his village nor the village of my own for this body to take its presence and so I go back. It is the hardship we all have experienced. It comes from the burden of the lands that have given to the point of exhaustion. This is the story of many who arrive at the city, and for these people, it is the reason for staying." At this he looked at Rose's husband and then at Rose, and he saw the dreading—a need to ask, a fear to know. "More should be said but there is nothing in the language which will do the preparing. Still I will say these things."

Rose and her husband involuntarily braced themselves as one instinctively does when expecting a collision.

"As I have said, I do not know how to use the words or even if there are words to choose." He paused before continuing. "In the world there is danger. As you know it, a snake could hide in the grasses and then bite you. With the long or the quick suffering that follows there may be the dying. There is the danger of drinking bad waters or the eating of spoiled foods, and the danger of falling and with this the breaking of bones. There is the danger of the diseases that come as they drift with the winds. Fear is in these dangers, but I believe that if each of these fears was a stone and they were stacked one on top of the other they would not rise to the height of the fear that you will find in the city. As tall as your fears may be, they will not come to the knees of this new fear. In the city there is a need for large carefulness. Snakes are disguised as people and they are everywhere. There is disease, awful disease, and it has many faces and does not hide in the corners and there is much loss of blood. Dying is every day. Even with all of this, you cannot go back. You can never go back. Nothing has changed since the leaving."

The walking continued and later they prepared to sleep on the side of the road under the enormous stars of the bewildering earth. Rose, while setting up for her sleeping, spoke. "*I heard much and though I am anxious about the going and full of sadness with the leaving, I am somehow pleased to have this time with you. Perhaps this meeting was meant to happen. Still, we do not know of your name.*"

To which he replied, "I too am glad for the knowing, but I cannot speak as to whether this is part of some grand design or if it is, as much seems to be, an accident. I do not see a great deal of the God in these times." Then he told them his name. It is one with no English meaning. It speaks of all which is solid and brings forward the images of the wood and the earth, not the whole Earth, but of the clays and silts and pebbles that form the grains of the soils. In this recounting he will be called "Ned" which seems to evoke some of these qualities.

This tall and thin man named Ned, along with Rose and the husband of Rose, walked for several days. In that time there had been conversation, not of their destination but of the stray dogs who ventured near and of the butterflies and the different birds. Nothing more was said of what had been or might be.

During the traveling, Rose and the husband of Rose came to find out about many things, one of which was the road itself. Still a full two days away from the city, the road gained a new texture. It was now covered by a blanket of dark stone. This, of course, was pavement. Although this had been spoken of by those who visited their village and by the teacher at the school, it had never been experienced.

The cars and the trucks became many more and their quickness increased. Some who passed used their horns as if to say "do not get in my path, I am a charging beast, and I am coming." There was only a small need of this as many of the travelers had bare feet and as tough as their soles were, the blistering heat of the road during the day was to be avoided. So except in the early parts of the morning and the last lights of the evening, they did their walking on the roadside, choosing pebbles and sharp stones over the hot, black smoothness. At least there was less dust.

On their way, they passed a village. They did this after winding up a slight rise and rounding a corner. There had not been any possibility of seeing what was coming until their arrival. In the ways Rose and her husband had come to understand, this was not a village. Rather it was a collection of broken-down houses made of mud and sticks and metal. People silently watched. There were no friendly nods or gestures which said, "Hello and good luck on the walk ahead." No invitations were extended. No "Please have some tea and share this shade offered by my house as it intercepts the sun." This did not happen.

Equally difficult to comprehend was what appeared on the other side of the road. Before them stretched to the limits of their eyes a vast expanse of the tallest grains either of these two had ever seen. A high fence of sharp wires bordered the lands. This, like the fertile grounds, also disappeared beyond the use of sight.

They stared with disbelief at what was before them. The tall and the thin man named Ned, seeing their incredulity spoke, "Do not try to cross into the field. Do not go there. Some are doing the watching. They drive in the cars and trucks and if they see you in this field, which seems more like a country's size than a field, they will do the shooting. This will be done not to scare you but to kill you. Should their aim not be straight and they miss, or if the bullet hits you and does not cause you to fall and only makes the bleeding, do not think of this as good luck for their dogs will catch you. In the ripping and the tearing you will have wished for a straight shooter."

"How can this be, such richness, such beauty, such abundance and ..." Rose paused and looked to her right at those with the vacant eyes. She tried to continue but found no words. At first her look was one of puzzlement as she made every effort to fit these images together. Then at once she understood, and when she did a great blanket of sadness came and fell over her and nearly crushed her with its weight. Its threads were heavy and made of the tears and the suffering of many, including those of the hollow-eyed people who lived in such conditions and who spent the days working this field. "How can this be?" she asked. "It is said that God has no favorites."

The tall and the thin man named Ned, seeing before him the destruction of the spirit, replied, "Child, I mean no disrespect to you or for what is said in your village, but it is not the God I am familiar with. There are those who have wealth and comfort and who own the rich lands and the buildings, and there are others who have come to know the greater pain and who can never escape from the massiveness of that misery. The only mercy bestowed upon them will be the mercy of a short life."

THE IRISH DAYS AND THE INNER VOICE

James, still on the road to personal discovery, cloaked himself in yet another ethnicity. The Irish days arrived. Not only did James assume the typical role of a North American Irish immigrant but also in the true fashion of what defines Irish, everything became a story. This singular fact could explain why he stayed Irish for so long. The lyrical textures of his voice combined with the pleasures of making meaning from these tales comforted him, much as a blanket gives security to a young child or a stone house provides protection from the raging storm.

The stories became allegories for James, each with a purpose and all perception and meaning were clothed in the soft tones of Gaelic ancestry. It was lunchtime again. He and Phil were conversing.

"We walked by the cliff, my father and I." The "a" became an "ah" and the "I" assumed an "oi" sound, and the Irish prevailed. "At first we stayed together hand in hand, but as the path narrowed we let go of each other and we walked in file, me three paces behind him. When he looked back, which was often, he would call his encouragements. 'Are ye keeping up, lad?' We were already half way up to the point, and you could still feel the salt in the air. Hundreds of feet high, yes hundreds of feet from the sea spray, yet some form of magic lifted the smells and penetrated the nostrils. Not like a knife, because a knife is an unwelcome intrusion, but like the aroma of a flower's scent which quietly invades and captures you in its wonderful essence. In such times, one is not unhappy being a prisoner. The gulls towered above us, sailed above us, their shrill cries telling only us about their place within the world and the timelessness of their pursuits. 'Are you all right, boy?' My father stopped and turned again. 'I'm good, dad. But how long, how far till we're there?'

"'Well, as I see it, when we wind along the upper path occasionally the sunlight will find its way through the trees and cloak us. We may set aside our immediate purpose and stop and enjoy some of these moments. Length and time then become two different elements. So I cannot tell you how long, only how far. It's a distance yet.'

"We walked and paused and resumed our trek. That was the pattern until we reached our destination. At the top it was as if we could see forever. And though there had been some before and likely many after, at that moment we were the first, my father and I. That was a great day."

Phil jumped in. "Good story, James, but as all things Irish, how much is of real substance?"

James, not leaving his Irish lilt even for a second, continued. "Everything happens, Phil, to you and to me and to everyone else, but the threads of magic in our memories make the meaning. That was a good day, and that good day just keeps getting better." He took a breath and gazed out for a bit. They both did. "I know you, Phil, and sure as the sun shines and the winds blow you, too, have memories where reality and perception appear to challenge each other."

For a while there was silence as both looked inward. Phil slowly and deliberately cracked his knuckles. Then he spoke: "It happened to me once. Every year the family packed up the car and made the trek to visit my grandparents." Irish is contagious and though there was no accent, he, too, became a storyteller. "I always looked forward to that time. They weren't rich, in fact exactly the opposite, but they had a small cottage by a lake, and that's where they chose to live out their lives. Tied up to the rickety old dock was a bright red rowboat. My grandfather with his ulcerated legs, and my grandmother after her stroke, were in no position to row a boat and never again would be. Yet every year when we arrived, the freshly painted boat was tied to the dock, waiting for my brother and I to get in and explore the wonderful world before us. Out we'd go safely attired, in our big old-fashioned pillow-like orange life jackets which were puffed out so far that it made it difficult to reach forward and bring the top of the oars back to our chests.

"We were anxious to rediscover the hidden bays and old sunken trees each of which had been given its own special name. 'Look out for Dead Man's Hook!' I would call as we approached a submerged tree, the one with five gnarled branches reaching toward the surface like a hand patiently waiting to trap an unwary explorer. 'Let's slip into Destiny Bay and get our bearings,' my brother advised. On a blistery afternoon, I remember swimming clear across the waters, my brother and I, our father in the boat, cheering us on the whole way. That night at dinner, laughing and smiling and sometimes slapping the tabletop, he recounted every stroke, every pause, right until our rubbery legs victoriously found lake bottom. That was our last visit together. My grandmother died before we could return, and my grandfather, needing to be less lonely, moved into an apartment near us.

"As it turned out I never went back that is, not until years later when a business trip brought me to an area fairly close by. For some reason, perhaps curiosity or sentimentality, I rented a car and drove into the hills and found the lake, but it was no lake at all, just a big pond. There were no large or hidden mysterious bays, and the distance between the north and south shores was certainly not worthy of my father's stories. I stood there for some time, quite astounded at what lay before me, and tried to reconcile my childhood memory with these waters. That memory had nothing to do with reality."

There was a breath of space where no words were spoken, and then the Irishman stepped forward once again.

"On the contrary, Phil, you have two memories. The first is every bit as real, every bit as valid, as the second. This is where reality and truth merge. When you were a boy, it was neither a lake nor a pond, but rather a wondrous world. It seems to me, as we grow older we lose our ability to make meaning from our experiences. Instead we are burdened with clinical and isolated observations. As our years advance, we become more preoccupied in a quest for purpose. In doing so we end up searching far and wide, when all we ever need to do is look within and reaffirm the magic of our own stories. I believe it is there where truth flourishes and destinies can be fully realized. Trust your inner voice, Phil. Trust your memories. The perimeter of the lake is not important."

MOTHERS

 Hope offered tea and bread and the fruits of the season. These had been prepared by the mother of Rose who was amazed and filled with inexpressible gratitude. To have this doctor come to her home to visit her Rose, her wonderful, gentle and kind daughter—that was truly something to thank the God for.

 Whenever a child is in pain, there is suffering, not only by the child but by all who know or come into contact with this being. Even a passerby, who does not have knowledge of this young soul and sees the misery, will be engulfed in huge sorrow. But the greatest pain of all resides with the mother. This cannot be explained. Mothers in the face of no earthly hope for their children pray for the miracle. The mother of Rose looked into the eyes of the doctor and saw the truth. She observed the tenderness by which each of the soothing strokes *was administered by this woman, and she knew. Yet she continued to pray.*

The translator, also a person of great heart, stood in the near darkness and watched these moments unfold. He saw the tormented, trapped, and beautiful spirit fighting the battle that could never be won. He witnessed the anguish of the mother, the sorrow of the doctor, and the desperate grief of Hope. In the dimly lit room, he was thankful for the gloom as it spared his eyes from some of what was before him. For years he had worked with the people of different languages and as their translator he understood the important words. Still, if someone on the street had stopped him and asked him to describe what he had just experienced it would not be possible for him to form a reply. He could only say that there is a young woman who has horrible pain, and a mother who knows and feels this hurt in all of its detail and a doctor who moves with tenderness, and a girl who is filled with love. But this would not in any way tell what needed to be said.

So this translator shared the darkness. Though he did not know Rose and had never witnessed her kindness nor heard her stories, he cried deeply for he knew what was before him was the greatest of losses.

Rose, with a damp cloth placed against her forehead ever so gently by Hope, listened to the words of this doctor and felt the presence of her mother and tried to reach out to reassure each. This was what Rose was. But all strength had forsaken her and it was not possible to move or even speak. She returned to her memories and once again found the walking time.

The tall and the thin man named Ned spoke. "There is a difficulty I am having. It has been with me for much distance."

The husband of Rose replied, "What is troubling you, my friend? We walked these many days together and together slept under the beautiful stars that shine over this vast earth. In the short time we have known you, you have become a brother. What is your burden?"

This conversation happened in the strength of the day. The sun's brilliance unmercifully assaulted them. As they could no longer choose their times to walk, they were forced to endure the attack. Generally energy was conserved in these periods and talking was kept to a minimum. Stopping here and there to sip from the containers which held the dirty waters, they moved forward in a perpetual state of near dehydration. They conquered more hills, and traversed much flatland before the tall and the thin man named Ned spoke.

"Have you thought about the staying? There are those who sleep where they can on the streets and huddle near the houses, but this is dangerous and is not to be advised. A badness is in this land, and even if you possess nothing some will kick you for the fun of the kicking. Others will do more. The houses, one or two rooms of mud and sticks, are owned by the few who rent to the many. For the privilege of living there they charge you beyond what you can pay. So others also move in but the spaces are not generous; there is much crowding. When I arrive, I will look for a place to take my bones and weariness and find people to help with the paying. I do not wish to hear of your affairs, yet I know of no other way to do the necessary learning. Since it is you who invited me to say

what needs to be said, I ask this. Do you have some money, and would you desire to use it to do the living with me?"

The husband of Rose spoke, but not before looking into the eyes of Rose to discover her thinking. "We are very poor and that is the reason for our going. Still, we have kept a small amount of money. We trust you as a brother and we will live as a family."

With the unknown comes a fear. This is a separate type of fright, quite distinct from those associated with life-threatening circumstance or the kinds of phobias which plague a person. Fear of the unknown is more properly thought of as an anxiousness, and human responses to anxiety can and do vary considerably. Much is dependent on temperament as this governs the perceptions of those involved in the discovery.

In the transition between not seeing and then seeing, between not knowing and then knowing, different approaches are possible. Some carefully register the details, taking specific inventory much as a warehouseman might when entering a vast storage area. Others see the parts but only in ways to help them understand the whole. It is said these are the ones whose lives move with feeling.

The eyes of Rose's husband shot side to side and up and down. This did not happen in a random fashion. Rather it was done with an intent and quickness which was uncannily efficient. While doing so, he and Rose walked slightly behind Ned. They did not allow themselves to be more than one and a half paces away as there was a sense of security in being close. Together these three followed a skinny short man who moved quickly, not as an antelope but as a rat, running and pausing, looking around and then scurrying some more.

The path before them was narrow and the thinness was broken into five parts. On each side rose mounds of discard. Filth of every description, human and otherwise, formed the contents, which were of things that either had absolutely no value or, worse, had acquired negative value. The piles were not here and there but existed as long snakes that came half way to the height of a man and whose length was equally impressive. Beside these snakes wound two dirt trails, the width of each being so restrictive as to require single person travel. If there was to be a passing, one had to balance on the back of the snake to allow for this. This needed to be done with care in order to avoid falling. A general understanding surfaced; each side would be reserved for those moving in opposite directions. As for the ditch, which claimed the middle, there was no describing the smell, and there was no relief from it. Sewage and the seepage from the snakes formed pools of oozing sludge. Beside the pathway stood a form of housing, structures made from whatever was available and stabilized in ingenious manners. Ropes, wire, and nails were used in these shanties which incorporated the obvious physics of things that lean into each other. That was some of what the husband of Rose saw.

Rose's vision, however, was of profound sadness. There was a giving up in this unhappiness, and the small birds that moved about on the snake of refuse provided no songs.

All walking abruptly ceased and the rat man pronounced, "This is it! This is your home, this is your palace! For as long as you pay the money, you will be the kings and queen of all you behold!" He gestured with a mock sweeping of one arm and smiled an awful smile, one which exposed a disease rotting out his gums. This had already claimed the majority of his teeth. Although it didn't, blood seemed to move freely from his eyes.

A makeshift door swung open and the three went in and stood in a single dark space. Their eyes worked feverously in order to make the required adjustments brought about by this movement from the brilliant white light of the outside to what was available in the cave-like atmosphere. A tiny glassless opening offered a small amount of relief from the gloom. This could not be viewed as a gateway to reverie as through it came an invasion of flies and foul smells. The entire space was two human lengths wide and three deep; the height required the tall and the thin man named Ned and the husband of Rose to stoop.

"What became of those who were here before?" Rose asked. The three turned to the rat man but he had already disappeared. No matter. Everyone knew.

BOATS

Time unfolded and, as is its habit, it unfolded differently. It would seem no apparent relationship exists between the duration of an event and the importance ultimately ascribed to it. In an instant, a life can change or the metamorphosis can be elongated, lending itself to detailed observation and subsequent documentation much as when a tadpole becomes a frog and the often-marveled transition of caterpillar to butterfly.

When it comes to the human species, any application of a time/change proportionality scale appears to be accidental. For James, outward changes continued to mirror staged progressions; internally this was a different matter. Insights built one on the other in almost indiscernible ways. The "eureka" story of Archimedes, soaking away the stresses and worries of his working day at the public bath, when he suddenly comprehended the relationship between mass, volume, density, and measurement held no parallel for James and his life. Those seeing James on a regular basis may not have appreciated his evolutionary nature. Even his best friend, Phil, and his wife, Melanie, would be hard pressed to discover the variances though by sense and feeling it might be understood. However, if others were to see him only after the elapse of lengthy periods, they could identify these changes, much as one can say this is the same world and the same location within the world, but this is summer and that is winter.

"Look at those gulls!" James spent a good twenty minutes in quiet observation, watching them soar and glide with seeming effortlessness, their white bodies made even more impressive under the brilliant sun and the backdrop of a clear blue sky.

Melanie, lying motionless and bathing under the radiance, glanced upwardly and saw them, but not as James had. "Nice," she said and shut her eyes in efforts to return to her own form of release.

The all-inclusive cruise proved to be just that. Everything which could be provided was provided. The shipping company's slogan, "Eliminate decisions, eliminate tensions", was accurate. Technically decisions still needed to be made, but nothing that significantly impacted a life. Would one partake in the endless smorgasbords or would it be à la carte? Which port tour to take? Which coffee location to occupy?

Initially tension was applied to these choices. They were worried over as if they held an equal importance to those made at home and at work. But as the days drifted, the energies used to make such decisions diminished. James continued to watch the gulls while Melanie soaked in the rays of the warm sun. Both had arrived intent on reading the books and articles they had meant to consume earlier, and were it not for daily demands or the excuses of having them, they would have. On occasion they looked up from their deck chairs to see the distant shorelines and the ever-present azure blue sea, and to confirm the existence of paradise and their place within it. This was to be their life for two weeks, not including the travel days on either end.

Tonight's menu included beef bourguignon, one of James' favorites, but how could one refuse the Dungeness crab? If done correctly, and heretofore nothing had led James to believe it wouldn't be, the dish would be worthy of consideration.

Such were these boat days. He chose to live them in the sun for as long as his aging body allowed. His tolerance of the near star had diminished since his youth and, of course, he needed to consider the cancer connection and the nagging ozone thing. Apparently there actually is a hole in the sky where none used to be. The environment had become one of the dominant stories. Global warming added to his concerns.

In his more lucid moments, James read. Initially he chose from the analytical and descriptive articles he brought, but he strayed, choosing from the fiction best seller lists, the favorites of the multitudes—tonic for an overtaxed mind. James finished a few more pages, put down the book, showered, formally dressed, and ate the crab. It proved to be excellent, though he couldn't help but wonder about the beef bourguignon

Despite everything, James' mind was not successful in its efforts to discover true rest. His already intense search was magnified. The process resulted in immediate dividends, as insights began to present themselves and the relationships between ideas started to become apparent. The picture gained clarity, or at least it became clear there was, in fact, a picture. He returned to his stateroom for a short nap, but instead of sleeping, he began to think. The first thing his mind focused on was reading. There was no tangible reason why this was so, it just happened that way. It might have been because the stack of books and articles on the side table drew him in that direction, but that would be speculative. Perhaps he was influenced by a greater force or directed internally.

"There are only so many stories," he mused. "In the important literature, characters are often dysfunctional yet captivating, each on a voyage of self-discovery, each struggling to overcome something, and each moving inexorably forward to gain a measure of personal insight. Most of these stories end prosaically, almost poetically. They are designed so the reader will stop, put the book down, and marvel at the beauty of a simple truth." James thought about this and he found the notion interesting. His mind continued to move in unpredictable ways.

'Interesting,' James thought, has numerous interpretations. One can say the pink and yellow room is interesting. It means the combination of colors is unusual, perhaps disquieting. Mathematical formulas are interesting to mathematicians and some scientists, but are passed over by many others. Sports-cars are interesting to sports car enthusiasts. The lives of actors and actresses are interesting. The proof of this lies with the lucrative sales of entertainment magazines. Collectors find things interesting: paintings, books, butterflies, spoons, coins, stamps, sports cards, china, antiques ... the list seems limited only by the number of items in the world, though a collection of bacteria or fungus might be stretching that thought. Interesting applies to the unknown. The quest to discover cures to the host of debilitating and terminal illnesses is of interest and, by extension, interesting. It is a word used to describe a name, picture, story, tattoo, conclusion, cloud formation, flower, insect, dress, hairstyle, problem, idea. The application of this adjective is without parameters and this fact, in itself, is interesting. But specifically, what is interesting to James? Such was his stream of consciousness as he lay in his lower-deck stateroom staring at the ceiling. He burped. Efforts at digestion were continuous and uncomfortable.

It was interesting to James that people could be happy talking about the so-called smaller things. He had not mastered the art of conversation; he got by at functions but it didn't come naturally. For James, discourse required serious exchange. Sometimes, while in restaurants, he would overhear others. Unless he was fully involved with his meal or own discussion or consumed in an introspective way, it could not be avoided. After all, people in these places are often seated less than an arms-length away. As he discovered, for some, words simply flowed. There was comfort in the language which somehow reflected contentment with life.

"This is good blueberry pie," she said.

"Uh huh," her partner offered back. "Reminds me of the time when we did the U-pick thing. Remember that?"

"Boy, do I," she smiled. "Do you think Jolene could have gotten any bluer? We picked two buckets full and I'm sure at the weigh-in the lady at the scales considered charging us for a third. She stared at Jolene the whole time."

They both laughed, and James had thought it was over. They would move to more meaningful, thoughtful discussions or drift into individual worlds. Neither happened. She picked up the pepper shaker. James was half convinced she was going to pepper the pie.

"Remember when we ate at the Red Dog? Every table had a different shakers—cows, ducks, goats, pigs, frogs, and sheep. The pigs were good. I liked the pigs."

"My favorites were the tree frogs. They had those weird looking yellow toes and huge bulging eyes." His eyes widened in some humorous effort to mimic the look.

Effortlessly they moved to the next subject and then another, all the while stuffing themselves with pie and whipped cream. They laughed, paid the bill and left.

"Interesting," James mused as he recalled this time.

Work interested James. Even after many years, water flows and the application of technologies still held their appeal. This was good because it consumed a large piece of his life. Diverse cultures interested him. He found politics interesting; bizarre, but in some perverse manner, interesting. The fact great disparities existed between the rich and the poor captured his interest. He recently read an article on Arctic pollution and how the toxins produced in the industrialized world were layering the north. This was of concern and, therefore, interesting. In a similar vein he thought it interesting that deforestation in the Amazon climatically affected Africa.

Unpredictably, his list took on an elongated form and he spoke out loud as if the room was a listener. "It is interesting how varied, yet interdependent, the life force on earth is. It is interesting that in the face of overwhelming evidence there are those who continue to ignore this. It is interesting how, for some, personal happiness may never be truly achieved while there is knowledge of another's needless pain."

James saw the darkening seas, the crystal twilight, and if a person was able to discern beyond that, he did. He found the place where vision moves so far away it leads to a space within. How this is achieved cannot be explained. Even references made in wizardry and witchcraft or the projections of quantum physicists are not able to accomplish this. At last, James was beginning to understand some things about this world and his place within it.

The air conditioning hummed. Someone could be heard walking down the hallway. Digestion continued.

CONFIRMATION

"It is as if they walk without hearts. All their spirits are submerged in the gloom and broken in ways that allow for no repair." Rose spoke to her husband as they moved through the maze and across the unmarked borders which unmistakably defined the city limits and the beginnings of their living place.

In the times before the sun came, they did this walk and waited in lines and in groups in the hope someone would say to the husband of Rose, "It is you and your strong back that is needed. If you work hard you will earn enough to live for both today and tomorrow, and perhaps the next one." Rose also waited. Maybe she would be asked to run an errand or look after the boss's children or the wants of the boss's woman, or when many people are needed, fill the role of a man and lift the heavy loads.

In Search of Sticks

The husband of Rose knew nothing of damaged souls, but in his journeys he never failed to take stock of what was around him. As was his habit, he counted. He counted those with the distended stomachs, others with the running sores, and the people who stood in the doorway and stared into the light yet lived in the shadows. He counted the beggars who asked for the money, their bodies and minds having long forsaken them.

"Oh, brother, do you not recognize me? How is it you can walk by?"

"Are you not a son? Will you not pity a father?"

"I have three children and a fourth is coming soon. There is no food." He counted and he heard but he could not give.

And he counted those in the corners who beckoned him to make a purchase, offering what was left of themselves or selling different forms of escape.

When Rose ventured out by herself, which was not often due to the danger, it would be said that such beauty commands an excellent price.

This was the way of the life, and Rose got lonely wishing for her family and for her friends. She became sick at heart. The husband of Rose took from the small amount of the savings and went out into the nights to drink and to forget. This frightened Rose, and when she told him of this fear, he yelled; and in the yelling there was huge emotion and he hit her, not with one blow but with many. Rose crawled into the corner taking her aching and bleeding with her. She cried, but she did not do this loudly, instinctively understanding that the noise might serve to further enflame his wrath.

After there was no more hitting left in him, the husband of Rose didn't know what to do. He did not have any previous knowledge of such a person and this shocked him, so, once again, he took from the small savings and went out to buy more drink.

The tall and the thin man named Ned, who lived with them, came back. He was a knowing man and did the difficult calculations, and he worked into the evening for the businesses. This was done before he left and it is what waited for him on return.

He found Rose in the corner, curled up and spent as a small desperate child, huddled and afraid in the darkness. This kind man lit a single candle and helped her up and sat her in the one chair, and with the water he saved for drinking he cleaned her wounds as best as he could. There had been cuts around an eye and her mouth and there was much bruising.

"Why is it that I have been treated in this way?" she asked, her blackened and swollen eyes searching.

"It is not what you have done, child; this is the anger of desperation and it builds in many who come."

Rose spoke the words which were in her heart. "There is much to be afraid of. I have been told of the dangers to those who would roam in the darkness of a warm evening. I have heard the screams in the night and in the day. What has caused some to bring such hurt?"

The tall and the thin man named Ned looked at her and then away and shook his head. "I have tried to think of this myself, and I do not truly know. But I believe it is one of the last desperate acts of being alive. When all the laughter and the love has been lost, what else is there to do but to affirm and embrace the misery? In a strange and twisted way it provides confirmation that the heart still beats."

MOUNTAINS AND DESERTS

There is an old saying: "look to the past to understand the future." History is a teacher, and when considered in its true context, the statement is fundamentally valid. Successful application of the concept not only requires comprehension of the major forces which governed societies and their populations, but also an understanding and appreciation of the subtle pressures. Not many have accomplished this. For most, this kind of knowledge is made up of a rather disjointed and superficial delineation of dates, dynasties, and the names of their kings, queens, generals and religious figures, and then only as they existed in selected geographies. It would seem that true history lesson learners are few and far between.

However, some narrowed the task by dissecting a single and continuous strand, one which links earlier civilizations to contemporary events—leadership. Irrespective of time and place, leaders existed, do exist and, by extension, will exist. Whether they are made or are simply born is a subject for continuous debate. The personal qualities that define them captivate many.

It is said good leaders are visionary, constructive, wise, reliable, sensitive, confident, humorous, flexible, dedicated, humble, resilient, tough, assertive, balanced, focused, efficient, charismatic, controlling, imaginative, creative, innovative, responsible, empowering, interpersonal and proactive. They listen. While every one of these characteristics may not be exhibited, one thing is clear, great leaders are articulate. "Four score and seven years ago," "I have a dream," "Lend me your ears," "We shall fight on the beaches, we shall fight on the landing grounds, we shall fight in the fields and in the streets, we shall fight in the hills; we shall never surrender."

"Claire is in the hospital with appendicitis; she had an emergency operation." William Sanchez, cell phone in his left hand, whirled his long skinny right arm in some kind of wild erratic windmill action, one of several outward signs of panic. Other indicators included his totally flushed face and bulging eyes that refused to settle into their sockets. Through no fault of her own, the President of the Society for Human Justice would be a no-show. "You've got to go on James, right after this guy finishes! It's our turn!" William waved a paper in front of James' face. On it were listed the speakers and the order in which they were to appear.

"Jenny can do it. She's out there somewhere, but I can't find her," William said. For a split second both stared into the crowd hoping the girl with the lip ring and tattoos would make an appearance. No such luck.

"I'd just go blank and end up looking at everyone." William again swept an arm outward towards the several thousand people who were milling about on the lawn. Some focused on the current speaker while happily socializing, sitting on their blankets with their picnics. Banners of different sorts announced the various causes and fluttered and snapped in the stiff breeze. "You're it, James. No one else can do this."

James stared at William Sanchez, absolutely astounded at what he was hearing. "Are you kidding me? I can't do that!"

William's balding head, which hitherto had been bobbing wildly on his stick of a neck, suddenly was still. His dark eyes became quiet. "Yes you can, James."

"No way! No way!" James emphatically shook his head.

"You can, James, and you will. You've seen a few of these; you get how this works. We need you." Williams' steady, high voice took direct aim and pierced the skull.

In Search of Sticks

"How do you know?" James furled his eyebrows. Two deep vertical lines creased the space between them. He repeated, this time in a whisper, "How do you know?"

William Sanchez looked at him with his newly acquired eerie calmness and confidently affirmed, "I just do."

Less-than-enthusiastic applause followed the last speaker. It was of the polite variety. Thirty seconds later, James gained the platform, adjusted the microphone, and without any opportunity to gather his thoughts, began to speak: "I have climbed mountains."

Each amplified word, every syllable, was projected in such a manner as to demand attention. Techniques were not applied purposely; pause and emphasis progressed in a natural way. People stopped in mid-sentence and in mid-chew. Not knowing why, they began to listen. Though babies still cried and children continued to play, a strange and unexpected quiet took hold.

"Yes, I have climbed mountains, every step a journey. I lifted my foot and carefully planted it down, and in the rarified heights, considered the gain. I traversed gorged rivers and angry lakes, and with huge thirst I crossed over and survived the unforgiving deserts. I read of others who have embarked on much greater treks, across vast tundra, over the turbulent oceans and through the dense and dangerous jungles. One, on a single leg, set forward to run the length of a huge nation, and another whose legs did not work as legs any longer circumnavigated this world." James looked around. This was not the speech he had planned; they were not the words and phrases he had carefully crafted while speaking to Melanie at the kitchen table. They flowed from an undiscovered source. He saw the people who were spread across the lawn and though it was evident they had focused on him, he wasn't nervous. There was no anxiousness. He continued.

"Those journeys were difficult; the challenges that presented themselves were numerous and daunting. Enormous strength of both body and spirit was required in such times. Just when it seemed exhaustion would be victorious, each reached deep into the well of their soul to discover new, unexplained energies. Yes, there have been some incredible undertakings which taxed the totality of one's being; many are documented in the annals of history and legend. But there is a journey that lies ahead and it will not have the ease of an excursion by a meandering river and lush valley bottom and the scenery will not be magnificent. It will be a time of indescribable hardship. The fatigue that will be experienced will eclipse all forms of tiredness. The images that will be engraved into the minds of those who choose this expedition will result in personal disturbances which can never be escaped." James locked on to the people littered over the field of grass.

Someone shouted, "Amen, brother."

"Walk with me in these moments of vision, in this time for action. Hold my hand." James put out his left hand and as he did so he seemed to touch the fingers and palms of all who reached out, both those in body and in heart.

"Look carefully. Can you see us now? We are walking on the shoreline of the blood ocean and we are not stepping on stones. They are the bones of those who died for diamonds, of those who died for poppies, of those who have been sacrificed for ideological or religious excuse. They are the bones of those who dreamed of justice and succumbed to the violence of a society in neglect." James took a deep breath. He inhaled again. Everyone was still in his grip.

"If you wish to continue, I will take you to the river of tears. Steel yourself; these times will be demanding. The tears are from people who left us in terrible ways and whose faces are now mirrored in the flat calm of the blood ocean, and they have fallen from others who live in the depth of emptiness that is left behind. They have been shed for some who are disfigured and for others whose lives are shortened by terrible disease and by the parents because their children have no food. They are the tears of despair, erupting from eyes that have seen the emptiness of a black heart. As we walk together, you will shudder uncontrollably and your tears will add to the already raging waters.

Yes, we have, in our own way, all climbed mountains; we traversed gorged rivers and angry lakes and survived unforgiving deserts. But do not rejoice in these small victories, for what lies ahead will be incredibly more difficult.

On this journey we will not be sightseers. We will reach forward. We will stem the flow of blood. We will right the wrongs. We will dry the tears. We will fill the hearts." James looked out—for many seconds, for an eternity. "In the days and months ahead, let us do this together." Once more he reached towards the listeners, this time using both hands.

A spontaneous round of applause erupted and filled all spaces. People shouted; they whistled. James stood still, not knowing what to do.

A rotund individual came to the rescue; he took the microphone. "Ladies and gentlemen, let's hear it again for James A. Terrance from the Society for Human Justice! And, yes—I believe many of us are ready to walk with you." More continuous clapping, whistling and cheering followed. James, humbled and embarrassed, acknowledged the crowd with a slight wave and descended from the stage. The speech of Mountains and Deserts had been concluded. Legend would take care of the rest.

"James! Listen! You're a hit!" William Sanchez' immense wings enveloped James and he planted a kiss on the middle of his forehead. "Where have you been hiding?"

Before James could consider a response, people were gathering around, slapping his shoulder, and shaking his hand.

"Bravo! See you at the next meeting."

"Wow, you truly touched my heart."

"I can't begin to tell you what this meant to me."

Many others speakers followed, their comments lost to James in the general frenzy of words and touch. For James the rest of the day took the form of a dream, the kind that you know is a dream but just as sure as you know you're having it you also understand that when you do wake up you won't remember much, if anything at all. Speaker after speaker said what they thought needed to be said and the afternoon transitioned into early evening. It got a little chillier, picnic provisions were low on choices, kids became rattier, babies more demanding. People began to filter away, returning to their lives.

Still in a fog, James also found his way home, kissed Melanie, poured himself a glass of wine, and sat in front of the television. He turned it on and to his surprise there he was delivering his speech. He made the local news. Leadership was evolving; preparations for judgment day continued.

Randy Kaneen

ENDURANCE

Death came quickly but not beautifully. Sweats arrived; diarrhea and vomiting followed in rapid succession. Eyes sunk deep and disappeared into their sockets, and cold blanketed the skin and yellowness was painted on it. There was a thirst that could not be quenched and the voice abandoned certain abilities.

It came to the family who lived across the snake of refuse, to the husband and wife in the home with the red door, to two of the three children who played up the way, to the old man beside her and to many others. Bodies were wrapped and carried and thrown away. This was somebody's job. She had seen this too often and smelled its presence and heard the moans, the painful silence, and the cries of absolute despair. Such is the legacy that comes with the unclean waters. With these immense sorrows surrounding Rose, she continued to remember.

ഏഏഏ

The sun was hot. Almost every day it shone. Some of the times were hotter than others, but by anyone's definition it was always hot. The only shade available was provided by the unsteady walls of the falling down homes. There were no covered porches and no trees.

The act of living required unfathomable endurance. It was not the marathon, a race to exhaustion and then recovery. Personal bests were not recorded in this arduous journey and unless you count death, there was no finish line.

When work was not obtained, the only thing left to do was squat in the shadows and fight off the flies and the smells—battles that could never be won. This was almost every day—not once in a while, not on alternate weekends. It was every single minute of each day when employment could not be discovered, which meant this was most of the time.

On one sorrowful day, someone had broken into Rose's place and taken things, and in the hurry, the thief did not think, "This is of value and can fetch a price so I will steal it but this is not and will be left." In a small box that was stolen were the few photographs Rose had of her family. Rose endured the scorching heat and while doing this spent much of her time remembering.

"I am having difficulty with the detail. I dream of the face and with my hand I reach out and gently stroke the side. This is done in ways which do not surprise the face; I do not want it to disappear. I am desperate for it to stay. I feel each

of the creases the years have brought, and I touch the moisture of the eyes that cried during my leaving. But I do not see the face. Every night I try and have done this in many ways. I even pretended to go and then suddenly move in front but the face is always knowing and turned quickly and just enough so my eyes were not able to do the looking. I cannot remember her face." She spoke to the one who sat beside her. *"How is it I cannot remember her face?"*

Even though Rose had experienced hunger and immense sorrow and had seen things which challenged the nature of her heart and had cried deeply in some of these moments, there were still waters left within. Nearly imperceptible crystals formed in the corners of her eyes. She swiftly wiped them away as if ashamed this small thing brought forward such emotion. Her mother had been wonderful and loving; that was important. Remembering her face should not matter.

The listening woman sorted through her own splintered images before she spoke. "It is a trick of life. Everything on this earth continues to shift, even the memories."

Together they crouched on the dirt and shared the shadow. They were among the many that spent much of each day sitting and looking out. Some saw the children playing on the garbage; some saw hitting; some saw tears. There were those with eyes wide open who looked within. Others, affected by the drugs of false deliverance, sat and searched in a different way.

No schools had been built. Children cluttered the pathways and took refuge in corners. Many roamed in large groups. The youngest played in the ditches and on the snakes

In Search of Sticks

of refuse. Soon they would tire of such games and join with the others who were differently occupied. Rose felt the misery in all she passed and in those who passed her. She was affected the most by the torment of the children. Their coughs resonated in her soul and many coughed. Rashes and boils and other diseases owned pieces of their bodies and their skin was often like sandpaper. A boy walked by, much less than a man but more than a child. Rose did not know the boy, but in her travels she had negotiated many of the pathways and while doing so she watched and listened. Though she did not know the boy's name, she knew the story of the boy.

There was reluctance in his entrance to the earth. The arrival came slowly and the mother experienced much pain. A neighbor, remembering how this had been done for her brothers and sisters, assisted and then tied the cord. The snake of refuse consumed the bloodied afterbirth and the baby cried the small helpless sounds newborns make. He was brought to his mother's breast.

The fact he survived was a miracle and his continued breathing stood as a testimony to the extraordinary sense which accompanied his living. For the first few years he stayed with the mother. If she went down the path, he was carried; if she visited, he sat; and if his mother spread the blanket and tried to sell the small things she had made, he would be with her. This was his life. There were days of eating and of little or no food, and this too was part of his experience and he did not complain. The father left in the morning and came back at the night. Sometimes he returned as a father and sometimes as a frightening stranger.

The mother got sick and had many sores and coughed and became slight and weak. One evening her breathing stopped. The father quit coming, and a person entered the house, let some others in, took the boy out and told him not to come back. He was in his fifth year on this earth.

He went to the neighbor, who had been at his birth, but there was hunger and she was not well, and he was not let in. He walked the streets and consumed what he could find from the snakes of refuse, and curled in a corner and slept. This he did for much time, but he learned how to take from the cooking of someone's meal and run rapidly while moving in ways to make it difficult for the following. He discovered the way to ask in just the right sorrowful manner so people might give a small part of what they had.

Though he drank from the bad waters, he did not get the illness of thirst and dying. However, he was bitten by mosquitoes, some which brought the disease of cold and fever and shivering and often, of death. Earlier he had known one who, as himself, lived on the path but had not managed an escape. When the great shaking came to the boy, he found a corner and curled up for many days and nights where he shuddered and sweated and vomited. He felt he would die, but he did not. The story of the boy's endurance and the miracle of the breathing continued.

The boy wandered. He moved as a stray dog might, looking for any opening to steal whatever was carelessly left unguarded. During this endless walking he was found. Fifteen or twenty boys, some close to being men, passed, and for no reason, one pushed this small boy and quickly others did the same. They shoved him as a stuffed toy from person to person, and just when the hitting began, a voice commanded it to stop and before another blow landed, it ceased.

"Where is your family?" the voice said.

The boy replied, "My mother is dead and I do not know if my father still has the life."

The voice then spoke. "Where is it that you stay?"

The boy answered, "Wherever there is not the hitting or the chasing."

"How is it that you live?"

"I take from the people what I can and when I can."

And the voice grew a smile. "You will come with us and live in our large room. We do not pay the money to the owner but in turn we make sure people do not do the same for his other homes. We will teach you."

The boy who had lost his family had another.

He had much knowledge to acquire and he learned quickly. But these were not the lessons of a school. There was not any discovery about the making of letters and numbers or memorizing the names of the people of the government. There was no singing of songs. There were, however, many other important things to know, and in his way, the boy became a scholar.

He learned how to distract those who sold the goods so his newly discovered older brothers could fill their pockets and move away to be lost in the crowd. When one of these brothers was chased, stripped, and beaten so he could no longer be recognized as a brother, he learned that he never wanted to be caught. He came to understand about obedience and loyalty. He learned to be part of the pack and how to surround the prey, and to yell and scream and be excited at the smell of blood or the sight of another's pain. He learned life is dull and that things which broke up the tedium and provided escapes were to be welcomed.

The boy became familiar with sex and he found out about the sniffing of glue. He drank alcohol, but it required money and sometimes made him sick.

Rose saw this boy and others who walked by and she knew all about their lives. She was also familiar with those of the passing girls. Their stories were much the same as the boys, only worse. The girls were not as strong. Sex became important for them. It gave change to the day but it was also used as a gift and in return they received protection. Some of them had lightning speed and could steal and be gone in a flash. In this way, they brought back to the family. Others, even very young girls, found favorite places and sold themselves. What was earned was given to the head of their new family. This was the rule and it was not to be broken.

Rose and her neighbor sat in the shadows, escaping what they could of the heat and smells. Neither was certain of the whereabouts of their husbands. Perhaps they were looking for work, or they had given up and were doing the drinking and gambling. There was always the temptation of the women who stood in the doorways. No one had eaten that day, and Rose could not remember her mother's face. My God, the sun was hot.

STRATEGY

"Hey, James, nice speech!"
"James my boy, you sure did us proud."
"I gotta tell you that rocked!"

He arrived, hailed by many as he made his entrance, if not as a conquering hero then at least in heroic fashion. The monthly meeting of the Society for Human Justice was about to start and attendance was up, probably quadruple the average; this necessitated the retrieval of several stacks of metal chairs stored in a closet.

The speech of "Mountains and Deserts," though weeks old, was still not without effect. Talking continued. Regular agenda items were quickly dispensed with so they could get to the main order of business—that being James, his speech, and his stated intent to lead anyone who wished to follow on the road to the Promised Land. Many, in the metaphorical sense, had already packed their bags. Everything seemed electric. The air was filled with expectation and each atmospheric molecule contributed to a tension associated with this emotion.

James spent sleepless nights thinking. He had made the news; he had been interviewed. People talked to him at work and even some whom he had never met stopped him on the street to earnestly discuss ideas. Words of encouragement were accompanied by inferences of expectation. Throughout this time Melanie's remembered caution resonated in his head. "It can destroy you. I'm asking you, James, to be careful." She remained vigilant, watching and listening, examining his every move, checking for signs.

In earlier days James had thought it would be only a matter of letting people know about the reality, just as if he was at work constructing one of his analytical water flow reports. All that was required was a convincing and thorough document, one which detailed the extent of the issues and provided sensible solutions. Some might refer to these as 'innocent' times, while those less generous could ascribe the term 'naïve' to the era. After all, James was not the first to pick up a pen and formulate his thoughts into words. Letters, authored by different people, had been written. Speeches had been made. Many speeches from

In Search of Sticks

many people had been delivered, but real change had not been.

Last week, James, troubled and unable to sleep, found himself gazing out his living room window to the metropolis which stretched out before him. Streets lights formed near-uniform grids and within those spaces a myriad of houses and buildings sparkled. His left hand held a cup of decaffeinated coffee. Depending on perspective, it was either very late or very early. Though his body was weary, his mind refused to acknowledge this fatigue and continued its relentless pursuit.

"There will be resistors," he thought. "They might walk by on the sidewalk; perhaps sit near me while I'm having lunch. When I drive, they will be on the road, both following and passing. How can we recognize them? Sides are not easily distinguished; there are no uniforms."

It became clear to James that in volunteering to lead he was taking others into a form of conflict. The speech of "Mountains and Deserts" was nothing short of a battle cry. War had been declared and though weapons of mass, medium, or single life destruction would not be accessed, there would be causalities.

A general needs to understand and appreciate tactical choice. The element of surprise is favored by many. Just when one is convinced something isn't going to happen, it does. The speed of its arrival is meant to frighten and overwhelm. For the proponents, the result is never in doubt. Some leaders advocate offense at any cost. There are those who promote complicated plans, while others look to simplicity. Maneuverability is desired and, when available, can be used to advantage. Good generals are aware of the terrain; they understand the psychology of battle and the building of and the breaking of morale.

Much needs to be considered while commanding on the field. James had volunteered to lead and people wanted to follow. But what kind of leader would he be? Time, as in all things, would reveal its secrets.

"Now, ladies and gentlemen, hold on tight for the second part of our meeting—the person we have been dying to hear from, ever since he made the speech of 'Mountains and Desserts.' It is my distinct pleasure to introduce someone who no longer needs any introduction—James Terrance." Claire, the president of the Society for Human Justice, was speaking.

It is said "when one star rises, another falls." Perhaps this is an illusion. Maybe it doesn't fall at all. Maybe it's just that with an additional luminary emergence there is the perception the brightness has waned. Claire was committed and remained strong. No discernible signs of jealously were evident. Her appendix had been removed and with the intervention of fate, James had made the speech of 'Mountains and Deserts.' Wishing this had been different would not change things. She smiled openly so all could see and applauded as loudly and as long as the others.

He came to the front and once again words flowed with confidence and conviction. "We are peaceful people, but from this moment forward you will become warriors. An enemy is out there and it has certain controls which are not easily relinquished. We have treated them with kindness and have negotiated with them. In doing so we reached out and searched for common ground. All possible ways to make progress were tried. But what is there to show for these efforts?

"Unfortunately the nature of our successes can, in relative terms, be compared to the size of the smallest particles of matter known in the universe. They are beyond theory, but for most people, they are so minute that their existence is still a question of trust." James stopped, picked up his stainless steel mug, and for more than a few seconds studied it. Without taking a drink, he set it back down. His eyes became clear and pierced the air. He spoke calmly and directly, but not quietly.

"We need a new strategy. We will not carry weapons but we will attack. We will be the soldiers of knowing, of reason, of compassion, and we will be relentless. We will be the most feared army this world has ever known." James once again picked up his mug and this time did partake of the liquid. He continued.

"I have come to realize some deliberately confuse issues for personal gain. They subvert the truth.

But we will wave truth as we would a flag, and be a force to be reckoned with. The people will see this Flag of Truth and it will become their flag, and their loyalties will be to the truth. It will fly in front yards and on balconies and, indeed, in all the winds of this world. This revolution will be universal, and it will be final." His voice resonated with huge strength. For emphasis, the flat of his right hand came down as if to hit the table before him but stopped short of impact.

It was too much for the audience; they rose to their feet, breaking out into a round of spontaneous clapping and cheering. James looked outward and humbly let the applause take its course. Then he put his hand up as if to say, 'I am not finished'. People returned to their chairs. "Yes, we will tell the tales of inequity, but what truths will be told? How shall they be presented? Who will we inform?" The intensity that was a part of his delivery abated. "We need to talk. Bring your ideas to the council. Present them with clarity and with the passion that is building within you. Next week, when the executive members meet, the process will begin. We may discover the pathway to our own salvation."

At that point he nodded to Claire who on cue bent down to pick up a pole with cloth wrapped around the upper third. Together they unfurled a large rectangular flag: a green triangle at the bottom, a gold one at the top, bisected by a wide band of white. There was a collective intake of breath. James announced, "Ladies and gentlemen, I give you the Flag of Truth." Then came the inevitable and audible release. "Within the embodiment of a flag are at once the small deeds and the universal visions. A flag represents values, and serves as the rallying point for ideals; it provides a focus for belief and gives a sense of belonging. While watching it snap in the stiff breeze, one can be captured within its embodiment. Flags are far more than pieces of decorated cloth. In our flag, the Flag of Truth, each part symbolizes things that are important in human society. The green area concerns itself with education and health. The gold is poverty and holds the hollow and desperate faces of all those who truly do not have enough. And the band of white is you and I. This is the leadership—dedicated people who will focus these concerns."

Everyone jumped up and applauded, whistled and shouted and in doing so annihilated the decibel level of the previous outburst. If they had an anthem, it would have been sung.

The details about how the meeting ended are not clearly recalled, but it did somehow conclude. It is remembered that people moved to the Flag of Truth. They talked excitedly to James and to one another and there was an extreme reluctance to leave. The speech of the "Flag of Truth" took its place in the annals of history.

A RETURNING

    Sitting in a chair while selectively and quietly reflecting on one's life and its purpose, can lead to meditative peace.
    But the retrieval of the past knows different roads. When the continuation of an existence hangs in the balance such as in a near drowning or a head-on crash, it is said life flashes before one's eyes. These flashpoints are formed from those memories laced with the most meaning and do not necessarily present themselves chronologically. However, when the end is predicted and the pain and the sadness build inexorably to an inevitable conclusion, the process for review is almost always more orderly, deliberate, and detailed. Peace is not guaranteed.
    The wind blew in from the east, and it came as no wind had ever come before. It arrived in surging anger and in outrage, and its piercing screams announced a destructive

intention. Almost all living creatures cowered and those who could form prayer did so delivering constant supplications: "Please God, let the roof and the walls hold." "Please God, save me from this wrath." "Please God, spare my children." "Please God." Hope, and the mother and the father of Rose did not fall on their knees. Though they could feel its presence and hear the assaulting voice, they were not afraid of this wind. No greater pain existed than that which was before them. They continued to apply the damp cloth and hold the hand and direct a singular prayer. Though Rose was in the last of her times, she still remembered.

As it had done to many others before her, an enormous tiredness visited Rose and her skin bore the marks of an invasion. She tried to hide this but it was not possible to do so. First, no longer able to get the work and then no longer able to do it, she lay on an old blanket on the dirt floor. She shivered and she waited. The husband of Rose, who had succumbed both to the drink and to the women in the doorways, understood the grief he had brought, and taking from the memories of who he once was, he sought out the last of the savings and with this bought food and water and carried them to the house. While Rose slept, he held her hand and tears flowed. He cried for his own weaknesses and for the immense sorrow which enveloped his wife, and for the script that had been written foretelling the story of his doom. He kissed her forehead, caressed her face, and left for the final time.

The tall and the thin man, returning in the darkness of the evening, found these gifts, and at once understood. He knelt by this young woman and gave her some of the water and told her all of what must have happened. "The time for the returning has come," he said.

And Rose, feeling the leaving of her husband and the failure of her life, wept freely. Through these tears she replied, "It is my wish to once again see and touch the face of she who bore me, but I have made this journey and it is long and difficult. I fear there is not enough energy left in this body to take the steps needed for the going back."

The tall and the thin man reached forward and drawing from an immense depth spoke, "I will tell you this, and just as you know that there is a harmony between the sun and the moon and the Earth is their grateful child, you also know that I am a truthful being. Your body will not be picked up and taken uncaringly away by those who are paid to do the disposing. You will once again view your mother and your father and your cousin Hope of whom you have said much. As I know them through your stories, they will reach out to you and touch you, and with the greatest of tenderness, and with the most profound form of love, guide you to your own peace."

Rose raised her head and looked at the tall and the thin man named Ned and spoke, "I cannot do this; I do not have the strength of a broken bird."

To which he replied in measured words, "Do not worry my innocent one, my wonderful friend. I have thought of this and arrived at a plan."

In the days that followed, he talked to the people of the businesses and told them of his need to be gone for a time. Each in turn allowed for this, not willingly, and not happily, but this was a knowing man and his skills would be required on return.

In Search of Sticks

The tall and the thin man named Ned then took from his money and bought an ancient wheelbarrow. Wooden handles joined to rickety wooden sides. Wooden spokes attached themselves to a wooden wheel around which on the outside was hammered flattened tin, salvaged from old cans; someone's effort to provide more durability. The tall and the thin man judged it to be generally sturdy, and so he made the purchase. He returned with it on a late afternoon and put in blankets and the food and the water that had been left by the husband of Rose and he added to this.

In an early hour of darkness, he told Rose of his plan and asked that she lay in the wheelbarrow. But Rose would not agree and said, "I will walk from here. This place shall not detect my weakness. It will be deprived of seeing the victory of killing yet another spirit."

So the tall and the thin man pushed the wheelbarrow behind the erect, stately woman and under the light from the first piece of the moon they negotiated their way past the snakes of refuse. Once having found themselves beyond the city and its festering surroundings, Rose, with the help of this kind man, lay herself down into the wheelbarrow. She was exhausted. Though it was warm outside, a blanket was wrapped around her and this provided a form of comfort. For a time she fell asleep and mercifully, for a time, she left this world.

At the beginning the ribbon of pavement was relatively smooth and this fact made the going less painful, particularly for Rose. The tall and the thin man did not do the lifting for the work, and he did not possess the great strength nor did he have the thick layers of yellowed skin on his palms. His hands began to bleed. These he wrapped with cloth. An aching came to his back and arms, and he did his best to ignore this. As was the practice, approaching vehicles honked their warnings, but the tall and the thin man kept his space as if not hearing. Moving to the side would require going over the stones and the unevenness of the earth. Each bump would shatter through the wood and blankets and into the bones of this friend who lay helplessly before him. He would not add to the pain. Soon enough dirt and rocks would form the base of the road. Some of the vehicles swerved well ahead of the passing. Others bore down and came so close as to almost do the hitting. This action spoke for itself, "I did not collide with you but be warned: next time I may not be as kind."

The fourth night did not hold the moon. In the true blackness of a moonless night, no one can safely move forward. Even with the help of the countless stars, one cannot see to the end of the first step. All travel needed to be achieved in the day. The sun came fiercely and searched out the body of Rose and waters poured profusely from this sick angel. The tall and the thin man often paused to help Rose with her thirst and comfort her in her exhaustion. There was no shade to be discovered, no places to rest. When he stopped, he protected Rose as much as possible by placing himself between her and the sun as she lay in the wheelbarrow. The pain grew in the tall and the thin man's arms, and a massive throbbing and stabbing came to his back and shoulders. His legs ached with each step. He did not speak of this and he did not speak of the rawness that had become his hands. But he was not silent.

Whenever Rose woke, she looked up and saw the tall and the thin man. His sweat oozed from every pore and dripped down his face forming numerous rivers; the tip of the nose and chin became the formation points for uninterrupted waterfalls. But as he moved ever forward, he spoke with energy so Rose could hear the stories.

"Almost every day I passed the great mountain. Where the people walk, the soils rise in such gradual ways from the path that you would not know it as a mountain. Only from the distances can you truly understand the explosion of this earth. It is from these places where you are able to see a massive blanket of different greens, and above this a big ribbon of rock, and even, at times, a crown of white. As a boy I thought of what a wonderful victory it would be to reach to the top of the world. I grew older, and still dreamed of this but each day was filled with its own set of things. Years passed and I had not done the climbing.

"Then it happened. I put food and a coat in a cloth bag and strapped that to my back and I entered into the bush. At first the forests were dense and it was difficult to find a way through the sticks and the leaves. I kept going upward. I was scratched and bitten but this did not seem to matter. After all this time, and after all those dreams, I was finally climbing the mountain.

The bushes became less and suddenly there were none. The rocks took the scorching heat of the sun and threw this at me. Hot and tired and drenched from sweat, I drank from the water that I carried. But in this stopping, I did not look back. I saved this looking for the top. My feet became wet and cold and sometimes my body sank almost to the knees into the snowy whiteness. I was determined and excited and kept moving ever upward until everywhere was down. From the thin airs I drew a breath and another and yet one more before finally turning around.

"I saw from whence I came, and viewed the amazing bigness of the lands below. Within the vastness, I located my village and the one beyond and when I looked even closer, I found a third which I had heard about but did not really know of. I was seeing as the God might, and briefly I was overwhelmed.

"As overcome as I was, I realized that even though I could see as the God, I did not want to be the God. Seeing the village did not mean I knew the village or the feelings of the villagers. Observing these lands did not include the hands and the feet understanding the soils. This view was remarkable but it did not compare to seeing into the gentleness of the human heart.

"When the time came to return, I did not do this with sadness. Rather I left with a new sense of being. I understood my life would be a search. I was meant to look into the world for the discoveries of beauty—and I have found these in many corners. They are with the mothers looking after their children and in the fathers working beyond the life of the sun to help their families. I found it in the smile of a child and even discovered beauty in some of the falling down mud and stick homes which stand by the snakes of refuse. It is in a guiding hand and in a kind word and I found it in you. My gentle and dear friend, I wish to thank you for such a wonderful gift. This helping in the going back is all I am able to offer in return. It is a repayment, but it is not enough. It can never be enough."

In Search of Sticks

In the walking, he told the many stories of his life. When these were completed, he spoke of that which had happened to others. Rose listened to the tall and the thin man named Ned and the presence of his voice was a powerful equalizer that helped with the agony of her body and the suffering of her soul.

The journey was torturously hot and slow. In this slowness, people passed and in the passing they saw Rose curled up in the wheelbarrow. Astounded at what was before them, almost all offered something from the nourishment they carried.

Many would say, "Your journey has been long and your hands and arms and back are telling of the pain. Let me help you with this burden, if only for a small amount of the way." Though he took from the food and the water, he would not allow the pushing of the wheelbarrow. This could not be done. There may be a wavering of the carefulness and a stone might be hit or a hole encountered and with that a tilting and a falling and Rose's pain would be even greater. He would not chance this. Anyway, Rose was not a burden.

On the last part of a day, the tall and the thin man named Ned met some people on the road who were going to Rose's village and also knew of Rose. These people quickened their pace and told of this returning to the mother and the father. They, and the cousin of Rose, hurried out.

The father picked up his daughter and with such love and caring and tenderness, held her, and walked with her. With the crying of the mother and the silent tears of both the father and the cousin, Rose was carried to her home.

Hope persuaded the tall and the thin man to follow, and he saw that the wonderful stories Rose had told had all been true.

Even in the midst of this immense sorrow, the mother and the father and Hope and many others tended to the tall and the thin man named Ned. His wounded hands were wrapped. They thanked him for his help and were grateful for his spirit. They asked him to stay but he did not. As he already knew, nothing had changed since the leaving. He took from the generous offerings of food and drink, and for the longest of moments, stared deeply into Rose and, feeling the need, gently touched her face. Tears fell. The tall and the thin man once again began the long walk back.

The screaming threatening wind stopped as quickly as it presented itself but the flow of the waters that came from the many eyes did not. The days of true pain had only just begun.

THE FLAG OF TRUTH — THE UPPER TRIANGLE

The committee of the Society for Human Justice met in the evening, and while sitting in the unmatched chairs began the daunting task of mapping out a common vision, a New World Order. Decisions about which issues and ideals to weave into the fabric of their Flag of Truth consumed significant energy. The process was not without disagreement.

"I don't think you should say that." Though James spoke in quiet ways, a certain confident tone resonated in his voice. The speech of "Mountains and Deserts" had created the foundation for leadership; James unconsciously built on this.

"What do you mean, I shouldn't say that? Who are you to tell me what I should or should not say?" The hostile challenge came from a multi-tattooed young man. He sat opposite James.

"Sorry, Rafael, let me rephrase. Yes, of course you can say it; but I know you, like the rest of us, want to address the problems around poverty and disease, and you've already said you understand the need to enlist the help of others in order to achieve this. Some statements are less than helpful in this regard." James maintained his calm voice.

"I don't want anyone telling me what to say or do! That's the problem with this world—everyone wants to control you." His glare matched his verbal intensity.

James presented another explanatory effort. "It's up to you, but in my opinion using blame words like 'fat cats', 'bourgeoisie' or 'capitalist pig' only serves to put some people on the defensive. It's as if they, personally, are responsible for the shortcomings of civilization. We want to solve for future generations, not dwell on any past injustices, perceived or otherwise. This is about truth, not ideology." He stopped momentarily, more for effect than the need to formulate the next thought. "If we are going to discover solutions, we have to work together. We require allies. The world is desperate for some unity." As if he needed one more spike to nail down his position he added, "Phrases which alienate just aren't useful."

Having emphatically made the point, he ever so slightly loosened the intangible strands defining his control. "You do know, Rafael, I'm not saying you're completely wrong. You make some good points. I just don't want to give anyone any excuse for dismissing our ideas, the ones you and I and everyone else here have in common." The many-tattooed man, understanding the face-saving gesture, appreciatively nodded.

James looked around at the array of body piercing jewelry, and those caught in the time warp of the sixties; work needed to be done. Rightly or wrongly, perceptions are important.

The next moments were quiet. The building's walls did not effectively filter the outside sounds. Vehicles were heard passing in both directions on the busy street. One could almost smell the exhaust and feel the hurry.

As was envisioned and presented, the Flag of Truth had three parts: two triangles and their mutual hypotenuse, a wide diagonal white strip that bisected corner to corner, lower left to upper right. Each section stood for an idea. Though they could be considered and comprehended in an isolated manner, the fact the three concepts existed on the same flag symbolized their interdependency.

Those who sat around the perimeter of the table had been charged with the duty of debating and clarifying. The upper triangle represented poverty and the issues surrounding it. The threads of this cloth held the stories and the faces of those who experienced its desperation. While looking at the Flag of Truth, one would not just think of the statistics, as impressive as they are. Instead, one would also see the people and imagine or remember their stories.

An elderly gentleman started to speak. He dressed according to his generation: plaid short-sleeved shirt, tan pants, and well-worn walking shoes. His thick forearms spoke of a past spent in construction. The story he told was said in such a way that, though he did not say he had experienced this, it was apparent to everyone listening there had been a personal connection.

"It's not safe like it used to be. That's for a fact. I read the papers and I seen the stuff on TV and you ain't even safe in your own home anymore. But I can tell you this—as dangerous as it is here, it's a darned sight safer than in some parts of this city. There are areas in our cities you should never set foot in, not if you think seein' tomorrow might be somethin' you want to do. And these places are crowded and they're not small.

"There ain't no prison walls and there ain't no guards but not many seem to escape. You'd think it'd be a simple thing, keep crossin' streets until you're outa there. But it don't work that way. It's like the wives who get beat up but never leave. Maybe they feel they don't deserve more or are just plain afraid or they believe the hell they know is better than the one they don't. All those people livin scared, doin' drugs, gettin' hit or doin' the hittin', and almost no one leaves.

"When I look at the Flag of Truth, I see their faces, their pain and their desperation. Poverty surrounds them and it's not the type about not havin' the big flat-screen TV or the good car, but the kind that destroys spirits. I see a kid called Gabriel, who was named for the angel but suffered because of the mother's addictions before and after his birth …"

Claire, the president of the Society for Human Justice, spoke at length and with great passion about a visit she had taken to a part of the world where the scenes of poverty were almost beyond description and perhaps, for some, beyond belief. At times, while speaking and remembering, Claire shed tears—this surprised her for it had been a number of years since she had been there.

Everyone who sat around the table understood that in the speeches to come and in the references about the Flag of Truth, many of these stories needed to be told. Perhaps in doing so they would touch the hearts of those who could help make a difference.

James contributed only in small ways. For the most part he watched and nodded and agreed. Story after story unfolded. Almost everyone present shared something.

James was pleased. The approach was simple: statistics were to be followed by stories and together these things would force people to open their eyes. In outrage, changes would be demanded. Government officials, desiring reelection and knowing about the Flag of Truth and the immense army of voters behind it and at the ready, would want to be seen positively channeling their energy, expertise, and resources. This would be done in ways which captured votes. "Yes," James silently reflected, "the roots of the grasses were reaching deeper into the soil."

The evening transitioned to night, but there was still more desire and need for further conversation. No one wanted to go home. The truths that would form the parts of the flag represented by the lower triangle and the shared hypotenuse remained, as of yet, undefined. But the hour was late; another meeting would be required. This was scheduled.

THE DAY OF THE ENDING

Life clings to the body. When a great sickness arrives and progresses or nourishment is too little, a thinness presents itself and this has no description. The skin becomes transparent paper and still covers the bones but this is done in such a manner that it reveals them and the way in which they are put together. People having seen this shake their heads and say, "Today will be the day of the ending," but the dying does not come. Another day passes and perhaps many more and each time those seeing the tightness and hearing the troubled sounds from within, make the same prediction; still, the living continues. Life does not give up easily, and it did not do so for Rose.

The mother of Rose sat with her daughter, and the father of Rose was reluctant to leave to the fields, and every day he hurried back. Neighbors and relatives and friends also did the watching. The cousin named Hope stayed the long hours and when the mother or the father had need for small sleeps or for going away, Hope was always with Rose. Her breathing grew shallow and eventually came in such a way as to almost not be found. But as one breath faded and disappeared, somehow another would follow.

Hope and the mother and the father and the rest of the family of Rose heard the last breath and waited for the next, and when this did not come there was disbelief. Even in the face of the immense struggle which brought forth the skeleton, there had always been the next breath. Minutes passed before it became clear this would not happen. Then came despair and crying but also relief. The gentle soul of Rose would suffer no longer.

After the offering of prayers and the saying of the good-byes, a huge sadness blanketed the family of Rose and others who truly knew her. Seasons passed and it could still be felt; for some, the emptiness would never completely leave. Time does not heal all wounds. Those who say otherwise are not being truthful.

You wish that after the loss misery ends and personal pain ceases; in the new beginning or the next chapter contentment and happiness prevail. For neighbors and friends this was possible, but when there are blood ties, further strengthened through the closeness of the doing and being together, this cannot be the case.

The father of Rose went to the field with his sons and he worked feverishly, accomplishing that which required the energies of three younger men. In this way he tried not to allow for the thinking, but this did not happen. Even in the exhaling and the inhaling, images appeared and these were of his beloved Rose. She was seen as a child and a young girl and a young woman, and they were the happy scenes and the proud moments, but the last ones of pain could not be brought forward, for they would cause further collapse. The brothers of Rose worked to match the pace of their father and tried to move his mind to other things in order to soften the hurt. This was done by asking questions or giving observations.

"Will the rains be enough to encourage the grasses?"

"The sun is full, but I believe a gentleness is in it which was not here yesterday."

"Do you see the patch over there? The grains are much bigger than those surrounding them. It is where we put the droppings from the beasts. If we had more, there would be a greater giving. Think of the abundance!"

The father heard but gave no responses. He provided no additions. Even so, there had been some success in the plan and for the smallest fragment of time, his mind held less pain. But then one of the sons spoke: "Do you think this harvest will be greater than the last one?" This was said in error. It had become known that one should not speak of last year or even of the handful of years before. Such talk would bring forward memories.

Though Rose had been away from the village for much time, the feelings never left. The few photographs of Rose were a treasure to the family and through handling and searching, the valued pictures became worn. During the celebrations and hardships which happened since her leaving, there were thoughts of Rose and it was always imagined she was safe. In this thinking, it was allowed to be believed she and her husband had grown prosperous. With this dreaming, the prosperity would extend and include the birth of a grandchild. As part of the same vision, Rose returned to the village and the grandmother made a fuss over this dear little life, and the grandfather pretended not to overly care but allowed for bouncing on the knee. Later in this scene, he sat contentedly in front of the house, gazing outward while smoking a cigarette.

But it became known that during her times of absence, Rose had lived in danger. Instead of peace and contentment, a nightmare of despair dominated. This understanding brought much pain and guilt to the father. How could he have been happy while his daughter suffered so? How could he have smiled or laughed when she was gone? For the rest of the day he punished himself with huge work.

As for the mother, her days also found little relief. No amount of work or talk from the neighbors helped. Hope came every day but often for hours no words were exchanged. They would tidy the room and in the space see the place of the suffering and the dying and remember.

The worst was in the evenings, when Rose's mother and father sat alone. The bleeding of a sorrowful heart can never be stopped. Sometimes it spurts and gushes, while in other moments it drips. Though the flow varies, it is for always.

THE FLAG OF TRUTH — THE LOWER TRIANGLE

The days became incredibly hot, and the heat was accompanied by an air thick with water. Those reporting the weather confirmed the obvious—records were falling as if dominos had been lined up and the first one pushed. Temperature variance between night and day was little, as was the relief. There were no breezes and an inversion trapped the gases which came from vehicles and industries, adding to the stifling atmosphere. Anyone who could retreat did so, finding comfort in artificial, air-conditioned environments.

"It is what it is." James took a forkful of lettuce and crispy peppers. Some of the raspberry vinaigrette salad dressing oozed from the right corner of his mouth. He dabbed at this with his napkin.

"Complaining Tuesday" had arrived. When you're not the boss, not every decision is going to be the exact one you would make. Phil and James had been careful with their criticism, discreet with their vocalizations. They never blew off steam in the office; hence the invention of "Complaining Tuesday," a weekly lunch affair held only between these two trusted friends.

Some Tuesdays had more faultfinding than others, but recently James didn't add much to the conversation. It is difficult to be critical about work and restrictive circumstance when he knew the statistics, those that summarized a different style of life. He understood their meaning.

"I tell you, James, something better give, or one day they'll be looking for 'good old Phil'—and I won't be anywhere to be found." Empty threats, Phil wasn't going anyplace anytime soon. The combination of age and experience had caught up to him—pension prisoner: employee number 009576.

"Yeah, we definitely need change, I couldn't agree with you more. Things have got to be different. There's only so much a person can take." James offered this affirmation, but was referring to another circumstance. He finished his garden salad. None of the lunch crowd had ventured out to the sidewalk tables; it was just too oppressive.

That evening at the meeting, James found himself in intense conversation trying to define the lower triangle of the Flag of Truth. There was no air conditioning. All those present sweated, some more profusely than others. In spite of the fact water visibly and continuously exuded from pores, everyone persisted. This was a significant time.

After the welcome by President Claire, James began. "Okay, let's review." He pointed to the Flag of Truth which had been carefully draped over a couple of chairs, the simple design there for everyone to admire—gold over green triangles separated by a band of white. "As I recall, the top triangle is all about poverty, the kind of scarcity where there is little food and hopelessly inadequate housing. Searching faces are imprinted on this flag and the dominate emotion is desperation. You can see these people in their ghettos, hiding behind invisible walls. We will speak about their lives, the endless scenes of violence, abuse, and addiction. When we focus on the upper triangle, we will tell their stories. By doing so, we will fuel the outrage and our army of followers will grow." He drew a deep breath. "This is some of what was spoken of at the last meeting." The summation was eagerly affirmed.

"I also remember that the gold triangle is more than this. It holds the stories of those who live in a state of virtual dehydration and starvation. In these lives there is extreme anxiousness; this worry is not about their ability to pay the rent or make a car or furniture payment, but about their ability and their children's ability to exist at all. When we fly the Flag of Truth, when it stands beside us on the platform, we will point to the top triangle and speak about these people. We will say their names." The strength of James' conviction mirrored the intense heat of the day. He took a large gulp of water. He drank, more to replace that stolen by the atmosphere than to assuage any immediate feelings of thirst.

"We are here this evening to talk about the Lower Triangle." James pointed to the green portion of the Flag of Truth. "What does it represent? As we look at it what will we think of? When we talk about it what will we say? What is the relationship between the lower and upper components?" He looked around. He asked but he also was prepared to guide. True leaders are never without plans. These may be altered though the essential frameworks usually remain. James continued.

"In my thinking, the green triangle should focus on health and education. It is about what needs to be in place in order to change the lives of poverty stricken, destitute people, those whose stories are woven into the gold fabric of this flag."

No one questioned James. No one said, "How come you get to say what the triangle means?" or "Who made you king?" James was a leader and he led. Following, at least at this point, seemed the right thing to do.

Anyway, room still existed for debate and as it happened, there was a great deal of it. The conversation moved six ways to Sunday: socialized medicine, universal health care, public versus private education. There was no direction and little agreement. If anyone had recorded this and others later listened to the audio, it would be thought this all took place at the bar around many pitchers of beer. The more alcohol consumed, the more disparate and strange the discussion. Just when the conversation seemed to be going nowhere, James assumed control.

"We are not here to debate solutions. We are here to discover truths. In the process, we will not only provide numbers but also tell the human stories the statistics represent. We must limit the use of adjectives. The essence of these narratives will resonate with the listeners in such a way that they will be carried forward and be retold and told again.

"Questions will be asked, solutions demanded. More and more people will make this insistence. Our flag is the Flag of Truth; it is not the flag of opinion or solution. That will come. When we point to and talk about the green triangle, and focus on education and health, whose lives will be described?" James had purposely let them muddle through the first hour. They needed him. If this wasn't apparent before, it certainly had become evident. This might not have been voiced in so many words but it was understood.

Stories began to flow in rapid succession and they told of being caught in the web. They were about those who did not attend school because of little encouragement or no insistence at their homes.

Others spoke of unique children who are unable to learn due to the lack of special supports. Some did not receive the important guidance, their possibilities narrowed with violence, drugs, and early pregnancies. Each of these stories had a face, each a name. They formed part of the Flag of Truth. But the names sometimes changed. Michael and Jason and Serena and Melody became Snake and Terminator and Sleaze and G-Bitch.

Certain members talked about education in the developing world. Much information was forthcoming. Almost a billion people are illiterate. An incredibly large numbers of them are children. Some are tied to looms or work in sweatshops or spend long hours in the fields and cannot go to school. Others do not have the possibility because they are either part of an ethnic minority or are girls. Violence is such that sometimes no one dares take the risk and attend. Many schools are overcrowded and for those lucky enough to go, nothing is guaranteed beyond grade four or five.

These people existed and do exist and after the discussions and the recounting of events surrounding them, their faces were emblazoned in the lower green triangle of the Flag of Truth.

As for health, a multitude of stories surfaced. There were the accounts of aunts and uncles, friends and acquaintances who had frightening diseases and who couldn't get a timely diagnosis. Often treatment was delayed. Sometimes the medicines which had been prescribed were not the most effective but rather the least expensive. Also described were the long waits to have hips and knees attended to or arteries cleaned and hearts unblocked. There is no denying these personal tragedies and their individual sufferings. The people who experienced such heartbreak formed part of the lower triangle.

Stories emerged about life in other countries and continents. The narrations were amazing. Sometimes living beyond thirty or forty years was considered fortunate. Pictures of cholera and malaria could be found in many places, and at times, the faces of leprosy and those affected by debilitating parasites came for a group photo.

A handful attending the meeting had lived in a few of these locations, not as residents or visitors, but as volunteers. Listeners sat with eyes wide open and jaws clenched or gaping. Everyone continued to sweat.

Some spoke of the nightmare of AIDS, and in the words which followed there was both sorrow and outrage. Many diseases were mentioned and each of the described afflictions had, in the developed world, a cure or prevention or a control that would ease pain and extend life. Not so in this other world; the faces of those who suffered appeared as ghostly apparitions, and in the heat and humidity, made their appearance at the table. Then came the associated stories of broken families, anguished parents, orphaned children, and weary grandparents. The questioning eyes belonging to all these victims crowded both triangles."

Upon leaving, the sense of urgency that accompanied this exiting was overwhelming. Everyone's insides twisted as if they had been subject to the sustained and relentless turning of a vice. But they left with a common belief and purpose. The stories emblazoned on the Flag of Truth needed to be told and if people truly heard, the number of those enlisting in the army of the Society for Human Justice would swell.

Beads of sweat continued to make their appearance and freely fall. Heat was not the only factor which brought forth these waters.

WORDS

On this earth, there is the movement from light to dark, and they are named "day" and "night"; there is also the changing of the seasons, and together these are called "time." Within time exists life and within that there are demands and opportunities and routines.

Hope's life progressed and followed the usual patterns. Schooling was nearly finished and she was doing more of the working in the home. Her age brought forward the speculation of marriage.

A young man, who did much visiting, found ways to talk and to be of assistance. "I can help you with the carrying." Hope was returning with full water containers when he 'just happened' to be walking on the same path. He was strong, and he carried the load as if it was a feather.

This was done in such a way as to make certain Hope would notice his strength. She did.

When they arrived at the home and the waters were set down, he saw the door had need of repair. "If your father allows for this, I can fix that door. I have learned this skill from my father, whose job it is to do the building." He was a gentle and shy person and his voice mirrored those attributes.

Hope replied, "I will ask him. He is a proud and able man and with the hands of my brothers, tends to our home. But as I understand it, doors are difficult and he may welcome the opportunity to work and to speak with you."

While the life of Hope moved in the familiar ways of people, the village began a different form of talking. A sense of unease blanketed the countryside and it spread nearer to them. At first there were the rumors and with it the not believing, but persistence accompanied the words and this fact demanded a heightened form of attention.

"This cannot be real. These things are made of many nightmares, each bound to the other," said one.

The second agreed. "Yes, it is a twisted dream and it is told in ways which bring fear. Just as the stories about visiting frightful spirits are designed to widen childhood eyes, these do the same to our adult form."

The third was wiser. "In the speaking of different stories there are often exaggerations, but within them are the small truths and as we say it, they are the grains. But when a story is spoken by many and the things that are said have similar kinds of words and sounds, then I believe there are more than just these grains in the talking. I have been doing the listening. It is a time in our world where we must be

In Search of Sticks

alert." This was said as all three sat together in the quiet of an evening; they played a board game which required much strategy. The last of those who spoke proved to be the most skillful.

The farmer sees the lands in many ways. While reaching down and holding the soils, he will discover if they are hard or they have a softness that can be easily worked. In the moving of this dirt between the thick fingers, he will ask himself: "Is this the earth that does well with the holding of the waters? Is this the soil that is good at feeding grasses?" And he will look around at the whole land and find out if there are piles or fences of rock because picking up stones is forever. Even as they are gathered others are coming from below to take their places. And there is much more concerning the growing that the farmer will think about while walking in the fields. As far back as stories can remember the land has been seen in just this manner.

But others began to move through the countryside and view it in different ways. They tried to discover if things of value had been hidden. Some stopped by the cliffs of rock, hit them with their hammers and with this breaking, wrote in a notebook and took the pieces. Others chose from the gravels and after the washing in the pans looked for that which would bring fire to the eyes. Planes crossed the lands and did so again and again; it is said the pictures they took saw below the skin of the earth. Sometimes a discovery was made and machines and drills followed and these required the energies of many. That is when things began to change for the country and its people.

The mines were small in the first instances and the riches, though important, were not enough to raise the eyebrows of those who truly knew of the wealth of the world. Many farmers were no longer able to grow the crops needed to feed their families and still have some left to sell in order to gain money for necessary purchases. So they sent a son or a daughter to the mine and the wage received, though small, helped in keeping everyone together.

But the people who ran the mines did not think or care about the farmer and his family and they did not do the things to assist in protecting the body and the soul. In the mines there was need for the grinding of rock and with this came large dust, and afterward, and during a difficulty with breathing. Coughing followed and later much spitting of blood. There were those who set the explosives but were not careful enough, or who had not been taught the right and the wrong ways to avoid death or the losing of an arm or a leg. Some had the job of mixing the dangerous things which would allow for the separation of the gold from the crushed rock. With this blending and handling, their young bodies no longer held their promise. They shook and the quickness of thought left them. There were others who, in the hard work, lost an eye when a hit rock struck back and sometimes a crushing happened as a weight of the ground fell. Living together in the unclean place and drinking the waters poisoned by the mines brought forward the sicknesses.

In this mining great damage came to the earth and its people, but if one died or could not do the work yet another arrived, perhaps a brother or a sister. If the family was to stay together, this was required.

In Search of Sticks

This is not the story which is told for the single instance. It is one that can be said for the many. More discoveries were made, and each time it followed that similar wounds were experienced. In parts of the country mines existed less than half a day's walk away, one from the other. And they were so numerous that it would take more than the cycle of the moon to visit them all. Vehicles zoomed back and forth between them.

Naturally there was much talk of these new mines. But the most disturbing conversations were about who owned them and what had been done to secure the control.

THE SHARED HYPOTENUSE

While walking on a trail in a moonlit night or under the full spectrum of the sun's rays, one may arrive at a fork. If this comes to pass, the choice will be either left or right. Perhaps, as noted by a famous poet, the path which has experienced fewer feet could be picked. Then again, it might be determined the beaten trail is the one to take.

The meeting of the Society for Human Justice, the last of three, concerned itself with the concept of leadership. This was about coming to the fork and deciding. Unlike the bard who wrote of a single opportunity, it is known that, for most, many forks will be encountered. In the course of life's unfolding numerous choices present themselves and decisions follow. The process for selection should be deliberate and careful. This is not choosing the chocolate in a box. A great deal of consideration must be put into the decision. Which road to walk on? Which direction to take?

Leadership is about making good choices while going down this highway. James saw the fork that lay ahead, and he read the signs identifying the different pathways. Printed on each of the posts were single words: "Predictability" and "Possibility."

Those at this gathering held a common vision and it had the Flag of Truth flying throughout the world. Tightly woven within the fabric are accounts of individual tragedies. Those hearing these should be shocked. But telling stories which are meant to convey the need for a difference and telling stories that motivate people to actually try to affect change may be two separate things.

"Leadership should inform but also guide. It must be bold and inspire others to push to the limits and beyond so what was once considered impossible becomes possible." James spoke forcefully. "This is why leadership has its own place on the Flag of Truth. Much depends upon the skills of those in charge, on their energy and integrity. Will the haunting, desperate faces now seen in the details of the triangles fade and disappear? Will hope be restored?" James pointed to the flag. "When we look at the white piece of diagonal cloth dissecting the gold and green, we will find ourselves and all who are like us. We will see hard work and commitment and persistence. We will see leadership. We will see victory." Pause and emphasis was effectively applied.

The meeting was short. Those who attended had already arrived at the fork and decisions had been made. The Society for Human Justice was set to take a very different-looking road. 'Predictability' abandoned—'Possibility' chosen.

Someone had brought a couple of bottles of wine. An array of mugs and glasses was quickly assembled and a toast made.

"To the future." James raised his glass.

"To the future," echoed the chorus.

DIFFERENT BLOODS

Each mine, by itself, provided a level of prosperity which cannot be understood by most. But together the riches would take a person almost to the limits of imagination. As it is known only kings and queens command such wealth. If one could control them all, each of the mines under the direction of one being, now that would be power.

The man who wanted to be president said he was a good man, and others at the rally who stood near him said the same.

Another came forward and the one doing the introducing told everyone he was a farmer. This person then spoke of a time when the man who wanted to be president had given him seeds to sow after the year of insects had left him and his family with nothing. He said the man who wanted to be president was generous and understood those who worked the lands. *This talking man did not look like a farmer. Even though he had farming clothes on, his skin did not show the signs of the all the time and everyday weather and his hands were not calloused. Still, it was said he was a farmer and why would one not be truthful?*

When the man who wanted to be president spoke again he promised he would work to help the people. He talked about planting the "seeds of fairness." A wonderful crop would be harvested and distributed to each and every individual. He would ensure everything would finally be fair for the people in Hope's village. No one could ask for more.

He said these things to those who, even in the face of the greatest hardships, did not complain to one another or to the God. To talk about fairness would mean there is unfairness, and as it is known, God does not have favorites. One cannot curse the Maker. It is as if one said the gentle breeze and the loving touch do not have value and there is no reason to be grateful for their moments in this world; that the times of abundance and laughter should not be appreciated. So it followed that if there was unfairness in their lives it was not because of the God. Someone on earth was to blame.

That is when the man who wanted to be president told them of the government, about the people who held the power. He did not use direct words which would mirror his education but spoke in the lyrical language of those doing the listening: "There is a man and he lives in the biggest of the homes. It is as if he is a king and not someone who must seek the confidence of the citizens. Every morning he rises to an amazing meal and every night the best cooks in the wide lands which form our wonderful country put together a feast for the ages. And he may say, 'Give me some of this and a bit of that and a mouthful of what is in the blue bowl. But when I am finished do not let another taste that which was prepared only for me. Do not give what is left to the beggars in the street or to the families who lost the fathers and husbands and do not throw it to the stray dogs. It must be buried. No one but me is worthy of such a meal."'

It was as if the air had turned to wood. With fallen wood, there is a decomposition process and while the course of the atmospheric decay did not extend into the decades as it does for actual trees, this did take time. Those who listened had to fight their way out of the thickness in order to understand what had just been said. Some of the words that followed were not heard. Eventually the voice of the man who wanted to be president found its way through the deteriorating barrier.

"Yes, the man who lives in the palace and who eats and disposes of the food is also the man who makes the laws that tell us what to do and what cannot be done. Is this a man you can trust? Is this a wise man? Is this the man who understands your needs?" His hands gestured as a preacher might. They reached towards the heavens. "And this you should know." There was a long pause as people, now once again hearing clearly, waited for the next astonishing revelation. The silence turned to a restless murmur of anticipation before the words came. "He is not one of us! He is not of our blood!"

This speaking was done in the circle of the village that had been there forever. By forever, this means since the beginning of memory. As the village grew in the number of homes and people, this spot remained intact. Not one part of the grasses and earth which formed the circumference and contained its area had been used for any other purpose. Within this openness things commonly important were discussed—food, land, shared buildings, and shared rules. The most difficult decision in all the stories of remembrance was made on these grounds. Hearing the man who wanted to be president talk about the different bloods brought forward memories of a story told by the fathers and mothers and the grandfathers and grandmothers. It was of those who came to know these lands in the earliest of times.

"Before the country got a name and before all of the rivers and mountains and the stars received theirs, twin brothers arrived to the Earth and, as it is recalled, they did not appear in the normal way with one following the other. Both spilled from the mother at the exact same moment. The father was a powerful man who controlled much. As was the custom, upon the passing, all of the land and accumulations went to the eldest son. So when the time of the dying of the father of the twins arrived, things could not go to a single child, rather, everything became the property of two.

But these brothers had never been able to find the vessel which held agreement. As children they did not see eye to eye on the games to play or the paths to walk and this continued into their adult form. One spoke, "I would like to grow the grains on this piece of land." And the other replied, "It is better for vegetables." It was said, "I would like to live in this house." But in response the brother challenged, "It is the best house, why should you live in the best house? Our father was a wealthy man who owned many houses and had much land but of all the things I have wished for, it is to live in this house." For years this continued until it became apparent there could not be the reaching of any common understanding except the one which resulted in the division of everything. The details of this had been decided in the circle of the village.

One of the sons took the properties and the buildings to the north and the west and the other had those in the south and the east. Because the neighboring countries were grasping, a large army was required. Only control of the soldiers remained in the clutches of these two together. The neighbors were brought to their proverbial knees as more territory was added. And that is how the one land became a country with two people and two bloods."

Everyone who lived afterward, in the untold years of births and deaths, did so in separation. Those who settled by the boundaries did not marry each other, as it was thought there would be no peace in such a family as there could be no agreement.

With the extension of this thinking, the sense of the different bloods turned into a belief in its reality. The notion of disagreement between people then became the assignment of right and wrong and, in turn, these were ascribed the absolute values of good and evil.

This message from the man who wanted to be president was clear. An unfairness had become part of the life of each villager and this was thrust upon them by the uncaring president with the different blood—by an evil man.

The invigorated crowd clapped and whistled in recognition of someone who understood their recently discovered unjust lives. Hope receded and sat under one of the great leafy trees. Her heart shook.

SACRIFICE

When one is burdened, and the exhaustive intellectual search for resolution brings no definitive outcome, and the body has signaled that the time for sleep has arrived, often the mind won't comply. Lights are turned off and in this darkness eyes are deliberately closed; but the sought-after stillness is not achieved.

James dreamed many dreams that night. The first brought him to an ancient people.

The stone blocks which formed the base of the temple had been shaped into rectangles, and this was done with crude tools by men who were tied together so they had no possibility of escape. Each of the thousands of the rocks used in subsequent rows had been similarly constructed. At the apex they placed a slab. It is not known how this was accomplished, but it is understood it would have taken the backs and arms of many to have raised such a weight. The temple rose beyond the height of any tree, or even any three trees, should the roots of one begin where the leaves of another ended. Black-robed, blood-spattered priests stood at the top, enjoying unobstructed views of the four directions of the world.

The ritualistic slaughter continued as one unwilling participant after the other was draped over the massive rock. Priests, taking turns, thrust downward with the knife and with unerring, practiced precision, lives were ended. Each victim's heart, once removed, was held up to the sun so it, too, could know of this sacrifice. The frenzied crowds below cheered wildly. If the daily journey across the sky was to continue, there would need to be an appeasement. Somehow it was known the Sun God had a thirst for large volumes of human blood. The now heartless victim's heads were severed and rolled down to the bottom where they were collected and placed on a rack specially built for such a purpose. Sometimes the dead were flayed and their skins worn by others as part of different rituals. This was not done for sport. The continuation of the cosmic balance needed to be ensured.

And there were further scenes of sacrifice. The eighth ruler of days was a God who was not to be trifled with. When angry, he sent lightning and created storms that brought destructive floods;

when satisfied, these same waters would come as nurturing rains. The kind and the amounts of the offering were critical as to which of the possibilities presented itself. In this case, a suitable collection of children's tears was required. Young souls cried from the fright of impending death, from whippings, and from other methods of inflicting pain such as what happens when nails are pulled out from fingers and toes.

More examples of sacrifice appeared in quick succession and they came from many lands in different continents. The testing of Abraham was also featured. James' restlessness continued. His next dream took him to a firefight in war, where sacrifice climbed beyond the level of offering up someone else's life.

"All clear!"

Using every bit of their intense training, the soldiers rapidly moved from room to room. This was no exercise, no game. "All clear!" rang out for the second time and the routine was repeated. Wall to wall, door to door, rifles up and at the ready. Danger was everywhere, extreme danger, but the greatest peril was affixed to those who entered first and did the shouting. "All clear!" resounded once more. Soldiers were darting to the next position when hell opened its door. Gunfire! The one at the front absorbed the bullets, four in rapid succession and with this he should have fallen but he did not. He slumped to the doorframe, no vital organs penetrated, no arteries severed. With timely help from a medic, he would live. For a split second three soldiers who had been on the move were framed behind him in the open doorway. Those who did the shooting sensed the opportunity and jumped out from their hiding place to assail them but as they pulled the triggers the one who was hurt somehow found the strength to jump in front of the line of fire taking the bullets. This time he fell. By then the three reacted and their rifles replied in swift succession, killing those who had just slain their comrade. Though all of this happened in no more than a handful of heartbeats, a great gift had been given and the ultimate sacrifice made. The three lived.

The next image was of a small girl being raised in a home where yards are fenced and gardens grow. At the end of the block was a park with grass, swings, and room to kick a ball. The scene progressed and she was fully grown but now lived with poor and diseased people who were not welcome in any neighborhood. She did not suffer from any affliction. She chose this company. Help was desperately required and she provided this in the form of medical relief and comfort. In doing so the possibility of her leading a life of neatly fenced homes and green parks had been effectively eliminated—yet another sacrifice.

James then saw some who had been incarcerated for voicing beliefs which were not aligned with the political and military might. Each hour of each day of the rest of their lives was a gift to the continuation of an idea. For these people, much was forfeited: no more listening to song birds; no more seeing that which brings wonder; no more smelling fragrant flowers; no more drinking coffee with friends; no more falling to sleep in the arms of a true love. The list of sacrifices stretches to infinity. Forms of torture replaced the losses.

A flood of images arrived: single mothers holding down two minimum wage jobs; migrant workers needing to be away from their families in order to earn the money to feed them; people helping the aged and infirm. Others reclaimed neighborhoods, saved rivers, rescued endangered species.

The review of sacrifice overwhelmed James. He needed an escape and this was found in the form of deep sleep. But not before he resolved to have a morning conversation with Melanie. It would be an important exchange.

The days of autumn had been extended, not, of course, in terms of astronomical definition, autumnal equinox to winter solstice, but in sense of feeling. The intense cold rains which normally arrive in the last weeks of November had not yet made an appearance. Instead there had only been an occasional shower and a few gray days where a steady mist brought forth images of fabled Scottish moors. For the most part, however, the skies remained blue. Many experiencing this were lulled into a false sense of security, somehow believing such times would never end.

So it came as a shock when, on Saturday morning, the heavens opened up and a cold wind bit at anyone who dared venture out. This should not have been a surprise. The days had been getting noticeably shorter, and the sun's rays had lost much of their intensity. The deciduous trees' time of brilliance had long past. Anyone who knew about seasonal variations and had been the least bit observant would understand the inevitability of what had arrived. Nevertheless, some seemed genuinely amazed at the onslaught of the inclement weather.

This is as it was with the conversation. One could see the signs but still not be prepared for the eventuality.

"Are you saying what I think you're saying?" Melanie struggled to come to terms with what she had heard.

They were in the kitchen, untouched cups of coffee on the table. Rain pelted the adjoining outside deck at such force that the drops, if you could call them that, seemed to bounce back halfway to the sky before returning for another assault. This doubled the visual effect of the deluge. Sometimes gusts took the sheets of water and deflected them, changing the angle of attack by as much as forty-five degrees. The feelings of security and calm, commonly associated with those enjoying protection from the elements, were not being experienced by either of them.

"It'd just be for a while," James tried to reassure Melanie. "A year, two at the most. We have enough reasonably quick access to savings in order to cover the bills. I've talked to human resources; I can take a leave of absence. No need to sweat; it's in the contract."

"No need to sweat! No need to sweat!" Even if a single word had not been understood there could be no misinterpretation; her tone said it all. "And what about our plans? Five years! Five years to retirement! Don't try to tell me that won't be delayed. Five years to take trips when we want, where we want, to go on long walks and drink coffee on any sunny day that comes along, not only the weekend, not just the holidays. Five years till we can sit on the deck, read a book, enjoy the twilight of a summer's night, and not give a rat's ass about work! Five years! What the hell happened to those plans?" The vulgarity in her language was a peculiarity but this was no ordinary discussion.

James had underestimated the situation. He began searching, not in a thoughtful way, but with a form of desperation not normally seen in him. "Phil said it might be good for me to follow through with this and at the same time sort myself out." Mentioning Phil's seal of approval was a major miscalculation and he knew it. The hole got deeper and to add insult to injury, he was doing the shoveling.

"Phil? You've been flying this thing past Phil before me?" Her voice, with the strong delivery and inflections, became a kind of weapon.

In Search of Sticks

James began stuttering and seemed to be in full retreat. He had nowhere to run, no place to hide. Just when he was on the verge of being annihilated she suddenly let up. Melanie, his long-standing, long-supporting, long and deep-loving wife knew James like no one else did or ever would. And as it had been known this weather would come, she also understood this day would arrive. The rains were relentless.

"James, James, James." Her voice became noticeably calmer with each repetition. "What am I going to do with you? What can I do with you?" She shook her head and half smiled. "This has been coming for a while. You don't go making the news, even the national news as many times as you have without there being something in the wind. That flag of yours is getting quite a profile."

James started to reply but Melanie reached out and with one finger gently touched his lips. "It's not your time to talk." She looked straight at him, eyes never wavering. "All those things I said about retirement? You know as well as I do that everything will be fine. Maybe there'll be a few less lattes, but we'll be okay. Heaven knows our lives will still be infinitely easier than those you are trying to help." She made a half-circle waving motion toward her husband: right hand in the air, wrist bent back, fingers to the heavens, palm upward. "James A. Terrance, I release you."

Silence. It was not clear of the duration; no one looked at the clock. Rain still fell ninety degrees to the deck and sometimes beat at the doors and windows. Melanie broke the spell. "While doing this good work, James, you'll be going on a voyage of self-discovery." She trembled visibly. "In the process of finding yourself, don't lose me." All inner strength gone, tears flowed.

James got up and hugged his wife; it was a gentle hug of immense power. "Not going to happen, Mel. Never going to happen." He would make sacrifices and a steady income would be the first, but he couldn't endure the loss of their relationship. It was God's gift.

RESULTS

After the votes had all been counted, the man who wanted to be president did not win the election.

The man who was president had soldiers in each of the cities and villages and these young men with their automatic rifles told the people what to do. In this telling, it was said not only where to do the voting but where to put the mark. And if one did not choose to vote that person was taken from the house, and either after the threat of the beating or with the beating itself the democratic right was exercised.

In almost all cases, more people voted than lived in each of the villages, a fact which could not have been explained should anyone have dared to ask. No one dared. Where the soldiers' presence was not as great some of the ballot boxes had been inexplicably lost.

Other things happened during and before the day of the voting, and they persuaded in ways which did not use words. In the cities and the larger towns where many shops lined the streets, an owner might speak in favor of the man who wanted to be the new president; a sign would invite the vote to go in this direction. But the next morning when this person came to his place of work, he would find the goods stolen and everything broken in such a way that the business was no longer able to function.

Some, the most vocal people, were beaten and the bones of their arms shattered. Eyes became swollen and closed with the many blows. Those who did not have any fear for themselves and who were comfortable with their place on this earth and their relationship with the God, were not intimidated by this violence. But if that person had a family or, in particular, a wife and a child, the directed threats and actions against them would bring even such a soul to his knees.

There had been many bullets and much blood, but this was not reported. One could, however, read the wise words the president had said, and see his smiling face on the front page of every newspaper and at the beginning of every television newscast.

The president was elected for another term. As it was told to the world, "The president enjoys the overwhelming support and confidence of his people." The ballots were quickly destroyed.

The man who wanted to be president was arrested and imprisoned. But with some help, he managed an escape.

THE MOVEMENT

As it happens, the geography is littered with Societies for Human Justice. The names of the organizations vary, as do their structures, but the general nature of their concern does not. They can be discovered in virtually every city. In fact there may be several, each existing in a different neighborhood and operating autonomously. Small towns have them, as do rural settlements where the identifiable center might be any combination of grain elevator, food, clothing, hardware store, diner or gas station.

People of like thinking appreciate each other's company and enjoy talking together. This is not necessarily because the ideas are new and stimulating, but rather these conversations serve as affirmations and, in the final analysis, confirm their own sense of worth. It is always good to know that, with the kinds of governance and actions which continue to define the world, one is not alone in his or her sanity. The range of issues discussed at these meetings was disparate: education, economic inequity, environmental stewardship, and health care, to name but a few.

The Flag of Truth proved to be a stroke of genius. Most who cared to look could find their personal story of concern somewhere on it, and the discovery process was not a difficult one. The gold and green triangles incorporated numerous profound truths, their just causes woven in the cloth. Despite some variance of purpose these groups now shared two things: their caring and their flag. With so many Flags of Truth unfolding in the different breezes would anyone dare to hope that, at long last, change was in the wind?

Even if these commonalities were firmly entrenched, achieving such a wide-scoped and massive vision as the one being hoped for by James remained a daunting task. Never in the history of recorded time, as well as that which has been relayed through oral tradition, had there been a truly serious attempt to change direction and right the ship—at least not on the universal scale being proposed. It existed in the aspirations and dreams of many, but no one believed, as James did, that abject and desperate poverty would one day be eliminated, that learning would be available to all, and that there would be medicine for everyone in need. Then again, those who had gone before had neither given nor heard the speech of "Mountains and Deserts."

Nearly three seasons had passed since he had taken his leave from work, and he had been busy—very busy. Responding to one of the many invitations, James headed to a town almost a full day's drive away. Not wanting to risk getting a ticket, he drove the speed limit. Equidistant poles by the roadside formed a perfectly straight line and these and the wires which connected them stretched beyond sight.

The immense flat fields of wheat bordering both sides of the highway were gold and nearing maturity. A slight wind bent the stocks of grain, and as the small surges of air eased each righted itself. The resulting swirling effect somehow reminded James of the ocean at the time of the changing of the tides. Despite it being close to the hour when the day had its hottest value, James forsook the air conditioning, choosing instead to role down the driver and passenger side windows. The sun baked his arm and this sensation and the dry warmth made him feel more connected to the earth. His recently acquired inner conviction had brought with it a sense of peace. This was strengthened as he listened to one of his favorite singers, enjoying both the lyrics and voice.

James had been driving for well over half a day when, sensing a discomfort associated with increased bladder pressure, he pulled over. Bathed in the warm breeze and standing alone under the blue sky which held only a few puffy white clouds, he breathed in deeply and smelled and tasted the air. The rustling of the grain made it seem as if the Earth was talking, or perhaps singing. Standing by the ocean of golden waves, he weighed out the possibilities. What would he say at this evening's meeting? Many options were considered, all rejected. He urinated into a depression just beyond the gravel on the side of the road. Small dust clouds erupted as the yellow stream landed. He decided he would tell the story of Alexandra.

It was as described: "Go down Main Street, turn right at the second light, continue on for three blocks, turn right again, take the first left and you're there—the white house with the gables." The town proper had about ten thousand people and the surrounding countryside held that number and then some. His invitation came with a dinner, an amazing chicken potpie with one of the best pastry toppings he'd ever tasted. James was the guest of Bob and Laura, a couple he estimated to be somewhere in their late thirties. Also sitting with them at the table were their two well-scrubbed, on-their-best-behavior kids, Joey and Sophie, aged ten and eight respectively. Bob and Laura welcomed him like royalty and seemed to hang on his every word. James had become a bit of a celebrity. This made him uncomfortable; he was no messiah and he didn't wish to be mistaken for one. Still, what could one do? The word needed to be spread.

Table conversation was energetic and dealt with serious issues though it did stray from time to time.

"So Joey and Sophie, what positions do you play on your baseball teams?"

"How did you know we play baseball, Mr. Terrance?" Joey was somewhat wide-eyed with surprise.

"I wish it were magic Joey, but unfortunately I'm no magician." He pointed. "I can see the pictures of you guys on the buffet. You're both in your uniforms and holding bats. I kind of figured things out from there." He chuckled.

"I play third and Sophie is in the outfield."

"Well, you like the hot corner, Joey. Good for you; you need great reflexes for that position. When I was a kid, I was in the outfield just like you, Sophie. It requires a strong arm." He pretended to flex his right bicep. "Hey, what happened?" he mocked. "Looks like I better show up at Spring Training." The kids laughed; their parents smiled.

Savoring the last delicious mouthful James proclaimed, "Laura, this is the best chicken potpie I have ever tasted. It's absolutely incredible. How did you get the pastry to come out so fluffy?"

She started to reveal her secret, when Bob interrupted. "Holy Cow, will you look at the time? I don't mean to be rude, but if we're not going to be late we better leave soon. We certainly don't want people to be waiting around for the guest of honor. Where in the heck is Melissa?" His head turned first to the right and then to the left as if the answer to his question was somewhere in the room. At that exact moment the doorbell rang and in walked their babysitter.

Almost fifty people had already entered the small hall and were milling about in anticipation when James arrived. Someone said something, waved a hand and quickly everyone found a seat. Following the mandatory and somewhat detailed introductions and acknowledgments, James began his talk. It would be remembered later as the "Matter of Record" speech.

"The story of Alexandra, who lived with a poor family in a poor land, is a matter of record. The birth was without apparent complication. The labor was short and the child slipped easily into this world. She cried and she fussed and she demanded in the customary ways of all babies, and at first everything appeared to be normal. Perhaps Alexandra would be one of the lucky ones but as the months passed certain signs began to suggest otherwise. Her bowels were continually loose and a puffiness came to her face. A general malaise accompanied all she did. She barely crawled and was well into her second year before she made her first effort to walk. If a cold or flu moved through the streets and into the houses it found a home in the body of Alexandra. On the occasion of her third birthday, she was not well and the family's small celebration was full of worry.

"Her father was a truck driver and drove from the city to different towns and back again. He was away for long periods and became lonely. There were indiscretions. He did not take precautions, and the disease he brought home resulted in suffering, not only for himself, but also for his wife and their beautiful child. This is the Flag of Truth."—James pointed to the flag which had been unfurled behind him—"it is not the 'Flag of Judgment' nor is it the 'Flag of Condemnation.' The father infected his wife and she, in turn, transmitted the awful disease to Alexandra. This is the truth; it is a matter of record." The eyebrows of James came together. Every word, every inflection, every facial expression seemed to be with purpose and all those present were captured by this speaker and by his speech.

"It is a matter of record that three out of ten babies who are born this way will have the AIDS virus. It is also a matter of record that there are pharmaceutical medicines that, when administered in a correct manner will considerably decrease the number of infected children. Instead of thirty out of every hundred condemned at birth, this could be reduced to as few as two. Twenty-eight young souls would be saved if only they had access to the right drugs—if only." James spoke the last words in a whisper and his eyes were full of sadness. He seemed to drift before snapping back. "That is a matter of record. Additionally, it is a matter of record that in developed nations, the administration of these drugs is standard practice. Alexandra was not lucky; she was infected and she was not born in a prosperous nation. Alexandra's seven years on this Earth were a full three more than might, under these circumstances, be expected. Whether or not Alexandra was fortunate is not for me to decide. The deterioration of her health is a matter of record, as is her slow and tragic death." The audience sat in stunned silence. Some wept. James walked to the Flag of Truth.

"Look and you will see Alexandra's face on the green triangle, the part focusing concerns about health and education. And she is not alone. The faces of other suffering children surround her." James paused, waiting for the audience to assimilate even a fraction of the reality. "I do not use hyperbole. I do not exaggerate in any manner. This is the Flag of Truth and the life of Alexandra and those of millions like her are all a matter of record."

James went on to talk about other lives, different struggles. He spoke until neither he nor his audience could endure any more. He drank a glass of water, poured from the pitcher and downed that. No one said anything. Finally James resumed.

"I understand your energy is needed for another commitment, a river you are concerned about needs saving. But there is this other matter I have spoken of. It, too, is a noble cause. I urge you to take every opportunity to try to alter this reality. There are letters to be written, petitions to be signed, conversations to be had, and votes to be cast." He looked at each, making contact as he did so. "I know that I ask a great deal of you, especially you who are already giving of yourselves, you who are in the midst of sacrifice. I ask you not to forsake your cause, but to embrace another."

The applause was long and loud. The audience was moved. Many stayed and talked well into the first morning hour when James had to leave. Melissa, the babysitter, needed to be taken home.

This was just one of the numerous stops James made in the past several months. There were many truths to be spoken about and they were all a matter of record.

Randy Kaneen

FURTHER FLAME

One of his feet pointed to heaven while the other was sideways lying flat to the floor. If you did not see any more, you would think this is a man who is sleeping. His blue jeans were too long and the excess length in each leg was rolled up to make thick cuffs. After observing this, it would still be believed that he is in a deep form of rest. The looking continued. The shirt had been pulled away from the pants, revealing the soft belly. The right hand of the man's fingers curled in such a way as to make a fist, but no menace was in the grip. The left one held within its grasp a large amount of shirt material and this accounted for it being drawn well above the waist. And if this is all you saw, it might still be thought this is a dreaming man and he is quiet now but he has had a nightmare and this caused the grabbing and the pulling of the shirt. The sleeves were short and viewing the redness and bruising of the forearms provided a different kind of thinking. These were not the marks one sustains in the normal course of daily work. The searching eyes then began to race and went directly to the head. The forehead to the nose had been bound with a cloth. This had been done to prevent seeing from this man who would see no more. Though you could not look into the eyes, it could be imagined they either had been shut in the tightest way possible or were bulged wide open. The mouth was jammed full with a wad of something, possibly a rag, to prevent large sounds from escaping. This may have been in response to the yelling from the pain which annoyed the ears of those who were busy delivering it. Perhaps it was done to silence the pleading for the continuance of a life. Listening to one beg for mercy can bother the inner sense.

The eyes of the looking man found that the final act had been achieved with clinical precision. A clean, deep slice ran from the top right-hand side of the neck and moved diagonally to the left and did so for the whole length. Though there was a feeling of slow motion while making these observations and recording this information, the entire process consumed no more than a second.

All of this was seen by a greatly distressed man, one who was being asked to support a position. The attempt at persuasion did not happen in the usual way—one person to the other with efforts at accessing and verbalizing intellectual argument. No energies were applied to motivate with a speech about injustice which concluded with the need to address the grievance.

The man who lay on the floor had been his friend and business partner. Together they had owned a gold mine. The one left breathing quickly agreed to keep operating the mine and to give to those who did the persuading everything they suggested.

After leaving the room he threw up the contents of his stomach and he continued the heaving long after nothing was left. A time later, he stumbled down the stairs and discovered the man whose job it had been to do the protecting. The top and front of his head were missing and his brain had fallen out. It did not ooze as is the normal description, but cascaded forward; it showed a reluctance to leave completely and somehow remained attached. He had died quickly. On a dead man's scale of fortune, he might have been the luckier of the two.

Whether one seeks power for power's sake or wishes to oppose the causes of oppression, there are large needs to access wealth. Even a loyal soldier requires more than the gift of a simple meal and a good pair of boots. The enemy was powerful and the fire coming from such people needed to be fought with further flame.

The man, who had lost the unfair election, and who had been imprisoned and escaped, still wanted to be president. In order to feed and pay his soldiers and buy the weapons, control of the mines was required.

"I am able to deliver you these in units of two hundred or more, and they can come here quickly. Within the week you will be caressing them." The salesman spoke in a dialect which could be understood but his thick accent provided an obvious sign that he did not live in this area or even a geography close by.

In Search of Sticks

"And why should I purchase them?" said the man who wanted to be president. He did not speak in the friendly tone reserved for the times he talked to the villagers. "I have been told of this one and that one and if I bought more than I asked for, the cost of each would be less. The time has come to decide. Why should I buy the kind of rifles you are offering me?" They sat in a room with comfortable chairs. A low rectangular table stood between the two.

The reply came without hesitancy. He accessed a bank of descriptors and phrases used to persuade. In another world, he might be selling cars or houses or washer and dryer combinations. "Should you have asked the manufacturer to design and produce a weapon for your exact needs it would not be made more perfect than that which you will soon hold." He paused and looked at the man who wanted to be president to make sure he had gained his attention. He had. "If this was a suit, it would be as if it had been tailored just for you and not produced for the masses. Imagine that the measurements of your broad shoulders and thick neck and long, muscular arms were absolutely precise and the chosen cloth was of such a quality as to set you apart from all other men." Flattery was adeptly woven into the sales approach. He stopped and took from the drink that was on the table, never really moving his eyes away from the man who wanted to be president. Choosing from the crate beside him, he held up one of the models.

"This can be used in the closeness of battle, or you may choose to add the longer barrel and conceal yourself on the top of a roof. With the more powerful of the two scopes, you are able to see faraway targets, and using the one bullet option, fire with such accuracy that you will almost always have the *pleasure of seeing he who once walked and opposed you, lying on the ground without movement. There are many choices in how the ammunition is delivered. Perhaps you would wish for this single shot or a two- or three-round burst. The full automatic fire is amazing. This liberates over six hundred of your bullets, and does so within the minute. What is lost in accuracy is gained in the massiveness of destruction. It is accompanied by the deliverance of great fear." Both the man who wanted to be president and the one who wished to do the selling smiled at this thought.*

"In all these cases you could use the same rifle and simply put in different trigger units as would be your desire. With the reinforced polymers and steel inserts it is light but still strong." He held one up as if to prove this. "This weapon is easy to take apart and clean and is made in such a way as to not be overly affected by sand and dirt. I have seen your army—I do not say this to upset you but this must be said—I would buy these because they are not only effective and reliable but also uncomplicated. There is no large requirement for training. For a bonus, I will make sure each rifle comes with its own carrying sling. Should you want that which holds a bayonet, this is possible." He stopped and with a confident stare looked directly at the man who wanted to be president. "I can be paid in gold. As I understand it, this is not a problem for you." Once again they shared a smile and the man who wanted to be president laughed with fearful force. Several hundred were ordered.

If the man who wanted to be president was to become president, his army would require more people than just those who joined the struggle because they were convinced of the need for greater fairness and better opportunity. Therefore payments and the ability to make them were critical elements. That is why the control of the mines was necessary and select killings were unavoidable.

Additional purchases were also made. The desire for guns was quickly joined by a wish for rockets and land mines and other explosives, and for the buying of vehicles. Some of these were purchased to hold his many soldiers and some had been bought for the commanders. A special one was acquired that was strong yet comfortable and this was for the man who wanted to be president. All of this required much gold.

With the access to money achieved, the narrative everyone knows about was lived once again. Soldiers fighting soldiers is one of Earth's oldest stories. In the thousands of years of mankind's existence, there is almost no day or time when this story has not been reenacted. Though it is full of familiar sounds, it is not an easy one to tell. There is pain and sorrow and a struggle for breath and also despair and sometimes jubilation. The times of celebration and loss do not exist separately, but as the wider sense of history records, it is part of a cycle.

There are soldiers who are conscripted and soldiers who volunteer for the cause and soldiers who join the army for payment and those who want the excitement or the power. Within each of these types are many stories.

But there is another account that needs to be told. It is about the people who choose to do the farming and the cooking and the laughing on the porch but are trapped within the geography of struggle. Hope's life would soon take another turn.

MOMENTUM P=MV

Linear momentum is calculated by multiplying mass times velocity; the larger the mass and the quicker the speed, the more the momentum. When the mass is not great and the speed is slow, it follows that the momentum is not considerable. The momentum of a series of objects is ascertained by adding the products: $p = m_1v_1 + m_2v_2 + m_3v_3$, and so forth. ($p$ = momentum, m = mass, v = velocity.)

James, with the help of the Flag of Truth, tried to build momentum. This required an increase in mass and/or velocity. Adding to the membership is the equivalent of achieving greater mass. How quickly those numbers rise then becomes velocity. It is the speed of the action. For example, one petition in a single location may gain twenty signatures a day, while two petitions in two different localities might garner forty, another in an additional place may be signed only five times in the same day but the cumulative speed still rises—velocity increases. Imagine thousands of locations, hundreds of thousands of Flags. Building mass and increasing velocity are critical constructive elements. The greater the momentum, the more difficult it is to stop or hinder the movement.

And this was well underway. James had been the guest speaker in numerous locations, and others members of the Society for Human Justice had also made contributions. The train, so to speak, had left the station; exactly how many cars from the various sidetracks would join the procession was as yet unknown. The momentum was dependent on the mass of the train, and, of course, the capacity of its engine. $p = m_1 v_1$

The Society for Human Justice's budget was almost nonexistent and whenever James drove to a speaking engagement, he felt fortunate just to recoup his gas costs. There were no speaker fees or ticket revenues and no five-hundred-dollar-a-plate fundraising dinners. For the most part it was James and the Flag of Truth and his petition and letter writing campaigns, the purpose for which was singular: request help from those who could deliver it. A simple and direct message accompanied all efforts—"There are enormous needs; please lend a hand."

And though the flag flew in some yards in the different communities and could be found here or there unfurled at the rallies, and letters were being written and signatures added to the pages requesting differences be made, the overall momentum did not overwhelm. Despite the increase in mass and velocity, the movement was easily overlooked and in danger of fading altogether. Pollsters, those paid to discern the direction and intensity of the blowing of the wind, had thus far failed to discover the Flag of Truth. As of yet it wasn't on any of their radar screens. The forum of public opinion was shifting, but not obviously and for all intents and purposes, not measurably.

James and his wife Melanie were drinking coffee. This time they had chosen to drive from their home to a place tucked away into one of those cozy neighborhoods, the kind with neatly appointed older homes, mature trees, and a street that boasted interesting boutiques as well as a liberal distribution of coffee locations. Their favorite wasn't affiliated with any of the chains which dominated the scene; it had a personality. Marino, the owner/operator, was an accomplished barista who roasted his own beans. Leaf and flower foam designs floating at the top of the lattes served as reminders that each cup was, indeed, a work of art. Together they shared a grilled Italian Panini and while drinking their coffees and nibbling at the food, they read bits and pieces of well-thumbed newspapers. At times they looked up, perhaps to comment on an article, or reflect on an idea. The gray chill of the day added to their sense of comfort. This was a good place to spend some time.

"You know, Mel, I'm not finding out what I thought I might. At least, not exactly."

"Whatever are you talking about, James?" Melanie looked up from her paper creasing her face in a way that suggested she had no idea what her husband referred to. She was having a bit of fun. Apart from discussions which revolved around their kids—their accomplishments, the difficulty of them entering the housing market and were they ever going to produce any grandchildren—James' conversations with Melanie went down one path. He had almost finished year one of his leave of absence and his newly chosen role consumed him. It turned out Melanie was fine with this. James was happier. What did or didn't happen in the world continued to trouble him, but his soul seemed far less tormented. Somehow the fact that he was trying to make a difference, even in the face of all obstacles, had a settling effect.

James smiled; he knew his chain was being yanked. Two could play this game. "My research on the mating rituals of the artic blue fox. What did you think I was talking about?" They both laughed then James began in earnest.

"At first I thought the problems in the world, all the troubles in paradise, are a result of peoples' lack of caring. But I'm not finding that. In the meetings I'm invited to, I tell the real stories and there are tears. There's genuine compassion. You can see this. You can hear their words. You can feel it in the air."

Melanie waited for James to continue. They sipped their coffees; though getting tepid, the taste was still rich. "It's like this article here in the paper about a teenage girl who needed an operation but the family's health care coverage wasn't going to pay for the cost of the good procedure. A quick fix had been offered, one which required a revisit to the operating table every ten or fifteen years. The price differential between the one with the life time warranty and the one that would subject her to surgical repetitions wasn't a whole lot but the family didn't have the cash. In the meantime, the kid is limping around with the intense pain associated with this degenerative condition.

"Just when it looked as if they would have to go the cheap route, someone got wind of this and phoned a guy on a radio station. Within twenty minutes, callers had contributed five thousand. An hour later the total amount had been raised. There are no shortages of good people. The caring is there. The question is, how do we get them to act? The radio thing worked well for the one kid and her family, but when the problem is tens of millions strong, then what?"

Melanie shifted her approach. Her support for James had never wavered but thus far she had limited her participation to providing nods and affirmations. This time, though, she pursued the conversation. "I think you're right on, James. So what is the answer?"

James was somewhat startled. Monologue had moved to dialogue. Without pause he picked up on this new approach. "I haven't got a clue. I've been thinking about this twenty four seven but no 'aha' moment. Not yet." His eyes settled as they searched hers. "Any suggestions?"

Melanie was also quick with her response; she had been witness to his daily efforts and his killer traveling schedule. "I'm not sure if it's a suggestion, but I can tell you this: you're not going to get this thing done unless there's more than just you and handful of others spreading the word. If your efforts are to have the effect you want and people are inspired to move from awareness to action, it has got to be happening on every corner of this country and really, for a problem of this scope, every region of the globe.

"I know something about this, James. Remember, I'm in the airline business. We advertise, and not just a little bit and never without a plan. Each communicative possibility is analyzed by people who are paid good money to do this. Only then are decisions made about which direction and what energy to apply to advertising initiatives. You and the airline company have something in common—you are both in sales. They have tickets to unload and you want people to buy into a need for change. But you've got to get modern James, move the communication approach into the twenty-first century. It's your only hope." She remained afraid for her husband. Unlike James, she was not about to risk drowning in the River of Need. Still, there was no denying that the cause was noble and she was proud of her husband's efforts. "Give me a couple of days to wrap my head around this. Maybe I can come up with a few hints."

Melanie would go home and think about mass and velocity. She understood their importance and their unique relationship to momentum. They left, both experiencing increased levels of energy. Possibly the caffeine had kicked in.

FORMS OF PERSUASION

The ebb and flow of power does not mirror the ocean tides where the timing of the rise and the fall and the amount of variance is predictable. The man who wanted to be president wished for greater territory, lands well beyond those which had the mines, and the man who was the president craved what he once held and with this reclamation, a measure of revenge.

When the man who wanted to be president arrived at Hope's village, he did not ask for permission. There was an assumption of control and no one questioned this. His soldiers needed to rest and to eat and this was achieved by placing them in the different homes. They did not wait for the welcome, and their arrival was not met with a sense of generous hospitality. No one said, "Please come in and sit awhile and share our drink and the small foods we have prepared." Rifles sufficed as the form of introduction.

Two soldiers strode in and sat at the table. "Woman, we will eat here. Fill up the bowls—and not half the way but to the overflowing." The man who did this speaking was young, and it was clear he enjoyed this ordering. They ate all of which had been placed before them and finished the amount that had not been served the first time. They did not mind the spilling. "Ugly woman, give us more drink!"

The husband, returning from the field, entered and seeing what was before him, stopped and stared and said nothing.

"Old man, it is certain you married this hag out of pity. She is revolting to the sight and her cooking is worse than the ones who are just doing the learning." They had the rifles and they laughed. There was danger in the sound.

And the husband did not know what to do. He was greatly angered by their words, but he dared not respond. In his mind he grabbed the larger of the two with his strong left hand and in the quickness of surprise, took the rifle and pointed it directly at the heart of the one who curled his upper lip on the deliverance of each command, each insult. Seeing what happened and the intent, the other quickly gave up his weapon. Throwing these soldiers out onto the dusty road he challenged each or both to a fight, and even set the rifles aside to make the odds more inviting. They did not do this because, without the guns, they are spineless cowards and as such begged to be let go and ran away, never to be seen again.

This did not happen. Instead the husband stood stoically, clenching his jaw and said nothing. He and his wonderful *wife took the speaking from this vermin and they gave all the food that could be consumed. And they prayed that there was no discovery of the young woman who lay behind the mattress. In the morning, it had been propped up against a wall as part of the readying for daily life. Hope did not move a muscle.*

Feeling the fullness of their power and tiring of this small game of terror, the soldiers from the armies of the man who wanted to be president left to do other damages. These were the early days of the coming and of the staying of the great evil.

The mines to the north had the need for many men. A vehicle drove down the streets which together linked the houses in the village. In a repeated announcement that used amplified sound, all the families were ordered to go to the circle of talking and not to finish the sipping of the tea or complete the cooking or conclude the doing of the chores. "If you think to stay in your home or hide at the edges of this village I urge you to reconsider," and in the next space was the sound of many bullets flying into the air. The message was painfully direct and in the moments that followed, people spilled into the streets and moved to the place where everything commonly important had always been discussed.

When it became clear they had all arrived, a young man was singled out and with the pushing by soldiers with the guns, was taken to the front. Not understanding what they were seeing, the crowd, in their apprehension, became quiet. A man, who was dressed differently from the rest of the soldiers but was still dressed as a soldier, used the microphone from the vehicle and spoke. "I can see, by the bigness of your chest and the large veins that are bursting from your arms, you are a strong man. You have been selected to help our heroic leader, the one who should be president. You will have the honor of working in a mine to the north of here. Take a seat at the back of the truck." He *gestured with a sweeping of the arm as if it was a gentle invitation.*

The strong young man did not immediately go and trying to pick his words he carefully spoke, "While I do not want to insult you and your great leader and I respect the high honor of being chosen, I would ask not to do this going. Instead I would like to stay in the village and help my good mother and father who are aged and failing and as such are also in need of my strength."

And the man who was the leader of the soldiers and who was dressed differently did not use the words to change the mind and say, "But my dear villager, in order to help us gain the freedom and liberate ourselves from the oppression that defines our whole existence would you, for the common good, reconsider?" He did not say, "Whatever the sacrifice and however painful this might be, your help is required." He did not say the things which convinced and he did not do the ordering. Instead he spoke in the kindest of tones and in this speaking asked to see these wonderful parents. When they came forward he took the pistol, a small steel item that had been holstered to his side, and raised it in the air. It glinted in the last parts of the evening sun. There was a loud bang and a falling, and the old woman crumpled and the old man, while trying to do the catching, was also shot. The strong young man screamed and ran to his mother and father and in this running he was met with a hail of bullets from the different rifles.

In the stunned silence, the man who dressed differently than the rest of the soldiers but still dressed as a soldier held the shiny gun and stood over the fallen son. He announced, "He was strong, but he was not smart." Fifteen other young men of strength were chosen. Nothing was said and no resistance was encountered. More "volunteers" were wanted but it wasn't the biggest of trucks and some of the soldiers also needed to return.

༄༄༄

It is the essence of ideas that they be open to analyses and interpretation. In the free world there are conversations about differing thoughts and sometimes these include efforts at conversion. During this process, some may be convinced to change sides and vote with this new belief. Others, still not persuaded, continue to provide support to another.

For the man who wanted to be president, gaining peoples' loyalty was not achieved in this fashion. No longer did he make an effort to persuade so people would see that, with his help, goodness had been done. No attempt was made to convince others he owned the righteousness of thought. An unjust vote had happened and an election victory stolen from him. He had no further interest in this process of persuasion.

The man who wanted to be president did not want an opposition, and he did not want to spend time and energy to do the campaigning and later hope for a fairer vote. Even if he could be successful, he would not be able to gain the support of ten out of ten. In any case, this was no longer needed. He owned the guns. What was required is there be no opposition. To achieve this, he created a deep fear. This thinking has its own form of logic. If ten of ten were truly afraid, there might not be any championing of his cause but there would be no opposition. Then only he, with the help of his soldiers, would have the power to rule. It is better to have ten out of ten fearful people than six or seven who do the supporting. The three or four remaining could become active in resistance. Such aggravation is not necessary. Fear is a great convincer.

There was randomness in the choice of victims, but a purposefulness in the attacks and a deliberateness in the selection of approaches used to bring the terror. The remaining people, including Hope and her family, picked up the young man and his mother and father who had fallen to the bullets and they buried them. They did this quietly. The technique of delivering the fright was working.

In the days that followed the occupation of the village by the man who wanted to be president, peacefulness and predictability gave way to a different forecast. There was crying in the night and the sounds of drunken soldiers roaming the streets. As awful as this was, the stories about what took place in other villages had not yet been equaled. But these were the early days.

The armies of the man who was the president attacked the armies of the man who wanted to be president. It happened just as the light came to the world. The presence of these forces and the events themselves should not astonish. This is how it has always been; someone takes something, but with opportunity, the one who lost it will attempt a *reclamation. It is a pattern that searches for the undoing of the perceived or the real injustice. The completion of this process can take days or months or years and it is not unusual for such a quest to take a lifetime or even generations beyond that. However, most often the first efforts to realize atonement happen quickly. Gunfire rang throughout Hope's village and echoed off the walls of the homes.*

PRIME TIME

The rumors are true: national TV advertising requires deep pockets. Thirty seconds on a decently viewed sitcom will set someone, or some entity, back a couple of hundred grand, possibly more. For a spot on a highly rated program, one can expect to cough-up at least double that, not including productions expenses. Those are extra. Not the kind which seems like an insignificant amount such as when one buys the large instead of the medium size product, but extra as in "Yikes! I think I will sit down and have that drink."

As well, there is the frequency/effectiveness factor to consider. Researchers have done their homework and their conclusions for the advertisers are not the happy kind. It turns out

In Search of Sticks

huge buy-ins usually don't happen until someone sees a commercial several times. So the massive budget should be tripled.

Newspaper, radio and magazine options are somewhat cheaper advertising vehicles which, if used appropriately, can get a message out. Still, when the targeted audience extends not only to those living within the reading and listening borders but also to others who reside well beyond, the cumulative cost of buying space and purchasing air time is astronomical. And the issue of repetition in order to achieve optimal results still needs to be considered.

"James, there's no chance you are going to be able to play with the big boys and girls. The money they have at their disposal is phenomenal." Melanie was talking. They were eating Thai. Tom kha gai soup, pad thai and chicken satay with peanut and cucumber sauce—nothing overly spicy.

"Time to review: remember the stuff we learned in school concerning responsible government? Well, they forgot to mention lobbyists. Naturally most politicians are concerned with reelection. A cynical individual might believe that even though the decisions being made are about right and wrong they can also be about lining up the votes. When these two things don't align the result is less predictable." She looked into James' eyes, making sure he was locked in. There was no need; his focus never wavered. "You don't have to like or accept it, but if you know how this works, then you just may be able to use the knowledge to good advantage. As consuming and slow as the process for recruitment is, the followers of the Flag of Truth continue to grow in number. You've got to get elected officials to not only understand the nobility of the cause but also believe the block of votes you represent is, or very soon might be, substantial enough to make a difference in their prospects for reelection.

So, as I see it, there are two issues here: increase your following, and increase the decision making pressure. We've already established that you don't have cash at the ready for ads to influence and bring focus, so I'm thinking it's time to talk technology." She looked deep into James' eyes, finding his troubled spirit and in turn this worried her. It created a sense of urgency in her tone.

The mere mention of this brought forth considerable angst. If there is an essential truth which can be attributed to technology it is that its nature is "ever changing." Charles Darwin, while advancing his theory of evolution, wrote of "slight successive variations" and "slow steps". However the technological era is one of rapidly developing growth. By far and away it outdistances the pace of all the evolutionary progressions ascribed to the various life forms.

Mankind's slowly evolving mind is now forced to wrestle with changes occurring at comparative light speed. James had been in wonder at the invention of the electric typewriter; he witnessed the birth of the computer, and marveled at its increasing range of possibilities. At work he had, by necessity, learned to use sophisticated programs and was thought of as somewhat savvy. Still, when Melanie spoke in detail about social media he was victimized by evolutionary restrictions.

They finished the soup. The galangal, lemongrass, and lime leaves were not consumed. For once, James wasn't talking.

"Your speeches are stirring and certainly well received, but so few actually hear them. Even though you are only experiencing modest increases in the number of supporters don't stop doing it. Take one more step and incorporate them into an interactive blog. Post each speech and encourage commentary. It's cheap to set up. I've looked into this, and a popular blog can get an unbelievable number of hits a day. When your following gets big enough, those running for office are going to sit up and take notice. Think about it, James. You've already got a great symbol with the Flag of Truth, you made some stirring speeches, and the Society for Human Justice is a good focal point. So use this and start blogging, get a Facebook presence, strike up a relationship with the Twitter generation. This could work." The pad thai was getting cold; no one was eating.

"And one more thing: new companies don't advertise half a dozen products at a time. They choose one, and if they are successful with sales, then they'll promote the second. They build on success. I think your concerns run deep and are so numerous that most people have trouble maintaining focus. You've got too many products, too many needs; you're going to have to choose." She paused before continuing. "Knowing you, you'll find this to be very hard indeed."

They finished their meals in silence, James in reflection and Melanie in emotional exhaustion. She was helping her husband and at the same time, trying to save them both. James reached over the table and moved his fingers across the back of her right hand. He understood.

People are not equipped to deal with too much information. Menus are not the length of novels or even short stories. Going to the grocery store? A list is useful. If this is not referenced, there is every chance an item will be forgotten. Companies generally don't set more than three goals. Multi-tasking people wake up in the dead of the night, fearful they didn't remember to do something. Melanie was right. Her husband would need to choose.

In the advancing evening, James sat in the half-light and considered the numerous needs and while staring into the void, once again broke through barriers. He visited the faces on the Flag of Truth and found himself in a massive camp of people, all who were in a form of waiting. Anguish was the discernible emotion in their fireless eyes, and their bodies spoke of no fight or resistance, only resignation.

In Search of Sticks

Some are able to come to terms with their difficult moments on this earth and through studious or naturally acquired wisdom, learn to accept. If any of the tens of thousands in the camp did achieve this state of being, it was not apparent. One should not confuse the feeling of acceptance with that of giving up. In James' vision, the word "refugee" was tattooed on each of the forearms and written in indelible ink on all hearts and souls.

Waking from this half sleep, James knew what had to be done. He understood where future energy would be directed. His vision did not change. There would be a better world. Children would go to school. People would get their medications. Babies would be saved. Slums would be altered in such ways that they would no longer be recognizable as slums. A newfound respect for property and an appreciation and celebration for differences in race and belief would surface. From the ashes of destruction would come forth scenes of contentment and prosperity. Peace would reign.

If he had a magician's wand and could utter the right spell all of this would be accomplished in an instant but the age of Merlin had long past. His vision did not change; the plan for its accomplishment did. Momentum is vital. Increases in mass and velocity result from the layering of successes. All energies would need to converge—refugees.

Randy Kaneen

A MIRACLE

The word "miracle" comes with many understandings. There is the miracle of birth, and anyone present at the event will not question the application of this term. Stories of miracles are varied. Some describe the reappearance of the holiest of figures long past, the unexplained healings with the new sight, the throwing away of the crutches or the vanishing of the disease. And there are things in nature resembling in appearance or in print that which is held to be sacred. At times these are considered miraculous. Then there is the miracle of survival. Vehicles plunge off cliffs and into the ravines below and against all odds, some live. There are those who walked away from planes after they fell from the sky. With hurricanes and tornados and other types of destructive winds, people are buried in debris and hurled through the air and though bones are broken, hearts still beat. Some *inexplicably escaped from massive floods and consuming fires. Others who have been struck by lightning are spared.*

In the battle, it became apparent that the man who wanted to be president was overmatched and he needed to retreat and regroup. But in the slowness of the stepping back, a message would be left to the farmers and the shopkeepers, and to all their families. The man who wanted to be president was disappointed with their lack of support, and of course there is always the need to apply the blame.

Those who heard the shooting and the exploding became concerned and fearful and wished more than ever for an escape. With the agony between the choices of dangers, the neighbors of Hope made a decision: in the quietest way possible, they left the home. During this leaving they also met up with another family intent on the exodus, and while moving, they tried not to be where the soldiers were. This was difficult because with the chaos, many of these fighters ran in different directions, deciding on the best approaches and places to do the defending.

For the villagers, it all went well for the first of the times. After turning a corner everything changed.

The seven soldiers stood for a moment and seemed startled. It was their thinking the enemy had arrived, but after seeing these families, the uncertainty and fear turned to sneers, and their swagger rapidly returned. They had the only guns.

What happened next has no detailed memory of a beginning, but for the one who lived through it, the ending will never come. In the permitted memories, this is known. There was a loud bang and a son who stood by a father fell, and in the falling, screamed in an awful way. Afterwards a demand was made for money and all of what was carried by those doing the leaving was hurriedly put down in a single spot.

And then a soldier did the asking: "Why are you going away?" With the answer it was explained that the bullets and the explosions had made their homes unsafe and their only wish was to find a less dangerous place. This was said by someone as a father and a mother cradled their dead son. They wept.

One, whose words flowed from the mouth like so much drool, spoke, "You should not be leaving your homes. It is an insult to us who have been here all this time, protecting you from harm. This has not been easy, and all we asked in return for our efforts were some bits of food and a place to lay our heads to find sleep."

And though there was not the smallest particle of truth in what was said, the father of the family whose children still lived quickly agreed. "We are ever grateful for your assistance and wish you every success in the struggle that is before you. When you have achieved the victory which will surely be yours, we will dance in the streets and invite you to the festivities and honor your skills and unselfish efforts."

The reply was immediate. "We are needed in another place; we do not have the time to be entertained by this crawling. There are not enough moments to take pleasure in the deliverance of slow pain and the writhing agony which is sure to follow. And though the daughters are inviting to us, we are too hurried to enjoy them. This is your lucky day; we are required elsewhere." Following a terrible laugh the guns delivered many bullets.

In Search of Sticks

Her name was the same as the mother of the great prophet and she had been in this world for a full season beyond eight years. As the bullets entered and she fell to the ground, it was as if a leaf had left the tree, floating, floating, ever floating, eternally suspended in the air until the earth opened its arms to receive it. In their hurry, the soldiers did not stop to check to see that every killing had been successful. The girl lay motionless with the others, and her blood pooled on the hard soil. Gaining strength, the sun reached into the streets to illuminate them and in doing so revealed the most recent deeds of humankind.

Thousands of flies were the first to make the discovery, and they drank from the drying blood and took uninterrupted, leisurely walks through gaping mouths and nostrils, and gorged on the spilled insides.

The struggle for dominance moved to the west, and hearing the shift much as one listens to the lessening of a storm's thunder, some carefully ventured out.

The man who did the finding was in search of anything to help feed his family. He had a good soul and as such was stopped in his tracks by that which appeared before him. Many times in previous months, he had seen what the great evil did and what it left behind. But this is not like the hot humid air or the sound of the barking dog, and he could not become accustomed to it. He wanted to drop to his knees and scream to the God. Instead, he rushed to those who had fallen. As he turned one body over, the blanket of flies simply shifted to the others. In the careful checking, he found that the intent of most of the bullets had been fulfilled, but there was the faintest whisper of life in a small girl.

This village was not big but the numbers had grown, and so unlike before, not everyone was known. She was not recognized, but in the examinations which followed he believed he had some knowledge of one of the men who had perished. He also knew of the place the man had lived, so he hoped someone there might know and help this small girl. The blood which had been flowing from the places where the bullets entered on her left shoulder had miraculously coagulated. He wrapped the wound, taking the cloth from one of those who had done the dying. She was carried with much carefulness as he cautiously picked his way through the streets.

Though the fighting was some distance away there was a chance the soldiers, who were still moving about, could stumble upon him. If they saw him trying to help, he most certainly would be killed. His responsibility was to look after his family and so he needed to continue to do the living, but he wouldn't leave this little girl. He couldn't. As he had said to his wife who one day had been weeping in despair, "The wicked will not prevail; they may have the guns and they will deliver the terror, but goodness will triumph. The victories are told in the small tales and in the sheer numbers who do not sell their souls."

He did not realize her entire family was numbered with the dead he had just left and no one came out to take the child. But the father and mother of Hope saw this man carrying the small person and rushed to their neighbor's home. They gently took from his arms this girl whose name was the same as the mother of the great prophet.

The doctor named Sylvia, who had tried to help and to comfort Rose, had left after her second year of service.

Afterwards, two doctors were at the clinic but one had been accused of healing the enemy and was killed in a most painful way and the other, seeing this, fled. The building was ransacked, medicines and bandages stolen. No longer was it possible to go there and gain help for those whose lives were in desperate need.

So she lay in darkness at this home and her presence was kept secret. This is because there is a kind of convincing which provides pain and holds in the balance the continuation of life. In such circumstances people will say what, in the normal existence, would never be voiced. With the tortures it might be said in desperation that, "The neighbors over there are the ones who oppose you," or "In that house they are regaining the health of a life you once tried to steal." Upon hearing this, these evil people would then rush into Hope's home in order to finish their job of killing and also end the lives of anyone who chose to help. So no one else knew of the injured girl, and Hope's family prayed that the soldiers would not choose to come to their door.

In the changing of control, there were those caught in the crossfire of attack and counterattack. Some were killed or maimed by the guns and explosions or by the fires which burnt the homes. Hope and her family and the child who was rescued from certain death stayed and waited and even when it was known the man who was president had been the clear victor, there was no celebration. The man who was president was disappointed with the support of the villagers who were not of his blood, and of course there is always the need to apply the blame for the momentary loss of the lands.

The first of the hours were critical, though they would not be the last of the serious times. The bleeding had stopped but the wounds had to be reopened and cleaned of dirt and the eggs of insects; a bullet needed to be removed. Two had gone through this girl; however, a third lodged in a bone. With the hot knife the father of Hope adeptly found and extracted it. As this was happening, he spoke in the quietest of ways. "Do not fear, my child, this pain seems large now but it is needed if you are to have less suffering. We cannot take away all of the hurts. Still, we are here to help in ways that are possible." Though this young girl breathed indiscernibly and showed no response to her surroundings, she needed to be held as she twisted with the entry and the searching of the blade.

She was given water and helped with the swallowing and Hope, as she had done with Rose, caressed her and tried to cool her feverish body with the damp cloth. She burned and the sound of breath returned, but it came in gasps.

Hope and her mother and father and the rest of her family took turns throughout the days and nights in helping with the cooling, the drinking and the feeding of the small amounts of broth. And when it was Hope's time, she told this young girl many stories. They were of the soft warm winds and golden fields. She spoke about her wonderful cousin Rose and the compassionate doctor and the wise teacher and the happy village. She talked of the tall and the thin man with his knowing and giving ways and his kind and gentle spirit. At the end of each of these times Hope told her the story of a brave person of pure heart who rescued an angel whose name was the same as the mother of the great prophet. After four days, the fever broke.

BLOGS

The way this works is: something is written—a statement made, a story told, a position taken. What might have been previously thought of as a voice in the wilderness has, through the discovery of a reader, found a listener. In the course of conversation and through the use of other technological communicative options, readership increases.

The blog got off to a quick start. This should not have been a surprise, as there were already followers from those who had heard the speeches—"Mountains and Deserts," "The Flag of Truth," "Matter of Record," and scores of others delivered by James or members from the Society for Human Justice. Once aware of the blog, many made the cyberspace journey and visited. The potential for dramatically increasing momentum had never been greater: $p = mv$.

In the blog of the Flag of Truth few adjectives were provided and no conclusions drawn. It is easier to say "a great injustice has been perpetrated" rather than detail the precise gaps in the process. Opinions, however, can be quickly assailed whereas it is far more difficult to challenge facts.

The organizers of a rally said it "attracted over 150,000"; police "estimated the crowd to be about 70,000." If this was to be reported in the blog of the Flag of Truth, it would be achieved by accessing clinical terms: "using an aerial photograph and applying a density grid, it was determined that at its peak the rally attracted 123,000, with an error factor of plus or minus 7 percent." Each reader would then be able to draw his or her own conclusions about significance, confident that hyperbole or other forms of leading or misleading vocabulary had not entered the reporting arena. In the blog of the Flag of Truth, things could be believed.

Human Condition and The Flag of Truth
Blog Entry #1
Posted by: James A. Terrance
September 23: 9:37 p.m.

This blog will supply statistics; it will provide quantifiable information. People reading this blog will extrapolate and bring forth their images of human condition. Many will see pictures of despair and disillusionment. The faces of ignorance and desperation woven into the fabric of the Flag of Truth will appear. In their minds they will hear the songs. Most will be laments. Readers, understanding the statistics, will be distressed. They will be sad for the people and their struggles and for a world which has allowed the continuous unfolding of this story of human tragedy.

In the past, speeches given by myself or others from the Society for Human Justice have referenced facts that pertain to conditions throughout the entire world. Efforts to bring attention to these issues have, to date, achieved very little. I believe our energies have been directed towards a target whose circumference is too large. We need to narrow the focus while heightening our outrage. Victories will be realized one at a time. Triumph will follow triumph and we will establish ourselves as a people to be reckoned with. The images embedded in the Flag of Truth show us that the needs in this world are considerable. What, then, will be the first thrust? It is a difficult question.

I was suspended somewhere between dreams and reality when it came to me. A series of visions presented themselves. I saw the faces of the needy and of the desperate. One image appeared time and time again. It was of a young girl, not quite a woman but much more than a child, and when I saw her she was in different places and also differently occupied—helping, walking, hiding, searching, sitting, waiting, hoping, crying. Then I realized I was staring square into the eyes of 14,774. A notation in a book had recorded her arrival and with this simple act she became a number.

She was a refugee, one of millions in the world. I came to understand that our first quest would be to change their lives.

Together we will succeed, after which we can move to another story embedded in the Flag of Truth. But before we venture forward be warned, comprehending the real meaning of these statistics, and realizing the stark reality is a deeply disturbing process. Let me begin.

What exactly is meant by the word "refugee"? The Council of the European Union's position of March 4, 1996, article K.3, notes 'the determining factor for granting refugee status in accordance with the Geneva Conventions is the existence of a well-founded fear of persecution on the grounds of race, religion, nationality, political opinion, or membership of a particular social group.' Probably accurate, but does it enlighten?

In Search of Sticks

For the purpose of this blog, the term 'refugees, is used to refer to people who have been forced to flee from their homes. Should they have stayed they could have become casualties of the violence that was either around them or was advancing upon them. The continuation of their lives in this environment was very much in doubt.

This blog will not distinguish between the two categories: those who crossed their countries' boundaries in order to escape—'refugees', and those who left and now live in encampments but remain within their counties' borders—'internally displaced people.' Despite the fact the world differentiates and gathers statistics separately, one would be hard pressed to identify even a single variation in their day-to-day lives.

Here is a stat:

Depending on the source there are between eight and ten million refugees in this world: internally displaced people may number upwards of twenty-one million. In round figures, we are talking thirty million souls.

All of us from the Society for Human Justice, who believe in the Flag of Truth, remind you that the intent of this blog is to dispassionately present information in order to instill within you your own passion. We have assimilated these figures and understand their true meaning; we know the human cost. Do you? Will you? We invite you to respond, to tell the world about your interpretation, to recount your experience. By doing this and reading what others have written, two simultaneous realizations are possible—things need to change and our burning desire must be to bring about this change.

Consider using a thematic approach: Food, Water, and Shelter. If at all possible, try to keep your comments and descriptions specific. Be clear and concise. Short may be the more powerful form.

Thirty million, now that's one stat worth thinking about. But what does it mean? Tell us. Tell the world.

Click to respond

CHOICES

In the land where Hope lived, the seasons had only small variations. Within the differences, this was the hottest of times. There were no clouds and the sun summoned forth the fire that is its essence and with this, unmercifully assaulted her home.

Those inside, in as many ways as possible, pretended not to be alive. With doors and other openings shut and movements governed in silence, they suffered much thirst as the temperature soared. This was necessary to ensure that the place they had lived in harmony with these many years, now appear abandoned. It would be dangerous to arouse the curiosity of either those who drove up and down the streets shooting whenever the opportunity presented itself or others who roamed in groups and whose appetite for the deliverance of pain had not been satisfied. There are some who, having spilled blood and brought forth immense fear, can never again be satiated.

In the deepest part of the night, the father of Hope and her older brothers crept out to discover and bring home whatever they could so life might be sustained. The well Hope had once happily walked to now held many rotting corpses and of course these waters were full of disease. The fields had been left unattended, the crops had withered, and with the passing of each day the inevitable wasting process which results from malnourishment grew increasingly visible.

It was recognized that the butchers of the man who was president would not suddenly depart. Still blaming the people who had been trapped within the violence for the loss of the lands in the first instance, these soldiers did not allow those who survived an opportunity to reclaim some of the life they once had. Though Hope and her family were aware of the dangers that lay ahead, they also knew about the limits of suffering. An escape was planned. When they moved into the night in order to achieve the outskirts of the village and the road which led away, they did so for the chance of living; fear of dying was no longer a dominant emotion.

In the darkness they had been lucky. They picked their way through the destruction; not knowing what was around the corners, they were cautious with their steps, careful with each breath. Every situation could not be fully assessed. The luxury of time which would allow for a weighing of options was not available. Everything was done instinctively and fluidly: "take this road," "do not go there," "duck in here," "halt," "run quickly," "crouch down!" The young girl whose name was the same as the mother of the great prophet needed to be helped. She was still weak from her wounds and there was the added burden of the reawakened nightmare.

Within the hour, they found themselves at the outskirts of what was left of their village. But they didn't stop. The deep black of the night was losing its intensity and this would be followed by inevitable progressions to gray. Roving militias still guarded the perimeters, and sometimes for sport they beat down the vegetation in the hope of finding someone who was hiding.

As the distances increased between those who were escaping and the boundaries of the village, the level of safety rose. The young men with guns were lazy, and though they had been ordered to patrol these roads, they did so by driving quickly. They did not look carefully at the lands on either side, and at a certain point they stopped and drank. When it was judged enough time had elapsed to not arouse the suspicions of their commander, they returned and advanced their forms of terror with far less effort.

Those who had managed an escape took from their waters only when necessary and then just a mouthful at a time. In the daylight they lay in the tallest of the grasses or behind some hardy shrubs, and did not move. Cloths were sometimes held over the mouths of babies and young children. They did not want the crying to be heard. With the careful exodus others were encountered who had also left. They walked together but only for small moments. It is not wise to have too many people in one spot. They can be more easily seen.

Some of those escaping were no longer able to summon their voice. These travelers were not mute, but they did not speak. Though they knew the stories about their families, their friends and neighbors and themselves, it was not within their abilities to tell them. Others, in some kind of desperate effort to understand their experiences, did nothing but talk.

"Whole groups have disappeared. This is a truth written in the books about different peoples and their times in this world." The man who was Hope's revered and kind school teacher spoke slowly, each word separated from the other. Once he had talked with speed and energy, but now he experienced a difficulty with the formation of sounds. As he walked, his steps were taken in ways that suggested the action of first moving one leg forward and then the second was not natural. Instead this required an unusual concentrative skill. He did not once look at those with whom he spoke. Though he would have known some, including Hope, it was doubtful he had the capacity to make any form of recognition. It was early evening.

"The pages in these books told of many violent deaths, of whole villages burned, of towns surrounded and all within slaughtered. Enormous holes had been dug to hold the large number of bodies and to hide the sins of the people who did these killings. Sometimes places were built to burn those who had been taken from this earth, and ashes and smoke filled the air the whole day long. The reasons provided about why such things came to be were no reasons at all. As it was written, this was done because some did not belong to the same group or they worshiped the God in a different way, or it was believed the color of the skin told the value of the soul. And though I have read many things and given my students much information, I did not tell them about this because I did *not believe it to be true." The teacher labored forward, not speaking for a while.*

"In all of the writings there was a single word used to describe these happenings. That word is 'massacre.' It is said at this time in the life of the world and in this location ten thousand people were massacred. There were other places where the deaths were greater and it told of the hundreds of thousands or even the millions being massacred. I have come to understand this is not the right word as it does not begin to tell the true story." And with that the teacher quit speaking. He continued to struggle with his walk.

Among those in flight was an older woman. Though she moved with the others, she seemed singular. No family member or friend walked beside her to help her with her steps or provide the strength which comes with being near to someone who understands the heart. A vast emptiness shrouded her and the hollowness in her voice spoke of the same condition. In life, as it has been experienced throughout the ages, she should have been sitting and playing with the children of her children. Instead she was on this trek, an undertaking which would tax even the available energies of people much younger. She was not certain why she walked. Somehow the God had left her breathing and she did not know what else to do.

"I was frightened and on the ground holding my knees together, as were the rest of my family and many other families. I cannot remember the time of the day. One almost always knows the moment when something happens which changes a life but I cannot recall this. We looked to the earth, not wanting to catch the eyes of those who stood above for

fear this act alone would be thought of as a form of challenge. The men who towered over us had taken drink and the drugs. A sickening smell that comes with the power of evil hung over everything.

"*A boy with a gun pointed it to my head and demanded I open my mouth. This I did and the steel was pushed into it. With a voice which had not yet changed into that used by a man, he sneered, 'Old woman, I should shoot you now. The world will not miss you. I doubt it even knows you breathe.' He said these things as if it was not the only time he used the words. Perhaps he had heard them from another, for they were not those which come from a boy. I waited but he did not pull the trigger. He moved the gun away and pointed to the next and then the next while the soldiers yelled and cursed. This was done as part of a game, and I could hear them betting. Who would be the first to die? The boy with the rifle shouted things I did not understand, and he danced all around. He was important to the game and enjoyed this fact. When he finally did the killing it was the second smallest boy of my eldest son who was chosen. His mother screamed and the soldiers laughed. The winner of the bet threw some of the money at the one who did the shooting. My son grasped his wife's arm with a grip that said, 'Do not move. Do not move to our dead son, for if you do you will surely be killed.' Even with this wickedness the hope was held that these soldiers might tire of this and some would survive. I prayed for my ending, thinking this killing would help fill their stomachs with the blood that was craved. Perhaps, through my death, someone would be spared.*

In Search of Sticks

"But they made up a new game and this was about how death should arrive. The voices became loud and there was arguing. This was not done in a way that spoke of anger but one which had a purpose—to bring the greatest trembling to those of us on the ground who held our knees. One stood above a young woman and said to the person in charge, 'Commander, I would like to save the bullets for the battles. Please allow me to hack her with my long knife, first a finger and then a hand and perhaps an ear, until there is too much bleeding and she melts in front of us.' And another said, 'No great leader, let me use the kerosene I have carried here. I will pour this over her and smoke a cigarette, and just before I finish throw the smoldering end to her.' One more who was anxious to join this game spoke, 'Wonderful and great warrior leader let us all use her and then with my gun I will shoot her in that place so she can never be used again.' And the one in charge made the young woman choose. She chose kerosene.

"In the end, every sitting person was killed by fire or cutting or shooting; that is, all but me. And when I looked up at the one in charge, he said, 'The boy is right, I doubt the earth knows that you still breathe. We who have the power are here to tell this earth it does not have control and is no longer in charge. It will not feel the loss of something it does not know it has in the first place. So why bother?' They all left. I did what I could with the bodies to make some of them seem restful, and I said my good-byes. Then I began this walk."

Everyone continued to move down the road and for a time no one else spoke and no child cried.

FIRST RESPONSES

Human Condition and The Flag of Truth #1
Posted by Julian M.
September 24: 8:46 a.m.

Great start for a blog, Mr. Terrance! I've been following this thing for a while and I'm already a big fan of the Flag of Truth. If I got your message right, it goes something like this: trying to fix everything which needs fixing means we'd end up fixing nothing. So, in order to prevent burnout and increase the likelihood of making a positive difference, we're going to go with one thing and then move on from there. Our single focus will be the plight of refugees. I have some history on this one so I'm good with this. But don't you think limiting us to 750 words is overly restrictive? I guess you're not looking for books. Believe me I could write one on this.

My life has brought me to two countries in Africa, and much of what I came to learn isn't good news. The experiences marked me. Rather than ramble on I'll take you up on your suggestion and focus on one thing—water. Maybe a couple of blog entries later, when no one is looking, I'll sneak in some things about food and shelter.

Here's the deal with water: humans may look solid, but as it turns out we're basically one big puddle. Trust me on this one, I did the research. Our blood is 83 percent water, muscles are 75, the brain is 74, and even our bones are 22 percent H_2O. So, you can pretty quickly figure out the water/life equations. They are simple to understand. No water = no life. Little water = life by a thread.

Picture yourself living in a big, burning hot space where almost nothing grows. In times past, these lands offered a basic amount of support for the nomads who used to wander through. But now you are a refugee and this is the only place you can live, so you're there. Don't think about taking a trip to a temperate climate—it's not going to happen. Forget air conditioning—you don't even know what this is. You're sweating big time and liters of water are dripping out of you, and through the process of evaporation more escapes unnoticed into the hungry air. You're going to need to replenish so you take your containers to the long line that has formed at one of the half a dozen pumping stations which are in constant use. A few people are in charge of giving out the water and men with guns are standing beside them just in case someone demands more or tries to jump the queue.

No one argues or butts in: everyone has seen what guns can do. The pumps go throughout the day and near evening they run dry. All you are given are five liters in total for drinking, cooking, and washing. The thing is, it's so hot outside you need to drink four of them just to exist in a state of semi-dehydration.

'Dehydration' is a word often accessed while speaking but many times it is used incorrectly. It slips off the tongue far too easily and comes to mean the same thing as thirsty. "I think I'll stop and get a cold drink, I'm feeling a bit dehydrated." Trust me; the speaker hasn't a clue about the true meaning of the word. I've seen dehydration. Brace yourself. At around 5 percent loss of fluid, the heart rate increases; the brain doesn't work like it used to; and the stomach is pretty much on edge. If the percentage is doubled, the kidneys experience difficulty functioning, many other vital organs start to shut down, toxins build up, vomiting occurs, vision dims and delirium sets in. Death is right around the corner, and for about two million children a year, that is their end.

Dehydration is not simple thirst. This is a huge problem in refugee camps. The lack of available water is a critical issue. Of equal importance are the proliferations of bacterial, viral, and parasitic infections all of which result in extreme diarrhea and vomiting. This of course only speeds the progressive effects of dehydration. Massive amounts of watery fluid escape from both ends. Remember the water/life equations?

Malnutrition starts to kick in, in a big way, when the little food eaten isn't in your body long enough to be absorbed. But that's another story.

Human Condition and The Flag of Truth #37
Posted by: Change Agent
September 24: 3:07 p.m.

People speak about life after death and in the same breath many will mention heaven and hell. They talk as if they are dimensions apart, as if an eternity of space lies between them and there is no common border. This is as it is envisioned in some peoples' minds but take a good look around—that isn't how it works on Earth. Here one can check out of paradise and walk into the inferno just by leaving a gated community.

Instead of one giant hell, the world has thousands of them scattered throughout the globe. It's as if an evil plant grew long ago and its seeds had been blown about by the four winds. They sprouted and the new plants matured and, in turn, their seeds were dispersed by these same winds. The pattern continued to repeat itself and more pockets of hell appeared.

Of course it didn't happen that way, but how can we explain the kinds of tortured lives many live—those who spend their days crouched on the sidewalks and nights curled up in the alleyways? Where is the explanation for the lack of available treatment concerning a host of curable or controllable diseases? Not to stray too far from the intent of this blog—refugee camps—how does one explain the existence of hell in paradise?

I never visited any of these camps but I have read articles and talked to others. As I understand it, the hell is more than abysmal housing and receiving the

> minimum amount of food for survival. It is more than being subjected to the hour by hour, day by day ongoing grief about the loss of a way of life.
>
> The hell is also loneliness and emptiness. It is not being able to truly celebrate their faith, work their lands or stop by the grave of one's father and mother. It is living with their pain, the hurt of others and the despair of having no positive future.
>
> We need to break open those gates of hell. We need to rescue these people. We need to give them back the parts of a normal life that are possible to return. Whatever it takes, we need to do this!

The number of responses kept increasing: 38, 39, 40, 748, post 983. By the end of the first day over a thousand had submitted comments. It was tenfold that figure when the week had concluded. James and the members of the Society for Human Justice were ecstatic. Correspondence had been penned from people living throughout the world. The Flag of Truth was indeed gaining a global foothold.

James sat in the living room reading from his laptop computer; stories were detailed—many unique, almost all illuminating. Twitter and Facebook and other social media sites also began to contribute their forms of conversation. Finally no longer able to focus on the print, he reluctantly drew his tired eyes away. The next steps would be critical—both for the refugees and for himself.

In Search of Sticks

SPECIALISTS

The walk from the nightmare that used to be their village seemed to stretch almost to eternity. Despite the lack of food and drink people persevered. At first the sequences were remembered. "The sun and the stars have completed five journeys since our leaving." "It has been seven full cycles when we found the brown waters we still carry and that continue to sustain us." By the time they met up with some who had escaped from a larger town far to the southeast, no one was counting anymore as there was nothing to distinguish the memories. One step followed another; they looked at something vague in the horizon and moved toward it. Having achieved that, they did this again.

These people, as Hope and the others did, travelled in a single direction. All chose to believe the thread of the story they heard –a town, a distance away to the northwest and just beyond the boundaries of their country, would provide help and protection. If only they could get to this place of friendship and comfort. People from the town and Hope's village joined together for a time in the walking and more stories were told. Some who listened doubted their ears, though they, too, had been victims of or witnesses to the forces of wickedness. Even when experiencing evil, there is a reluctance to confirm its reality.

A mother was first to talk. Her three children walked with her; the smallest one clung to her skirt. "Much thinking must have happened before these deeds were done. In the horror of the moment, I did not consider this but in the looking back I believe that, for things to have unfolded in the manner they did, all the details had been carefully planned. Methods were refined in the same way one builds an understanding of the loom and the ways of weaving or the pottery which is made through delicate turnings. With practice and the sharing of ideas, skills are developed and the art gains strength. They are the devil's own artists, whose purpose in getting together is to demonstrate diabolical techniques and expand the scope of twisted creativity."

People waited in expectation, wondering what possible horror would be spoken of. They dreaded these moments, yet somehow understood that this telling must be done. They had been chosen as listeners. In this type of conversation often a space exists between the start and the next grouping of words. The hot winds picked up the soils and the sands and threw them at their bodies. They kept on walking. At long last she spoke again.

"There are people who have dedicated themselves to understanding everything about the ways of flame, and they paint with fire. They have gained a knowledge and ability and this allows them to deliver a powerful and efficient terror, one which brings them obvious enjoyment. The house was large and strong

and many people had taken refuge between its walls in a futile effort to escape the senseless killings by those who once spoke of justice. I saw these killers from where I hid and though I did not want to look, I found I could not look away. It was as if seeing would bring comprehension to that which is incomprehensible.

At first they shouted, 'We are your friends! Come out and play and dance with us!' But no one inside spoke and no one left. I do not know of the thinking of those within, and I can only guess of the fear which took hold. Though my ears were not capable of discerning the words, my heart was. The air was filled with whispered, desperate prayers. These were not answered. More cruel taunts were hurled when suddenly a command was given to those wishing to do the burning and everyone swiftly moved to their positions. Each person knew his job and in the quickest of times a circle of flame surrounded this house. Every opening was also ringed by fire." Long moments passed and the mother didn't speak. The eyes of all of those who heard wanted to shed tears, but they did not do this because their bodies refused to give up the water.

"Some breathed in the volumes of smoke or took fire into their lungs and fell to the floor. Their corpses were consumed by flames and this was not felt. Those who leaped out of the door and windows in a desperate effort to continue a life suffered the most. They screamed with the pain and the awfulness of feeling themselves being burned alive. The soldiers who set the fires watched the writhing and drank and laughed. The house was reduced to ashes and all within tortured and consumed by flame. Only when it became clear that everyone had perished, did they leave. No bullets were needed; no bullets were allowed. These were the men of fire."

Somewhere in this talking, a sick child took his last breath. His father could not bring himself to leave this son, and so he was still carried for another piece of the long day before all who were part of this exodus stopped. In as dignified a way as possible, this young boy was returned to the earth.

After a time one more spoke, breaking the quietness which held only the small sounds of those trying to move forward. Remembering what had been said on the journey earlier in the day, he began to talk. "I also have known of some who practice the trade of bringing early ends to life and who pride themselves in using a singular approach for this accomplishment. They deliver a death that experiences no bleeding. Just as with the fire people, they choose to create fear and terror and do so without the use of a steel blade or a single bullet. If a nose gushes or blood is mixed with the vomit, this is considered a failure.

"One who described this to me spoke of broken fingers and arms and legs but this happened in ways where there would not be protrusions. The bones were not to break out of the skin and bring forth the bleeding. There was hitting though not with sharp objects, and not in areas which caused blood to move to the stomach and then escape through the mouth. The side of a skull could be struck. This was allowed. A strike to the front of the face was not, as a nose or a tooth might be broken. Then, most assuredly, there would be blood.

Unless the heart decided to give up, death did not come quickly for those who received this form of punishment. At first there was crying and pleading, but as the beating continued there was only whimpering, then no sound and sometimes a loss of consciousness. If this happened and there could be no reviving the one who had received the blows, the neck was snapped.

In Search of Sticks

"The people who came to practice this trade were prepared to spend much time demonstrating their considerable ability. Others were forced to watch, and when finally the last breath thankfully left one, another would be chosen from those who had been captured. Someone else took a turn to demonstrate prowess, to do the long and painful killing without bringing forth the blood."

More stories needed to be told: some of them about the herding of people; the stealing of daughters; the forced digging of the graves and the burying alive; the stripping and indignations before the killings, and the children becoming soldiers. But there could be no more listening, not this day. Descriptions of the victories of hell are not easily heard.

Hope and her family and the child whose name was the same as the mother of the great prophet struggled on. One step and then another.

TEMPERATURE RISING

The number of blog responses, Twitters, Facebook inclusions and other social networking communications increased in ways that James had not thought possible. It seemed as if arithmetic progression had taken on exponential form. Mathematically speaking, this was not true, but the rate of growth was such that it astounded many, including himself. A sense of urgency had been built into the words. There was evidence of understanding, of agreement, of a desire for difference and of the pressing need to achieve this difference. This was either expressed overtly or subsumed in descriptive language. James reflected on what he had read, "Facts and emotion in a mutually

In Search of Sticks

supportive balance, now that's a powerful formula."

He thought of Melanie. She had been absolutely correct, mass communication on the cheap was indeed worth the effort. What would he do without his Melanie? She was his rock, his comfort in the storm. How did the song go? "She is my everything." Many poets have expressed the sentiment, some more effectively than others. For a moment emotions began to take over, but his mind refused this pause. James continued his analytical quest.

All the speeches he and members of the Society for Human Justice had made in various cities and towns amounted to mere pencil marks on the canvass of change. The blog, however, contributed brushstrokes. Not that the times in the halls and small venues had been meaningless; those experiences built confidence. They solidified ideas. They focused vision. It was the birthplace for the Flag of Truth and that, combined with messaging technology, had the potential to bring about positive movement in the world. "Potential" was the key. It is a complicated word and not at all precise.

James drank the remainder of his orange juice and continued to tackle his plate of eggs and bacon. As he had been unable to sleep, he rose before his usual time, and discovering his hunger, made an American breakfast. The coffee was black and hot and the eggs runny. Toast soaked up the yoke which had escaped the first efforts at consumption. He glanced out the window; the day had dawned and presented itself in the early shades of color.

Melanie lay in bed, still moving alternately between the worlds of deep rest and dreams. "When she wakes up I'll make her a breakfast of her choosing." As was his habit, he talked to himself, not silently where the words are internal but audibly as if someone was sitting across from him at the kitchen table.

"I can't use a map to help guide me. No such publication exists. Perhaps I could check out the GPS, the one equipped with speech recognition and ask, "Where am I¿"

"Halfway between nowhere and somewhere," it would respond.

"And what is the destination¿" could be my pursuit.

"That's a good question," might be its reply.

James looked up almost expecting to hear his imaginary listener say something. After a few seconds he continued with this one-sided audible conversation.

"Neither a map nor a Global Positioning System are going to be the least bit useful if I don't have a clue where I'm heading. I'm a pathetic leader. Here I am, inviting everyone to walk with me down this road, but as far as I know, there may not be a road; in fact, I doubt if there's even a path. Everything is being cleared and built as we go along, so how will I recognize the destination when we arrive¿" He weakly gestured with both hands.

Drawing a long breath he concluded, "I'm a pretty sorry excuse for a guy who said 'follow me.' James A. Terrance has a blog and he has a Flag of Truth. Now what?"

"Now what, honey?" Melanie came in moving quietly, each step softened by her cloth slippers.

"Oh, nothing, I was just talking to myself." He got up and gave her a quick peck on the right cheek.

She returned the affection. "You can't call that a kiss." She firmly planted her lips onto his. "Mmm, bacon. I could smell it all the way to the bedroom and now I can taste it."

James laughed and proceeded to pour her a cup of coffee. "My lady, what can I get for you?"

"Why, bacon and eggs, of course. The smell of it woke me up. Thinking about eating it got me up. As always, eggs over easy, crispy bacon."

James was already hard at the preparation. Both basked in these simple moments of reverie. Soul mates.

Despite their best effort to make it otherwise, time refused to stop, or even slow. The protracted breakfast reluctantly concluded and they left the kitchen to move independently in their day. James continued to wrestle with demons and battle uncertainty. In doing so, he returned to one-way conversation. He took out the garbage and talked. He mowed his small patch of lawn and trimmed the side hedge, all the while conversing at great length. Everything James did that day was accompanied by solitary discussion.

The "now what" question weighed on him and he desperately searched for the intellectual road map, for clarity in his vision.

"Last week alone Google Analytics reported there had been some thirty thousand hits—all responding to the same issues, all aligned in their thoughts. People continue to interact with the blog. Tomorrow I will post another entry. Tens of thousands more replies are certain to follow. They share a belief that in some small yet exciting way, the directions of humanity will be altered. They also are convinced I know which forms of action will accomplish this—that I will soon reveal to the world who to see and what to do."

As the soliloquy was concluding, it finally dawned on James that he had at his fingertips the backing of at least a hundred thousand people. With the projections of growing support, this could eventually go to a million and beyond. "A million!" he exclaimed. "It's time to exert some muscle! I will not ask. I will insist. I will demand. I will lead." He reiterated, shouting over the noise of the electric lawnmower, "I will lead!"

The day was gray and none of his neighbors were occupied with backyard activities. His declaration went unnoticed.

James turned to letter writing. He ran the draft by the executive of the Society for Human Justice. A few cosmetic changes had been suggested and the modifications made.

"The letter looks great!" William Sanchez offered his endorsement.

The Society for Human Justice was becoming a recognizable entity and the Flag of Truth flew top center on the letterhead. It was a strong piece of writing addressed to his elected representative; the language was precise, and the issue surrounding refugees convincingly stated. It finished with a less than subtle allusion to a large, growing and restless voting public whose support could either serve him well or disappear and align itself with another candidate. He posted the letter without hesitation.

James didn't wait for the return mail. Patience had always been one of his strengths, but it was beginning to wear thin. At any rate he understood the drill. Correspondence received from his representative would be in the form of an acknowledgement and undoubtedly include certain phrases—"thank you for taking the trouble to write," "your letter is important to us," and "someone in the office will get back to you in as timely a manner as possible." Days later, after he was sure of the letters' arrival, he phoned.

"Good afternoon, the offices of Mr. Patterson. How may I direct your call?"

"I would like to speak to Mr. Patterson."

"I'm sorry sir, Mr. Patterson is not available. He is tied up all day. Would you like to leave a message?"

"Thank you. Please let him know James A. Terrance from the Society for Human Justice called." He left his number and then hung up. He had no expectation his call would be returned and three days later he was proving to be correct. Experience, once more, had been a first-rate teacher.

James called again.

"Good afternoon, the offices of Mr. Patterson. How may I direct your call?"

"I would like to speak to Mr. Patterson."

"I'm sorry, Mr. Patterson is unavailable. Would you care to leave a message?"

"Why yes, thank you. Please ask Mr. Patterson to look up the Society for Human Justice's website and check out the Terrance blog. I'm certain he will find this most interesting." James ended by leaving his phone number.

Human condition: Blog Entry #15
Posted by: James A. Terrance
January 04: 8:37 p.m.

Yet again I wrote my national representative. It was a respectful letter, and of course with all things linked to the Society for Human Justice and the Flag of Truth, it was informative, factual and unemotional. Anyone with a predilection to dispute ideas by attacking the emotional argument is out of luck. Instead they are faced with having to dissect, analyze and reflect. Many, once presented such information in a dispassionate manner, become passionate, highly charged supporters.

However, it appears some elected representatives have developed a form of immunity to reasonable argument. I say this because, for these people, facts do not seem to illicit a response, either positive or negative. My own representative did not provide a reply which offered any confirmation he has understood even a morsel of the information he received. Certainly he made no undertaking to use his position to effect change. Those massive misery counts we are too familiar with continue to increase. 'Dear James, thank you for your concern' letters are no longer going to cut it. Ladies and gentlemen, it's time to turn up the heat. This is not a call to arms but it is a call to action.

We are proposing to start an e-mail and letter writing campaign that has seen no equivalent. In every democratic country throughout the world, wherever our Flag of Truth flies, contact needs to be made. Make this a voting issue. Make this 'the' voting issue. It appears the only way we will get change is when voters demand it. Even if you are happy with your elected representative, make this crystal clear: your continued support no longer can be counted on unless, of course, there is hard evidence he or she is actively seeking a solution to help with the refugee crises—this blight on our world.

The facts concerning refugees are explicitly noted in the previous blog entries. Pick and choose; send that information on. Fly the Flag of Truth. Demand action. Be direct with the message—"Either get on

> board or look forward to your reentry into the job market.'"
>
> Millions of people sit in tents and makeshift houses, and they wait. They are not aware of what they are waiting for ... but we know they are waiting for us.
>
> Click to respond

WISHES AND PRAYERS

The walking could not to be described in the normal ways of moving from one place to another. Memories of this journey were rarely spoken of and for those who chose to talk, available vocabulary proved hopelessly inadequate. Not even vivid phrases such as "excruciatingly long" or "painfully draining" can bring forth the images of enormous loss and emptiness that prevail after the desperation for life's continuance has left. Who knows why some, in their exhausted and vacant lives, chose to move forward? Who knows why the poorly sandaled foot repeatedly placed itself in front of the other when all that was valued had gone? The heart beat; the blood moved; air entered the lungs, first in, then out. There are no words to tell of this walking in Hope's language, nor do any exist in the vast body of languages used in this world.

If history speaks of this at all, it will reference the exodus in ways which document the distances involved. This will be summarized in two or three sentences subsumed in a paragraph. Should there be an illustration, it would be a line on a map. Neither the physical pain nor the internal agony will be, nor can it be, detailed.

In the existence before this one, there was wishing. It happened in Hope's village much in the same manner as this occurs throughout the world. A child wishes for something—perhaps a toy. Then, as life moves, wishes change: more toys, love, true love, good harvests, greater prosperity, recognition, position, wealth and power, more wealth and more power. The progression seems to be without end. There are none who can say they haven't wished; there are few who can say they no longer desire. In the various places of earth's geography, the process is similar, only the details change. This is largely a result of different availabilities.

Without warning, one of the walkers began to speak. "I wish there was a cloud in the sky which would place itself between the sun and ourselves, and with this sacrifice give us the gift of small relief. It would be too much to wish for an abundance of dark clouds so overburdened that with their release we could fill our containers and drink deeply. Then choosing not to take shelter by those bushes, we would sit under the falling waters." He pointed to a few scraggly shrubs which had somehow managed an existence. "I cannot wish for this, as the God has not been disposed to do the answering of my prayers. I prayed for my wishes to come true. I prayed my daughters would not be taken away, and this did not happen. I prayed my wife would not be savaged *and this did not happen. I prayed the evil would leave and the house would be spared and neither happened. It must have been that I wished for too much."* He looked up. *"So now I pray for one small cloud."*

All those who heard, knew of this and felt the abandonment. It was mid-afternoon and above them the vast and intense sky was not interrupted by the presence of even a single cloud.

After much space, Hope spoke. *"On this long walk I have struggled to make sense of that which we saw and lived through. In doing so, I examined things as they exist in the different pieces of my mind, and I have come to a new way of thinking."*

There was a pause and in those moments many of the walkers studied her. Sometimes people are known because they can be easily identified. This might happen for someone with great beauty or a distinguished nose or birthmark. There are some who have not been given the special features, yet they are widely recognized and their presence commands attention. When Hope did the speaking, everyone experienced a heightened form of listening.

"We are not the God, nor do we live in the heaven, so we do not understand the reasons why no answers were given to our prayers. We have seen and suffered the forces of immense evil and the pictures in our minds and the feelings in our souls will be with us for always. But I also see those who, even in the face of the greatest persuasions, chose not to join the ones with their brutal ways. It is possible the God did not respond because we need to be looking elsewhere.

"Perhaps we should not beg for help from the greater force, instead look within. We have heard in the pieces of talking that some wait for us to complete this dangerous and torturous journey to the safe place so they can be of assistance. And it is my belief others also wish to extend their hands. I do not understand how this is known. It may come from the memory of the good doctor from the different land or from another place in my awareness. But I know this one thing to be true—there is a well of goodness in most souls and its depth is such that even in the face of intense cruelty it will prevail. I feel this."

Despite the various types of pain that their bodies experienced and had been permanently etched into each of their souls, these walkers appreciated the wisdom of the words. They believed, if only for the smallest moment of time, that things would be better, that prayers may be answered in different ways, that the slowness of the coming of help did not mean help would not come at all. Still many wondered, *"If it is to arrive, why did it not do so earlier?"*

The girl whose name is the same as the mother of the great prophet had not been able to regain her full power before the fleeing. At first she walked with the others but with the diminishing strength, her condition became increasingly fragile. At some point, she began to be carried on the shoulders or in the arms of all the members of Hopes family including Hope herself. During these carrying times, there was a new level of difficulty for those who held her but not one word was spoken about this hardship. With the passing of the days and the loss of the energies the frequency of the transferring from one person to another increased. The hot desert lands exacted a price from all who walked upon them. Still, nothing was said.

The vast expanse was almost uninhabited. Only a few small groups and their animals moved within its boundaries. These people understood the relationship between the sun and this form of the earth. But Hope's family had spent their days growing crops, and they did not know about the desert except by what had been told in stories, all of which came with a message—even people who are strong and able should fear and respect it.

Those in Hope's village had experienced intense heat. The capacities of the sun and the durations of the assaults were fully known. But there were times for sitting in the shade, and there was water to drink, and even some to splash on the face for cooling.

Seasons came where the God did not provide a radiant smile and the crops withered. In such times life could be conserved by not taxing the body with normal daily movements. On this exodus, there was little food and water and few opportunities to gain relief from the blistering sun. The demands, however, did not decrease. Rather, they grew in ways which would challenge even those who were healthy, both in body and spirit. That is, such people would be challenged if they existed.

A drop of water fell from one of the walkers and disappeared into the earth. A scream was heard, not by the ears but by the mind. It was the same cry that pierced the soul on the previous step and would do so again on the next. The death of his wife had been painful. Occasionally he raised his head in order to squint toward the horizon but almost always he looked down. More drops of water fell. Another step was taken.

One who drifted to the back of the loosely assembled group grew hotter. The heat in her body was greater than could be accounted for by the onslaught of the sun, and she began to talk in quiet, loving ways to her baby. The natural relationship between mother and child is wondrous, and those who witness this smile within. But no child was cradled in her arms. This woman began to sing a lullaby, a wonderful melody of peace and beauty familiar to all. It had been sung in most of the homes throughout the land.

Perhaps in some places, she may have been left behind so others more able had a better chance to survive, but this did not happen. Those listening were overcome both by the desperation of her circumstance and the memories of the song. They brought forth waters from their own small reserves and shared these with her. Because of this, she was not as hot, but with this reduction of fever, her baby whom she has seen and felt and caressed with song was no longer with her. It might have been wondered if, with their charity, they had helped at all. They stopped walking earlier than had been the pattern. It was well before the time of intense gray that happens before the blackness.

On this journey, the pains accompanying each life were experienced in excruciatingly similar ways. One aching day blended into the next. The assault that came from the sky was one of the few memories of distinction.

It was not clear why the man who was president tried to destroy those who moved from the violence. They carried no weapons and did not threaten his power. It may have been

In Search of Sticks

because of the different blood or the need to apply the blame. Perhaps it was their punishment for wishing to leave.

The arrival was not a surprise. In the silence of walking there came a sound and those not fully absorbed in their hurt looked upward and behind and saw the airplane in the horizon. It flew toward them; they had been seen. There was no point in hiding in the few bushes in the hope the pilot would fly by and not be aware of their presence. Instead, a strategy of chaos was implemented. This was done without thinking. People ran in all of the different directions and this made it difficult for the plane's bombs and bullets to take a large number of lives. If any of the explosions did the killing or maiming this would then just be a question of luck. But a small group had grown numb and in their anesthetized state they did not run; they kept slowly walking towards the horizon. Those people took the last of their steps. After the pilot got tired or bored or the bullets and bombs had all been used, the plane few off. The survivors ran to help, but there was nothing to do except gather the pieces of the bodies and with prayer bury what remained into the sandy earth.

Hope and her family and the girl who was named after the mother of the great Prophet continued with their walking. No one knows how many more days passed or how many more who had been wounded in body or spirit died on the way. When they did set foot on the lands of the neighboring country nothing identified the border, and so it was not realized this had been crossed.

Salvation presented itself in the form of four people in a small open vehicle. They asked in polite ways for these walkers to follow.

DANCING

James sat. His mind moved to a different time. "Step forward with your left foot, then, while moving fluidly, do the same with the right. Repeat again, leading with your left but this time step side right. You with me so far? Good. Now in a sliding motion move the left foot to the right foot. Don't hurry; do this slowly. Be graceful. Straight away touch the left foot with the right, remembering to raise your right heel ever so slightly. Ah, perfection. Repeat the pattern, only this time increase the speed of movement. Strive for effortlessness. Yes—well done, James! Melanie, you are an inspiration, what elegance!"

James remembered the choreography, the precision, the commitment, the automaticity. A decade earlier he and Melanie had taken dance classes. Those were wondrous moments. The state of being the two of them achieved individually and realized together amazed him. "It's too bad it came to an end," he thought. "The busyness in a person's life really bears reexamination."

Why this had been remembered while he sat in the receptionist's office, was not clear. Still, with James, ideas didn't appear randomly. There were links; everything could be connected—dot to dot.

The letters and e-mails from the avid followers of the blog kept coming, one after another, all directed to the offices of various elected officials in the different nations. If this was an effort to tie up the system, it could be viewed as a partial success. If it was supposed to serve as an irritant, the goal was absolutely accomplished. However, if the purpose was to bring about change by reintroducing the moral compass of human obligation, then the endeavor disappointed.

Contact was made, the kind that might be tentatively developed between two opposing factions such as what happens during the initial efforts to resolve a long-standing dispute. Those present at these events often choose to perform a figurative dance, one which tells the story of reiteration of position and attempts at persuasion, but never of a search for common ground. James was meeting with his representative, Mr. Patterson. The dance began.

"Mr. Terrance, please take a seat." The man in the expensive Italian suit stood up from behind the imposing desk, and using a sweeping motion, gestured toward a few comfortable chairs that semi-ringed a handsomely crafted, wooden coffee table.

James, who had just entered, did not sit but rather stood while the other busied himself putting papers in neat piles. Looking up and, seeing that James had not yet sat, he again implored him to do so. He spoke rapidly. "Please, Mr. Terrance, take a seat. I'll only be a second here. Some important stuff, I don't want to lose track of it. Can I get you coffee or tea? Perhaps water or juice?"

"Coffee, please. Thanks very much." This time James did sit.

"How do you like it?"

"Black."

"Then black it is." The immaculately tailored man spoke into the intercom. "Charmaine, would you bring in a couple of coffees please? Black for my guest. Thanks." Within a minute, the door opened and a professionally dressed woman in her mid-forties carried in two coffees. James thanked her as she left. One had cream in it; he judged the other to be his.

"Mr. Terrance, a pleasure to meet you." The man behind the desk had finished the tidying he felt necessary and, using quick steps, strode over to James. He extended his big, fleshy right hand. James rose, received and shook it. The two sat opposite each other.

In Search of Sticks

"You certainly succeeded in getting my attention. The e-mails have challenged a few of the office staff. They've had to find ways to deal with them, and I can safely say your letter writing campaign has killed more than a few trees." He laughed with confidence and ease. "Now, sir, what is it that you believe I am able to do for you?"

James, not expecting such a forthright approach, had been prepared to do a different dance before arriving at this point in the conversation. But he wasn't easily rattled; in his business life, he had worked with some highly positioned people. His nerves were under control, and he knew how to adjust. If the rhythm changed so be it; he was familiar with the steps to many different dances.

"Well, Mr. Patterson, first of all let me thank you for taking the time to meet with me. I appreciate it, particularly knowing how busy someone in your position must be."

Irrespective of the hurry this man seemed to be in, and his thinly disguised impatience with the situation, James knew about the etiquette such a circumstance demanded. Flow was required. He sipped the coffee. It had become tepid and had the taste which goes with the kind that has been sitting and warming for far too long. "Here's the thing, Mr. Patterson; you've received many pieces of correspondence and no doubt read some of it—or at least been briefed on the contents. There is a crisis in the world. People who lived peacefully but in the poorest of conditions have been brutalized in the most awful ways and forced from their homes. Those who did manage to survive the violence and the demanding exodus now live in the direst of circumstances, where life hangs by a thread of goodwill. They exist in tents and makeshift shelters, and in places which no longer have any meaning for them. The cemeteries of their ancestors cannot be visited, their farmlands are not accessible, and their homes have been destroyed. The mountains and streams and all things familiar have disappeared from their lives. The constituents who wrote you would have mentioned some of this." Even though he was not overtly nervous, his mouth was dry. The lukewarm coffee provided marginal relief.

The man opposite showed no acknowledgment and did not demonstrate any inclination to participate in the give and take patterns that normally accompany such conversation. He wanted this to be a solo dance. James continued. "Since you asked me 'What I think you can do?' here is my response. You are a persuasive individual, a member of our national government and belong to the party in power. In short, you have certain abilities to influence." James locked his eyes onto those of his representative. Mr. Patterson, for his part, had tried to avoid being captured, but the boldness of James caught him by surprise and it was too late. They were eye to eye. "You can use your position and personal talents to convince others to help structure and implement plans which will alleviate the pain for at least some of these innocent victims."

The elected national representative remained passive. His eyes became impatient and moved from the man in front of him to other things in the room. He knew there would be more to come. James, sensing the need to take this talking from monologue to dialogue, sat silently staring right at him. This would be a couple's dance. He sipped at his coffee. Any claim it had to heat had past. Mr. Patterson never once touched his cup. Understanding that James was quite prepared to sit for as long as it took, he felt compelled to offer a response. The dance had begun. 'Step forward with the left foot, then, while moving fluidly, do the same with your right.'

"Okay, Mr. Terrance. I appreciate you taking the trouble to come and brief me on this. Let me reassure you our government is committed to helping those less fortunate whether they live at home or abroad. We have many programs, too numerous to detail in our short time together." He turned his wrist and checked his watch to emphasize that the meeting was about to come to a close. "Some of these are detailed on our website, and I invite you to look into them. Modest sized projects, those which are joint efforts with another arm of government or a different organization, are not even listed. We are unswerving in our dedication to help people in need." He looked over to his intercom as if waiting for a call to come. It didn't. "Nevertheless, I respect your position on this matter. I will relay this sense to my party." At that the well-tailored and slightly obese man moved his fingers through his rinsed gray hair and rose from his chair.

This was the signal. There could be no misinterpretation; the meeting was concluded. He reached across to shake James' hand once more. "Thank you, Mr. Terrance. This has been most enlightening. If you wish to get a hold of me again, you know where to find me." He said this as both moved to the door. They were doing a slow step.

"Actually, sir, I believe it is you who will want to contact me. I'll leave my card at the desk." James' business background was proving to be of value; he understood how this worked. There would be other moves to make. Mr. Patterson might have wished it to be otherwise but this was not the end of the dance—not by any means.

THE PROMISED LAND

With stomachs bloated and skin wrinkled in ways that resembled the coverings of some who had lived well beyond the expectation of the time for being on this earth, it might be questioned how any of them continued to walk. This is the likeness of people when the food and water consumed is not nearly enough and has not been sufficient for periods which test the parameters required for survival.

The ones who came to meet those who had experienced the unforgiving earth were as shepherds herding a flock. No one was allowed to stray. One assumed the lead while others took positions on either side; still another played the role of the dog that would nip at the heels at any who lagged behind. When these weary souls who had done the leaving and the difficult walking came over the hill and saw that which lay before them, there was pause. Despite the prodding, their collective intake of breath demanded a halt. Someone whispered, "So this is the promised land."

While taking in the expanse they not only saw what was before them, but also what was not. There were no beautiful forests or streams flowing through valleys, and no lands waiting for strong hands and backs to bring forth their true possibilities. The grounds were nearly as arid as those they had crossed; only the existence of some small bushes and hardy grasses told of any differences.

Eyes moved to the houses. It was noticed how many there were, and an instant understanding came with this seeing—the pain which had visited the lives of those who just arrived must also be known by countless others. The sheer number spoke of the great evil that had been moving freely in the lands. All were small circle designs made of sticks with plastic sheets on the roofs. These were not like the homes they left with the two or three rooms and they had no corrugated metal to provide structure and offer feelings of security in the times of storms.

The walking resumed. A smiling man sat on a chair in front of a small tent. This is where they stopped; the man with the smile rose slowly and as he did, the smile disappeared. He fixed his eyes at those before him, shook his head, and began to talk.

When a speech has never been made before, there is pausing and searching and a lack of economy in the use of vocabulary; sometimes there is even movement from the intent as that which is spoken about has not yet gained focus. The one who had been smiling did not hesitate for a moment and sadly his speech was direct and without inflection. He had obviously given this far too many times. He spoke in a dialect which was mostly understood.

"Welcome weary travelers. You sacrificed much and achieved distance between your African home and these lands you find yourself in. You are now standing well within the borders of the country of your neighbor. This and other countries, both near and far away, are doing what they can to be of assistance. But in lending our hands, we need to do some discoveries. We will find out about any of the sicknesses and help with these needs. We want to know your names and the names of your villages and towns. Then we will put the information on a card for you to keep. You will show it to those who are giving away the waters and the foods. They will see the name and mark this down. In this way they will know you and your family have been cared for." The man once again smiled and held a card up for all to view.

His words had been carefully chosen and he deliberately left long spaces between the sentences. Even so, most looked at one another to discover if there had been an understanding. There had not. As the villages and towns grew in size, the knowing of all the names could longer be achieved. But if one asked, the name was always freely given. One did not need to reach into a pocket to bring forth a card.

The man with the smile was truly a kind man and though he received a wage for the job he did, this was not the reason he gave his service. His smile was freely offered in efforts to ease the grip of disquiet which had wrapped itself around the souls who stood before him. He understood the puzzled looks but had not been able to find a way to explain the system of numbering, soon to become a part of each person's life. So he continued. "Today is a good day. You are just the third group to arrive. Some days many more appear. You will not need to wait long hours to see the doctors. This is indeed a lucky day. For those who require the healing, there are people to help with this. After that, you will be asked the questions about your name and your home. Then your picture will be taken so you can carry a card." Again he held one up, waving it back and forth in the air as if by doing this once more there would be sudden comprehension.

The photographs were taken following the doctor's help because some bodies, even when receiving good foods and water and correct medicine, cannot recover. There are those who, after the tortures of the journey, arrive only for the dying. For such souls, what purpose could a picture on a card serve?

"May the God bring his blessings to each of you." The man with the smile said this with deep compassion. He then made a motion with his hand that told the ones who had brought these travelers to continue with their work.

The doctors did what was possible within the limits of their worldly abilities. They checked for different diseases and helped with the controlling of diarrhea. Infections were cleaned and dressed and parasites killed and in this process assessments were made. Some were judged as being capable of surviving in this new kind of world. Others would need special foods and medicines, and receive them in different ways and amounts, in the hope their lives might be sustained.

Those who were thought to soon know death were not abandoned. One who has endured such pain deserves at least the thread of possibility. The girl whose name was the same as the mother of the great prophet was weak and seemed near her end, but the doctors and others continued with their efforts. Hope and her family gathered around her and filled up the spaces. Because of this, there were fewer places for the doctors and nurses to move. The family was asked to leave but in the politest way possible they declined. In the talking that followed it was agreed one would stay and this person would touch the skin and sing the songs needed to be heard. Hope remained and it was discovered the miracle which had once visited had never left. In the hours and the days that followed, the girl's breathing became stronger.

"There are rules, and I have been given the duty to speak to you about them." A man who looked and sounded as if he had seen too much awfulness was walking with the group who, after seeing the doctors, were moving to the place where the people lived. His job was to do some of the telling and he held up a book.

"It has been written by those who continue to dream that the home you build should have the space of three and a half square meters for each person who lives in it." He gave out a long sigh. "But my world is not the one of imagination. You will be given one plastic tarp and one small piece of ground and told to get the sticks. These will be difficult enough to find. For those with families, you will be lucky if your completed home has half of that space."

Once again he held up the book. "It is also said that in places such as this, there should be one location to get the water for every two hundred and fifty souls. This is so you do not wait for large pieces of the day before your containers are filled. About fifteen thousand people are here and in the time it takes for the sun to arrive and leave the number gets bigger." He gazed out almost disbelievingly at the sprawling mass of homes. "In this place there are two wells and three trucks which hold water, making it five places in total for people to line up and get what is needed. For those of you who understand numbers, you will realize the problem. For those of you who don't, you will find out soon enough." He shook his head.

"The difficulty does not end with the places to get the water; it is also with the amounts. People who never lived here but have done the dreaming and put the words into this book, say each of you are to be given containers and together they should hold all the waters required for drinking and cleaning and cooking. It is said that every day these are to be filled to the overflowing. Containers we have, but water, not as much. We ask the wells to be generous to the limits of their ability to give. With the progression of the day the waters become more difficult to see through and by the time the last part of the light arrives, they are the color of dirt. All night, the earth works to fill back the spaces. In this book I hold, it is written each of you is to receive the correct amount of water for the healthy living. This is given as a number. Because so many are here, there is a tiredness with the world and this affects her ability to replace that which has been taken. The number for you will be less than half."

The man began to walk toward the place where the people lived, but after some paces stopped to look back only to find no one had been following. Seeing this, he did not raise the level of his voice to tell them to do the catching up. He understood and felt their confusion and returned. He spoke quietly, "If you come with me, I will show you some of what I told you about and other things which are needed to be known." Then, with an even softer voice that came as a song might, he entered the hearts of those who stood before him. "I lived some of what you know of, and I, too, left my village and walked into the desert. In the time I have been here, the seasons have already repeated themselves more than the fingers on this hand." He tucked the book under the stump of his left arm and held up his one good hand. "I truly wish I could say this place will bring you the happiness and joy you once knew, but it will not. What you see is not a town or a village. It is not a neighborhood. This is like nothing you have ever known. But there is some safety here, some protection from the great evil, and though your bellies may still experience hunger and your mouths thirst, there will be less dying."

The site where the living was to happen was then shown to them by this man, and in these moments they were told about how to build the house. It was to be made in the same way as all the other houses and it would be necessary to move beyond the perimeters of the camp in order to gather the sticks and the long grasses needed for construction.

This would require much walking, as the trees that had been nearest were stripped of branches for the building and the trunks carried back for the cooking fires. Those in the medium distance met the identical fate. However, beyond this, in the careful looking, one could notice other trees which still stood.

"It is best to go in numbers," said the man who was doing the telling and who would soon provide the exact spot for each of their houses. "There are people who move through these forsaken lands, just as their fathers and their fathers' fathers did. This traveling has been done by them since the beginning of remembrance and they are not pleased with our presence or the injuries caused to that which had struggled to grow. They do not say, 'Please leave our lands and trees and grasses that have always provided shade and food for ourselves and our animals.' Perhaps they did but their words were not respected, so now they do the injury. And they have a special violence for the women which we do not like to speak of."

He showed the places where people lined up for water. The lines were long and in the standing and waiting there was talking but no laughter. The locations for the division of the foods were pointed out. No one was there; everything to be distributed had already been given. The man who held the book again talked of those who wrote it and did the dreaming and how so much rice or wheat or corn and beans and oils and sugar and salt should be provided, enough to supply the good energy for a whole day. But just as with the water, no one would ever receive those amounts. He then talked of latrines and meeting places.

More needed to be said but he understood that these people had been besieged with this new knowledge and what was before them and they no longer had the capacity to absorb. So he took them back to a place where they could sit and rest and wait for the cards which would give them their names.

READY OR NOT, HERE I COME

The waiting game—a strategy implemented when it is thought that by doing nothing for lengthy periods of time, the likelihood of gaining a favorable outcome increases. The premise: inaction will, in fact, result in a positive scenario. There are numerous instances when sitting and waiting can prove to be a good thing. However, the tactic needs to be selectively applied and it decidedly tests the patience of those whose natural inclination is to be active in the pursuit of a goal.

James had been patient. He wrote the letter to the editor and he waited. He made speeches at rallies and he waited. He created a special flag and talked to many groups and he waited. He started a blog and was involved in most forms of social media. He composed more letters and e-mails and he implored others to do the same and still he was waiting.

Those playing the game often experience a growing sense of anticipation. When it is understood how critical it is that the sought after outcome be successfully achieved, the sense of expectation is further heightened. With every passing day there was more death, disease and misery. Souls hung in the balance. An anxiousness associated with deep tension had etched into the lines on James' face.

As he exited Mr. Patterson's office, James left a clear message about who would be calling whom. He had asserted under his breath, "They ain't seen nothin' yet." The days of being patient and playing the waiting game were over. He knew what had to be done. He would ratchet up the pressure, and more than just a notch or two.

Often as the lives of friends and colleagues move in different ways, drifting happens. This can occur even when people with the best of intentions set out for it to be otherwise. In the first few months, James and Phil managed weekly visits, either to break bread or enjoy at least a cup of coffee together. But with schedules and demands being what they are, things didn't always unfold in this way. Weeks sometimes turned to months and no contact had been made. Blocks of time passed when none was even attempted. This pattern is normal to relationship deconstruction and if continued these two would be reduced to exchanging intermittent e-mails, sometimes with an attachment containing the generic family letter. They had not entered into the final stage. There were times, though infrequent, where they still shared and enjoyed each other's company.

"Hey, Phil, how you been doing?"

"Never better! The boss has finally come around to recognizing my innate ability and is utilizing my considerable talents. Got a big raise, bought a new condo, and I'm thinking about getting a yacht. Not sure though—I've been known to get seasick."

"Yeah, right," James laughed. In recent times there had not been many occasions for laughter. He enjoyed the moment.

"No, seriously, I do get seasick." This time they both laughed. After a short moment to catch his breath Phil began again. "Everything's fine, thanks for asking. Work is what it has always been and always will be. Nothing much changes. More importantly, I'm still buying good clothes," he gestured at the quality sweater he wore. "My life is fairly copasetic. It's not complainin' Tuesday so, no complaints." He looked at James, "How about yourself? How have you been?"

James thought for a few moments before answering. "Different," he reflected. "Yeah that would be the word for it: different." He stared intently at his friend. "When did we last talk—two, three months ago? The course of this life of mine just keeps getting harder to predict. I don't really know how to describe it."

"Humor me." Phil remained loyal; he could still listen. "Go ahead, fill in the blanks. I've got all day."

By the time they had their third refill, the last one being decaf, his story had been told. The momentum of the blog and the meeting with his federal representative played prominently in the closing minutes of the narrative.

"Wow! What can I say, James? Spell my name 'boring' with a capital *B*. You've been busy. You're going to be in some serious personal crap when you get out of the fast lane and have to readjust to work with its pace and style."

James started to protest, something about maybe not returning but Phil cut him off. "Don't give me that; you'll be back. There's only nine months left on your leave extension, and I'm already painfully aware of the company pension policy. By my calculations, you've got at least four years of servitude to go, or all the work you did for them won't count for beans. You're not rich; I'll be seeing you at the office." Phil looked at James, who no longer challenged the inevitability. It was pretty much the way Phil said.

"In the meantime, I'm going to give 'em hell."

"That's my boy." The two raised their coffee cups as if they were champagne glasses. Phil gave the toast. "Here's to getting down and dirty."

Saturday, midmorning, sitting with a friend, the spring sun shining with a semblance of warmth, life was good. Their capacity for consuming coffee had reached its limit but their connection time had not. Needing more, they rose to take a walk. The sidewalks were starting to fill with shoppers enjoying their searches in the many funky boutiques that lined both sides of the street. A large park was close by and they navigated their way toward it. Someone over a century earlier had the foresight to set aside a substantial green space, which was now being enjoyed by the ever-increasing population. Ornamental cherry trees lined the boulevard; some of the pink blossoms having been released by the slight breeze, drifted to the ground much as snowflakes do.

"You ever thought of doing a stunt?" Phil wasn't keen on causes: his interest didn't signify a reversal of form. He was just trying to be of some service to a good friend. This was consistent.

"A stunt?"

"Well, maybe not a stunt, but something to get the guy you met with and others like him to sit up and note notice. With all the things you've got going: the flag, the petitions, the e-mails, the letters, the use of social media including that awesome blog, you should have gained some pretty serious attention, but apparently not. So how do you get the recognition?" He brought his left hand to the bottom of his chin and presented a thoughtful pose. "I suppose you could hit someone with a big stick but the law, quite rightly, frowns on this approach." They both smiled.

Phil stopped walking. He had always done this. The two of them would be striding along and talking together when Phil, wanting to emphasize a point, would come to a screeching halt right in the middle of the sidewalk. If James wasn't careful, he'd find himself three or four paces ahead before realizing his friend was not beside him. "All kidding aside there is absolutely no question you need to do something to grab some big time attention."

James stared at him; his eyebrows straightened as he tried to digest this thought.

Phil continued, "I'm not talking about camping in a tree or chaining yourself to a building. Nobody has to go on a hunger strike." Phil jabbed his index finger into James stomach, and in the process moved the conversation away from serious. "Though with the tire thing starting to happen, that might not be the worst idea in the world." He chuckled but quickly returned to the more sober approach. "All of that stuff is small potatoes, James. This needs to be a national protest, sea to sea, border to border; if it can take on a world dimension, so much the better."

The next moments were filled with discernible silence as these two carried on with their robust style of walking. They passed one of the large manmade ponds, complete with a giant fountain and scores of fat ducks and Canadian geese. Kids and old people had been constantly feeding them.

In Search of Sticks

"So, got any ideas?" James questioned.

"What? Do I have to think of everything?" Phil quipped. "Just be sure that whatever you come up with is easy to do, to the point and really big." He added, "Oh, yeah, and it had better be legal. I don't want to get a call to go down and make your bail." They finished their walk and went their individual ways. As always, they swore that, in the future, they would meet more regularly.

In the evening James phoned Claire, who, in presidential fashion, convened an extraordinary meeting of the executives. Two days later they were sitting around the table. There was no shortage of conversation and the talk moved randomly. Many of those present contributed.

"I saw this guy on the news once, and I couldn't believe what I was looking at. He actually had his lips and eyes stitched together. I can't recall the issue being protested but one thing is certain, that image won't leave me anytime soon." The speaker shook her head.

"I think we've all seen pictures of someone dousing themselves with gasoline and lighting a match, making the ultimate sacrifice in order to bring attention to a cause," said another.

The one sitting across from James assumed center stage. The staccato style of speaking was a result of his excitement. "Let's not forget the banner people. They hang those signs on tall buildings, off faces of cliffs and from the tops of bridges. A lot of things can be done. Think about the choices—sit-ins, pickets, rallies, demonstrations, blockades, boycotts, T-shirts, bumper stickers. There are hundreds of ways we could create focus." Just when it looked as if he was finished he threw one more into the mix. "And of course there's always the nudity thing; someone taking off their clothes for a cause can generate a fair amount of attention."

Another interjected, "Well I can't speak for anyone else but I am not sewing lips together. Banner hanging won't appear on my résumé, it's a fear of heights thing—acrophobia. Lighting yourself on fire, impressive as this might be, is not my style; and stripping down, at least in the case of yours truly, isn't going to accomplish a whole lot. We need a different angle, something unique."

Silence—it was the kind of quiet which said, 'now what?'

James had contributed little to the conversation. He didn't deviate from his usual pattern of listening and waiting. There was no set formula for his insertion but he seemed to always know when the time arrived for personal contribution. All eyes turned toward James; everyone waited expectantly. Once again he was challenged to rise to the occasion. He did not disappoint. James began with a question.

"What are we protesting?" Not waiting for a response, his second sentence followed on the heels of the first.

In Search of Sticks

"I believe speed is the big issue. Direction is important but possibly in this case it is of secondary concern. Many in this world are actually moving on the right path. We may not be in as much dispute as we think. Some efforts have been made to respond. Refugee camps have been set up and people are being kept alive. The gift of real hope, however, has not been widely distributed and few believe they will ever go home. This is because few do. The pace of repatriation is unbearably slow, and this is what we must protest."

James waited a moment for those around him to catch up to his thinking. "Ladies and gentlemen speed, or to be more precise, the lack thereof, is the problem. If they like slow, then I say let's give them slow." He looked at those sitting around the table, everyone hanging on to each of his words. "We live in a fast-paced society; how would traffic be affected if we drove the speed limit, or even five ticks less than the posted number? I'm guessing traffic jams, and dependent on the hour in the day, grid lock. Buying groceries? Spend a few moments talking to the cashier—discussions about the weather can take a while. Time to pay a bill? It's funny what happens to the length of a lineup when each of your motions gets a touch slower. You reach in to get the money and you methodically count it. Perhaps you try to find a check or credit card, but at first you're not successful. The government is going to quickly hear about this slowdown protest and I doubt they will be happy with it. I wonder what it will take for us to resume normal speed."

They had a plan. It didn't include death-defying stunts or high flying banners. No one needed to strip down. Even so, everyone believed the idea had a chance of working. Preparations would be made for the 'slowdown-showdown'.

I AM FINE

There were gifts, and these had been provided without flourish and without expectation of witnessing delight.

"This piece of plastic has the feel of a thick cloth, and though it is not overly big, it will, if correctly woven into the roof of the new house, keep you and your family dry in the season of rain. Be careful not to tear this, as the generosity of those who have given does not extend for a second instance. Even when the sun and the wind have, over the long periods, weakened the fabric in such a way that it no longer works in the manner intended, there is often not enough for another giving. In the times of the rains, the families in these houses cannot sit on their floors. Should there be a chair they will take turns using it."

The father of Hope accepted this gift and began making the speech of thanks but the man waved a hand in the air as if to say, "I do not want to hear this." The father became quiet and passed on the roll of plastic for a son to hold.

The man who had done this giving now looked carefully at the family before him and in a soft way so those in another piece of the room did not hear said, "I see by the tears in your clothes the journey has been difficult. Still, from this distance the cloth seems to be strong and can, with the right skill, be sewn together. We are told to give clothes only to those who require them, but I have come to understand that if you do not receive these now there is no returning later and asking for this generosity. So I will write in the book of a need. You may keep them until they are required, or use them for trading when a wish or a desperation surfaces." With this, he handed the father a stack of clothes but once again before the speech of thanks could be said the man went on to other things.

"Here is a pot for cooking and a pan to help with that. This day is a fortunate one. Someone has been unusual with their generosity and we have more to do this providing. These bowls are for eating, but there are not enough for all to sit and eat together as a family. The blankets will be useful in times of shivering when a sickness visits or the type of cold arrives that comes with the days of the rains. They provide a form of comfort as you sleep on the hard earth. These two containers you now hold will be needed every day when you stand in the lines to receive water. Do not lose them. Keep them close. Watch over them; even here some take." The one doing the saying and giving did these things quickly and the father could only receive the items and then pass them on to someone in his family. There was never an opportunity to say the speech of thanks.

"Finally, here are the cards with your pictures on them. This one for you, courageous and caring father, has all the names of your family on it: as it is written, your good wife, your loyal sons, and your two daughters." The mother and father of Hope counted the one whose name was the same as the mother of the great prophet as their own. This is as it had been since they received her from the man of pure heart who rescued this angel—their angel. "This card is to be used for the receiving of the foods but do not join the line today or tomorrow or the next day or even the day after that, as it takes time for others to know of your arrival. You will be given food after your names are in their book."

The building of the house was not easy. First they took the long walk to find the correct sticks and grasses, and they did this carefully as there was the fear of being found by those roaming through these lands. No beast did the carrying on return, so all who had arrived at the point of exhaustion were once again burdened. They had little understanding about how to do this building, as the houses around them did not resemble the ones in their village. But some who lived nearby and saw this need, helped in all the ways possible.

"When the wind blows, it almost always comes from this direction—and so more plastic should be on this side as it will help stop some of the air from moving through the walls. In the long walking you did, there was also climbing. This happened just a little bit in every step so it was not understood in the same way as when one sees a hill and moves up its slope. You are now much higher than where you lived in your village. It is as if you went halfway up a mountain, and so the nights are colder. With this coldness and the damp, chilly winds in the *season of the rain, you will be glad of this small protection."* An older man spoke these words.

"Because the wood had been recently alive, bending is possible; the sticks must be woven together. I can show you how this is done and then help throughout the day. In this way I may be useful. Though you may feel that it is I who offers this gift, I am grateful for the opportunity and am receiving as much in return." A man who appeared to be the same age as Hope's father did this talking.

Others came to lend their hands and their voices, and by the end of the third day, Hope's family had a house.

Many things were to be learned. In the early part of the morning before the sun had occasion to be present, they sat in the dark room with a single candle and waited. With everything they had experienced, their bodies were exhausted but sleep still did not come easily. When it did arrive, it did not stay for the long periods. They were filled with an excitement and a tension that came with not understanding and not knowing about this new existence. Also they missed the sounds and smells of their village.

It was their fifth day and this was to be the time when they would receive their food. They arrived very early to the place and lined up. Already some were ahead and quickly more behind.

"Where is your card?"

Hope's father held this out for the taking.

Seeing the name, the man searched through a large binder but did not find that which he sought. He looked up, *"When did you come?"* Upon receiving this information he, once again, made an attempt at discovery. *"Perhaps it is too early for your name to be written in one of these pages. You may need to return tomorrow."*

Just as he said this, the name was found. The man smiled and made a mark and ordered the food be given to this family.

"This is not an abundance and it must last. You will see the sun a full seven times before more can be provided so you should be careful not to eat too much in the first of the days. Even though the feeling of hunger will never truly leave you, it is best to do this."

Hope's father began the speech of thanks and the man, seeing the necessity to maintain some honor, allowed for this before doing the dismissing so the next family might receive. Everyone had come to help with the food, but only two were needed for the carrying.

Lessons about the lining up and knowing where to release the pressures of bowels and bladders were quickly learned. Other things also required understanding: should the family drink too much water, there would not be enough for cooking or for keeping their bodies clean; if they overly used the water for cooking or cleaning, then the intense thirst that comes with the heat of the day would not be satisfied; getting sticks for the small fire necessary for making the meal was a difficult and sometimes dangerous task.

This place, which was to provide needed safety before there could be a returning, must have already witnessed many cycles of seasons. Such was the thinking of all who recently arrived. The camp had the look of permanence. There were places for children to learn and for the sick to get help, and even a location to do the selling and buying if there were things and money to be exchanged. The cemetery's size was considerable.

It was also noticed that, for some, the bellies were too large and the cheeks and eyes too hollow and people did not wear the clothes so much as the clothes hung on them. There was a story in this seeing and it said, "Even though there is food, it is often not enough."

The manner in which many moved told the stories of beatings and of the attacks by fire and bullets and knives. Missing limbs and massive burns spoke of unfathomable horrors.

Styles of speaking added to the disorientation. People had come from large distances and a number of the words and even the ways in which they were spoken did not have the ring of familiarity.

Some eyes act differently than expected and do not record information in the normal manner – "The moon has grown now to half its fullness."– "As the foot touches the earth, a cloud of dust rises to the ankle." Instead, these eyes see feelings. Upon their arrival Hope's family saw fear in many who passed by, and it was not the fright which is short lived such as what comes with carefully moving by the dangerous animal; this fear is forever.

On the second day after the house had been built, a neighbor who had helped in the construction walked by and being polite asked Hope how she might be on this hot and cloudless day.

"I am fine," was her immediate response.

EVERY HOUR OF EVERY DAY

It was not a dream, but if it had been it would have exceeded the limits of every dreamer who had ever challenged the boundaries of imagination.

Day One:

"The traffic disruptions now being experienced by our commuters are apparently either happening or have happened or will happen in many major centers throughout the entire world. New York, London, Paris, Sydney, Tokyo, Moscow, Berlin, and Montreal are but a few of the locations named as targets for this action." While the television announcer read from his teleprompter, images of lengthy commuter tie-ups were displayed on the TV screen.

"Marianne Strabinski is standing by with a live feed from Los Angeles." A cameraman panned the scene before focusing in on the reporter.

"Yes, Jeff, I'm here in front of one of the many expressways that crisscross this amazing city. As you can see, the vehicles are moving but not quickly. This isn't gridlock and it's not a snail's pace. Maybe the speed is best described as being somewhere between that of a turtle and a really old slow dog." She smiled at her attempt at rehearsed humor and in the process revealed pearl-like, even teeth. No surprise.

"Interesting image, Marianne. Any idea as to what might be the cause? I'm sure there aren't accidents on the major arteries in every one of these cities." The newscaster's voice was steady and bold, much the same as most in the business.

"Well there appears to be a common thread. Some of the cars in all of the areas with traffic congestion have this bumper sticker on them." She held up one for the audience to see. "This is an image from the Society for Human Justice—the 'Flag of Truth.'" The camera zoomed in for a close-up, kept the picture for a second before retreating to its original scope. "Their website and blog call for a 'slowdown-showdown'. They are trying to bring attention to the plight of refugees in the world. To quote them, they are 'tired of the slow pace of progress, and it's time everyone got to know what slow looks and feels like.'" She gave a quick nod of her head, the sign for the announcer to ask his next scripted question.

"Judging by the number of different cities being affected, they may very well have succeeded. Is anyone saying how long this disruption will last?"

"The blog calls for an ongoing series of two-hour protests. Their intent is, and once again I'm quoting, 'that major cities go into slow motion for a couple of hours and experience a level of frustration at the sluggish pace. Perhaps then some will be more sympathetic toward the lives of those who are trapped in refugee camps where progress to create the conditions for their return has been abysmally slow.'"

"You talked about a series of protests. Can you expand on that?"

"Yes Jeff, the Society for Human Justice is calling for a different protest each weekday. Precisely what form it will take tomorrow is expected to be posted on their web site shortly. Stay tuned; there's more to come." She ended emphatically, stared straight into the camera, waited a second and signed off. "Marianne Strabinski, reporting live for Channel Ten news."

"And now to other stories," the announcer moved to the next item.

"People do the speed limit or a bit below and this makes the headlines. Amazing," thought James.

No phone call was received. Representatives were quiet. No need to be concerned. Two hours is an inconvenience, not a disaster.

Those living in the camps knew nothing of this effort. Their lives remained unaltered. Cemeteries continued to grow in disproportionate ways.

Day Two:

Just as in the traffic slowdown, the application of the second day's plan was subtly put into practice. The previous strategy called for a few clicks less on the speedometer; this time they requested a few seconds of pause. Nothing could be overtly identified as the cause, no opportunity for anyone to become the object of someone's anger.

"So, how are things today?" The order of this question normally posed by the cashier to the customer was reversed. The clerks at the cash registers were hoping to keep conversation to a minimum; they gave up making any effort at polite inquiry. Despite all attempts to streamline the process, the cumulative effects of some of the shoppers using those extra moments could not be overcome and the lines became longer.

"Just a second. I can't seem to find my credit card." A middle aged man fumbled through the contents of his wallet. "Oh, here it is." The transaction proceeded.

"Thirty dollars and seventy-five cents ... I think I have the correct change. Let's see." He started pulling bills. "Five, ten, twenty, another ten, that makes thirty." He reached into his pocket and brought forward a handful of coins. "Here we are: thirty twenty-five, thirty fifty, thirty sixty, thirty sixty-five, thirty seventy, thirty seventy-five. The exact amount, what are the odds?" He picked up his bags of groceries and left.

"Believe it or not, I forgot my code." She punched in some numbers. "No, that's not it." She turned to the person behind her. "Sorry, this is a bit embarrassing. I must be having a senior's moment." She keyed in her debit card number again and this time everything went smoothly. "Got it!"

"What do you think, I can only afford one?" Two DVDs had been placed on the counter. The line was a half dozen deep and someone wanted a movie critique.

The clerk looked up. "I don't know what to say: they're both good." Seeing the expectation that still rested with the customer she weakly continued, "I suppose it's just a matter of taste."

"Well, if it was your choice, which would you choose?"

"That one," she pointed.

"Oh, okay." A bit of a surprised tone accompanied the response. "How come?"

"Action. I like action." She was beginning to sound impatient. The lineup was several more strong.

"Right," he paused, appearing to submerge himself into deep thought for a couple of seconds before resurfacing. "I think I'll take the other one."

And on this went for a full two hours in stores situated in the same metropolitan locations which had previously experienced traffic flow issues.

But no phone call was received. Representatives continued to be quiet. No need to be overly concerned. Two hours is an inconvenience, not a disaster.

Those living in the camps knew nothing of this effort. Their lives remained unaltered. Cemeteries continued to grow in disproportionate ways.

Day Three:

This time the targets were government services. Both clients and employees were encouraged to utilize understated, barely detectable tactics which would result in losses of efficiency. As it said in the blog, "How long does it take for the application to be processed or the driver's license picture to be taken? There are quick ways to pay a fine and others which are not nearly as rapid. Submissions for permits and requests for variances all need to be reviewed. Regulations often require each detail be scrutinized for accuracy. Maybe this is the day people go by the letter rather than the spirit of the law and everything is accomplished while taking deep, noticeable breaths. Be slow, but not the kind of slow that would put a job in jeopardy."

Just as in the previous days, the length of the lines increased.

But no phone call was received. Representatives continued to be quiet. No pressing need to be overly concerned. Two hours is an inconvenience, not a disaster.

Those living in the camps knew nothing of this effort. Their lives remained unaltered. Cemeteries continued to grow in disproportionate ways.

Day Four:

The blog provided the details. "Financial services are to be affected on this day. This is a difficult one, and it took some time for members of the Society for Human Justice to work this out. We settled on a strategy that involves paying everything with cash. Credit card companies not only get money from each transaction, but also gain when interest rates are applied to outstanding balances. If the rate of this type of purchasing slows, there will obviously be a negative impact on the bottom line of some rather large companies' balance sheets. This slowing is not the kind applied day one through three, where the effects are visible. The protest, like all the others, is scheduled to last two hours. For one hundred and twenty minutes it is thought this action might bring some sluggishness or slowness to the economy, not a huge downturn, hardly a blip really—but perhaps enough to serve as a wake-up call so certain people will take notice."

Day four happened just as it had been outlined.

But no phone call was received. Representatives continued to be quiet, at least in public. There were no admissions about being overly concerned with the increased pressure. After all, two hours is an inconvenience, not a disaster.

Those living in the camps knew nothing of this effort. Their lives remained unaltered. Cemeteries continued to grow in disproportionate ways.

The whole process repeated itself, and the two hour slow-downs were extended to three. What happened on Monday was duplicated on Friday. Weekends were not targeted for any activities. Therefore, the events of day two, which had occurred on Tuesday, resurfaced on Monday.

Those waiting to see a reduction in participation, expecting the initial surge of enthusiasm to wane, were disappointed. The passion did not diminish. In fact, it grew in astounding ways. The media in their reporting never failed to make a link between the actions taken and the Society for Human Justice. As a result, traffic to their site and blog dramatically increased. With this came a corresponding growth in involvement, not only in the previously targeted cities but also in an extensive number of other centers throughout the world. The protest had become a movement. An uneasy sense visited some who concerned themselves with future voting outcomes.

Books detail how this works. Examples have been presented and analyzed and a single conclusion drawn: sometimes a kind of layering happens and this can go on almost undetected until the critical mass is achieved. Those who would choose to hold back the proverbial waters, whose wish is to maintain the status quo, are unable to do so, and suddenly the dam breaks. The rushing water covers the earth and soaks her soils.

The phone rang.

"James Terrance here."

"Mr. Terrance, this is Mr. Patterson's office. Mr. Patterson has requested that we arrange a meeting with you. What is your schedule like tomorrow afternoon sir?"

James, who previously had been afforded only the minimum level of courtesy and was brushed off in much the same manner as one might deal with a piece of lint, could have been tempted to let Mr. Patterson and the others twist for awhile. But James did not do this; he knew only too well what was at stake. People's desperate lives remained unaltered. There needed to be a decrease in suffering and this reduction had to happen as soon as possible. Every hour of the day counted. James would not be playing any mind games. He agreed to a 4 p.m. meeting.

"So Mr. Terrance, nice to see you again." James' elected representative, Mr. Patterson, rose from behind his desk, this time offering no pretense at being preoccupied. He strode over and his hand once more enveloped the one James had extended. "Can I get you coffee?"

James accepted and Mr. Paterson poured from the insulated carafe. Bakery goods had been arranged on a small serving plate.

"Cream? Sugar? Honey?"

"I take it black."

"No fuss, no muss, pretty much your style, I'd say." He laughed as he handed James his steaming coffee and proceeded to fix his own. Major volumes of cream and an indeterminate amount of honey were added to the cup. He stirred and sat down.

"Mr. Terrance, you've been a busy boy." Irrespective of the different tensions that presented themselves in the course of a day, words flowed easily from this politician's mouth.

"Whatever do you mean?" James couldn't help but smile and he did so with a measure of confidence.

Mr. Patterson, seeing this understood its meaning. The intimidation factor associated with position was no longer in play. Real negotiations would need to happen and it was clear the process wasn't going to be an easy one.

"So Mr. Terrance, all cards on the table, no aces up any sleeves?" He shook both his arms as if to demonstrate the impossibility of cheating.

"Sounds good to me. Though, if you don't mind, I'm going to play cautiously."

"I have no doubt you'll be considering your moves. I think we've all seen some evidence of that already."

On the wall opposite James hung a stunning clock. It was striking in each of its details: the brown red wood, the brass inlays, the delicate floral scene, together told the story of a skilled craftsman who had lived almost two centuries earlier. The pendulum was encased and its even movements were barely audible. The face of the clock was large and glassed and the black roman numerals seemed to jump forward.

Mr. Patterson, seeing James' attention momentarily move to the timepiece commented. "Just had it hung. It's old and beautiful—kind of like time within time." For a second he gazed without focus and then returned.

"Okay, I suppose first things first. I've been asked to talk to you and should the possibility present itself, negotiate—though, if an agreement is tentatively struck, I would need to take that to my colleagues for their input."

"Ditto for me. I came here on behalf of the Society for Human Justice and I'll be taking anything to them for perusal before there's any possibility of final approval. With so much in the balance I don't even trust myself."

The hours passed and each of the minutes was recorded by the remarkable clock on the wall. More coffee was drunk. Dinner was brought in but only partially consumed. Neither of them seemed to have much of an appetite. However, they shared a personal requirement for caffeine and fortunately there was a continuous supply. Both had a need to stay alert.

"I don't think you understand, Mr. Terrance. I'd like to snap my fingers and have the whole thing solved. Between you and me, I'm not happy with people having to live that way, either. Still, this isn't going to be easy. Whatever is decided I then have to sell it to the government. There's big money involved and as you know, in far too many of these places a lot of nasty battles continue to be fought. In a large number of cases it's not safe to return. I've been reading all this stuff on some popular blog." He gave James a bit of a wink.

For a moment James was taken aback. "Is he actually concerned? Is this an ally sitting across from him or is this just a ploy, a way to gain a measure of trust?" Such was his thinking. He told himself to remain cautious. "Perhaps you could remind them, Mr. Patterson, that we're up to five hours a day of disruption and this can easily be extended to a sixth."

With that, various maps of Africa came out. The homework had been done. Different camps and their populations had been identified and bureaucrats rank ordered them using three variables: safety, simplicity and government persuasion.

What occurred in the course of negotiations is not written in any record, and those directly involved had no distinct memories. This may have resulted from personal fatigue or perhaps it was submerged. What can one say about a decision which saves some while leaving others to continue to pray for their deliverance?

An agreement in principle was arrived at. The initial phase called for around twenty thousand people to be helped. Money was to come from different world governments and private agencies and each of the refugees from this camp would be given back some of what once was their life. The process would take about two months to put into place and be fully monitored and reviewed. Following this, more souls were to be taken down the road to partial salvation. An agency would be created and momentum was expected to increase as they strove to reach annual target figures. James, in return, had to "call off his dogs" as Mr. Patterson so colorfully put it, and things would get back to normal.

The pendulum on the incredible wall clock continued its movement in near silence. It was minutes past three in the morning when they shook hands and exited, walking out into the night leaving the grandeur of the government house behind. Floodlights outlined the impressive architecture.

Work still needed to be done. But first things first—James would need to meet with the Society for Human justice and, at least temporarily, call the dogs off.

Randy Kaneen

THE UNFOLDING

    Since the year of its beginning the camp kept growing. People continued to arrive who had done the escaping but the numbers coming in each of the days were not as many as before. Still, the number was never zero. There will always be different cultures and races or others who do not share the same understanding of the God. And up to this point in the life of the earth and its people, there are those who ascribe a twisted importance to these things and who sacrifice values in order to assert them. Therefore, the camp grew.
    Another reason accounted for some of this growth. Just because life as it had come to be known had been halted, it did not follow that all things stopped. There are natural progressions. There is marrying and the birth of children. But it could not be said, "The lands of my family are rich and with work and care and the right amount of rain and sun

they will also provide for you, me, and any healthy children which we might be blessed with." In this location, no one would hear the boastfulness about having a skill that could lead to a prosperous life. Plans to go to the city or to the mines in order to discover one's fortune were not announced; nobody was allowed to leave. Still, in this place without potential, young women and young men met. New houses were made and babies were born; the camp continued to grow.

There is life and there is emotion, and for almost all the two are inexorably linked. Emotion is a force; it is an interpretation and can dominate. It exists in a wide range of possibilities. Ecstasy, despair, love, hate, lust, anger, greed, ambition, and serenity are but a few of the words used to describe emotional states. By listening, watching and interpreting, one may find evidence of these as they surface. However, in the place where people who had crossed the desert and now lived, true serenity was never observed.

As much as feelings can shift in extreme ways, it is also realized they may appear as part of a progressive, predictable movement. Post traumatic emotions often present themselves sequentially. Initially grief dominates; this is followed by anger and depression. Finally a form of acceptance is reached as people, once again, begin to carry on with their lives. For those who escaped and had come to live in the camps as refugees, the succession of emotions in dealing with their losses had been experienced in similar ways; that is, all but the last one, which is difficult to attain. How does one truly accept and move forward when the life is trapped in houses of sticks and plastic and the interminable waiting is for always? How, then, does one break free from the chains of depression?

Just as he had done each of his days, the father of Hope rose early in the morning and sat outside chewing on the bread made the night before. He watched the darkness move to light. When the seeing had become such that walking might safely be achieved, he did not do this. The sun's rays grew in intensity; still there was no rising.

"Good morning, dear father." Hope's hand rested lightly on her father's shoulder. This touch was felt as it was intended and it spoke of a deep and great love. The father briefly touched the fingers of this wonderful daughter. She looked up to the cloudless sky. "The sun has no enemies today."

And the father said, "The grains in the field are wishing my presence. Perhaps the ditches still hold some of the waters given at the season of the rain. If I were there, I would move a few of the drops over the earth and offer small drinks to the grasses."

"Yes, dear father, you always cared for the land and it showed its appreciation by giving back to the best of its ability. Even in times when the rainfall and clouds were not enough, it still tried to show its gratitude for your kindness and skill by providing what was possible." Once more the father moved his hand to that of Hope's and for a time the two of them looked out together, he crouching by the door and she standing above him. She heard the voice of her mother beckoning for help to chase Hope's lazy brothers out so the room might be readied for daily life. Reluctantly, she took her hand away.

In a while her father would get up and find the father of Rose who had been given a place ten minutes from theirs. They would walk some and sit together, but the talk which used to happen about returning was not often heard. Many seasons had passed since the beginning of the waiting. They almost never played board games and most of their moments were silent.

"Where do you go, my sons?" Hope's mother asked her boys who had walked outside, each of them holding a piece of bread.

One responded, "This is not the day when the food is given. And as has been the pattern, Hope, and you and our new sister will join the line for today's water. We are going to meet others and we will walk. We will walk by the small market where people trade what little they have left to get clothes so their children will not need to run naked through this place. We will walk by the schools and see the students, some of whom have never known a village or their true home, learn their letters and numbers. We will wonder why they are doing this. Then we will walk some more and we will say things about how that one's life has changed with the drugs and another has become pathetic with the reliving of each of the horrors and people seeing us will understand who we are and will be careful not to get in our way. We will walk by the place where the burying is done and we will curse the God."

Hope's mother could not bear any more and moved to the one who had been talking. Grasping his arm and in a voice which was desperate to reach out said, "My son, do not curse the God. I beg of you not to curse the God."

"And why is that, dearest mother? Do you not remember the killings and the pain and how our lives have been taken away? Do you not recall the torturous walk and the

hurt which moved through souls? Do you not see the nothingness that surrounds us?"

Tears flowed from the mother in her reply, "I am not surrounded by nothingness; I am surrounded by my family, by my husband, and by you and your brothers, and by Hope and by a child who is a wonderful gift. This is not nothing. This is everything. Do not blame that which you speak of on the God. It is not God's doing. God does not have favorites." Her tears continued to fall.

Just as with the rest in the family, this son had been raised in ways that spoke of kindness and love. He drew upon all of this and seeing his mother in a state of crying, took both of her hands in his, and speaking softly, said, "You are right, this is not nothingness, and I will not curse the God." Then he left with his brothers.

Hope also found ways to fill her days but she did not pace the property. She moved differently. As in all things that involve connecting between people, the unfolding of each day did not occur in precisely the same manner as its predecessor, but there were similarities.

In the first piece of the morning, Hope and her new sister and her mother walked to one of the places where the precise amount of water was provided. This part never changed. They left at this time to avoid the midday heat which was often intolerable yet still needed to be endured. Also, one who helped them when they arrived had spoken the truth; the early waters were always better as they had not become clouded with small pieces from the earth. While waiting they talked to those in front and behind, but should one of them have wanted to speak to someone not in easy

In Search of Sticks

reach of voice, that person was never visited. Some men strode up and down the line and carried sticks. If somebody strayed, the reminder that this was not to be tolerated was not gentle.

In the next part of the day Hope walked her new sister to one of the schools and once again spoke about the kind teacher who had taught numbers and letters but had also said things to bring forward further thought. Hope had grown older and did not attend. Still she understood its value and each day accompanied her sister. As was the practice, she hugged her and told her how happy she was, knowing her sister would learn about this wondrous world. Hope never failed to meet her after school finished.

Some who walked by others chose not to truly look. The pain in the eyes, the knife scar, the disfigurement made by fire, the arm and the leg that was gone, the missing hand, the limp which was more like a dragging—all of these sights and others called forward unwelcome memories. People were passed who spent their days sitting on the ground. Hands cupped between knees, they rocked back and forth, back and forth. Seeing this also produced uninvited distant pictures. It is called reliving the nightmare, and it was to be avoided. This is one of the reasons why many who went from here to there did so with their heads down. Hope did much walking but she looked at everyone.

On one day, while examining souls, Hope once again found her beloved teacher. He aimlessly paced up and down the pathways which separated the endless rows of stick and plastic houses. Though they had fled at the same time and had done much of the desperate walking together, on the arrival people were moved in different directions and sometimes contact was broken. Hope's teacher strode along as if he was late for an engagement. She hurried to catch up and taking him by his arm said, "Dear teacher, how are you today? Where are you are going, moving with such speed?"

But he was not able to answer either inquiry. His memories of the great evil had not noticeably subsided and he spoke as if in a trance. "It must be remembered that this kind of knowing is different from knowing about numbers and memorizing the names of the mountains and the stars. Some knowledge comes with the uneasiness of other questions."

Hope had heard him use these exact words while in his classroom and at once she understood. "Come with me to my home and we will sit and have some tea."

The teacher replied, "Yes, thank-you, perhaps there I may find that which I look for."

The details are not important but Hope drank tea with him on many days, and she helped him remember. "You were always such a kind teacher, all students and their mothers and fathers held you in the highest esteem. Everyone was thankful for your wonderful heart." She would recount the stories of wonder and laughter and in this process something of who he once was returned. On one magnificent day, she walked to the school with her teacher and her new sister, and instead of leaving just one there, she left them both. Though he had not yet grown strong enough for teaching, he could help. The teachers, having already come to know the story as it had been told by Hope, welcomed him with much thanks and extended to him their deepest respect.

And while the brothers wandered, this is what Hope did with her days. She moved to the souls, talking to some, *and she gave freely of her spirit and if only for the briefest of moments brought light into darkness. She helped her mother and her father and the mother and father of Rose. In the pattern of her day, she would always go to the place where the people who had escaped were received. There she found those most in need and told stories and sang the important songs and stroked the skin.*

One day, in her purposeful movement, she discovered the strong quiet young man, the one who knew the proper methods to fix doors, and who, before the coming of the great evil, had found many ways to talk with Hope. Except for an enormous scar on the side of his head, memories of a wound he had sustained while rescuing a sister, he looked the same as when Hope had last seen him. With radiant smiles they moved to each other just as two souls sensing their common destiny might.

AN AIR OF CONCERN

"There's more than a bit of paper work on this one James." Mr. Patterson did the talking. "What we've set out to get done is not the easiest thing to accomplish. Everybody knows the gears in government don't mesh in ways which allow for high speed anything. Apply that fourfold. Despite the bravado and pretense at outrage by what seemed to be half the world, it turns out four is the number of countries who have agreed to help with this effort. Got all of that? Wait, don't answer. There's more." The necessary pause was less than half a breath long.

"Now remember the United Nations is involved. They're the ones who have been doing most of the refugee work on the site where we decided to focus our initial energies. So naturally they get a say. Are you keeping up? Consider that the government in the country whose people we are trying to repatriate, while not opposed to this process, hasn't exactly taken much of an initiative in the past five years. That's how long they've had the power to move on this. Put all of it together, and I'm sure you can figure this out. This is a big ship and it's hard to get it turned around and pointed in the right direction. Believe me, James, I'm trying, but I need more time." Mr. Patterson was phoning from the country's capital. Four months had passed without any tangible results. No one could say, "Because of what we did, that person's anguish is no longer part of the Flag of Truth."

James, The Society for Human Justice, and many of those writing on the blog were showing signs of impatience. "We respect all of your efforts Mr. Patterson, and hope to see a result in the next month. If, by then, there is nothing encouraging to report, we absolutely have the ability to pick things up from where they were left off. We can always offer persuasive assistance in the form of providing reminders to the rest of the world. Some people's memories tend to be short." It was a direct message, no need for clarification. The two exchanged pleasantries and the phone call ended. James, using the blog and accessing the various social media outlets, put everyone on notice.

The weeks passed but the words and sentences members in the Society for Human Justice wanted to hear had yet to be spoken. All communications were about the need for further extensions. "We ask for your patience." "We are doing everything humanly possible." "These things take time."

"We wait." President Claire spoke. "And all the while, the graveyards in the camps continue to grow. Some, too old and frail, passed away in their huts, their dreams of once again seeing their beloved homes and lands never realized. Their hearts which did not abandon them as they moved through the times of immense pain could no longer sustain their lives. Some died from diseases, and others found their own ways to end personal anguish." She drew in a breath which taxed the diaphragm, exhaled, and in the process heaved a great sigh. "James, I'm tired of being patient. What about you?"

The next blog entry called for an immediate restoration of protest tactics. Day one was a Wednesday and for a full twelve hours, traffic moved slowly. Even when the possibility of increasing speed presented itself, all limits were adhered to—minus five.

"Mr. Patterson, thanks for the call. How have you been?"

"Well, James, as it turns out, I've been quite busy." There was a space before the next words were spoken, less than a pause but more than what would happen in the normal flow of speaking. "Somehow I don't think you're surprised." A small quiet laugh ensued and James joined in the chuckle.

"Just trying to make a point. Nothing personal."

"I know, James, I haven't forgotten. And if it ever did slip my mind or move to the back of it I've got a feeling you would pretty quickly make sure it was front and center. But let's just get this one done for now, okay? It's better to build on success. Later can take care of itself. See you tomorrow; we'll talk some more then. Oh yeah, when you know your travel plans, text me. Someone will meet you at the airport; who knows, it might even be me."

"Okay, see you tomorrow," James, still fighting to regain his grip on reality, answered automatically.

The contribution of the adrenal gland is medically confirmed. Fight or flight. Tense situations in the business or personal world and the overwhelming sense which happens when there is a belief that way too much hangs in the balance are a few of the things that can kick this organ into overdrive and elicit the so-called adrenaline response.

From the moment he hung up the phone, James started moving. The combination of the circumstance and his ongoing passion to consume large volumes of coffee had an amazing effect.

First was the yell. Fearing the worst, Melanie came running only to find James walking in circles. He enveloped Melanie in a bear hug and told her the news. Then he fired off a series of staccato sentences. "I have to phone Claire and e-mail everyone. I have to change the blog and get a plane ticket. I have to pack. I have to phone Claire. Did I already mention that?" He embraced Melanie once more, did a little jig, and was about to launch into another jumble of nearly unintelligible phrases when Melanie broke in.

"It's time for me to get into gear and do some serious helping. Obviously I'm the one to buy the ticket. You call Claire. Then do what needs to be done with the blog. Together we'll pack. Ten days gone, maybe a week in Africa, some of the time in a refugee camp. I doubt if you're going to order door-to-door taxi service. There are decisions to make."

The flight was uneventful. He took the red-eye special, aptly named for the sleep value issues associated with night excursions. Even if this air travel had happened in the daytime it is unlikely the outcome would have been appreciably different. Relaxation was not on the list of possibilities. James was exhausted but sleep came only in small fragments. His mind refused to quit and the deepest forms of rest were never achieved.

"Mr. Patterson sir, good to see you." As had been suggested, he was, in fact, waiting for James at the airport.

"Likewise, James." The two shook hands. "Our flight leaves in a few hours. I'll brief you now and we can do some more catching up on the plane. A lot lies ahead of us; we don't want to mess things up."

"Do I detect an air of concern?"

"Let's keep it to ourselves, shall we?" Mr. Patterson winked. "I'm famished. After we get your luggage, let's do breakfast. I'll buy. There must be some place in this terminal that can serve up a semi-decent plate of eggs."

COLLISIONS

Forms of science, with the application of correct formulae, can measure different types of collisions: celestial bodies, atomic particles, vehicles .... There are those whose jobs are to reconstruct crashes, thereby providing a further level of understanding. However, any application of such expertise would not prove useful in analyzing the collision that James and Mr. Patterson experienced. Certain impacts are beyond anyone's ability to quantify.

While disembarking, the hot, dry heat was the first thing noticed. The air shifted around the two of them not as a wind or a breeze, but as a determined traveler, moving to a destination defined only by the direction on a compass. Seventeen people waited to meet them on arrival and they loudly inquired and beckoned and implored. There was no order in their speaking, and often many directed questions and comments at the same time. Why these people's presence was required was not clear to James or Mr. Patterson, but to the greeters each had a purpose. A tall, somewhat portly man dressed in flowing white clothes clapped his hands and all talking ceased.

"Mr. Terrance, Mr. Patterson, welcome to our country." He bowed. "Forgive this assault, but your visit comes with much excitement. In this land we have many officials and they have countless salaried relatives and"—he threw up his arms because he knew of no other way to explain what had just happened. "My name is Joseph. I have been educated in London and you can tell by the accent that I speak the Queen's English. Language is not a problem. It is I who will guide you through this maze and it is my hope you will consider suggestions I might make." Then quietly he told them, "A car is waiting for us, but the first thing to do is to discreetly give each one of the greeters a respectful amount of money and thank them for this wonderful greeting." This was done.

When two cultures are in danger of colliding it is best to follow someone who knows the road and understands the science.

In Search of Sticks

❧❧❧

While doing the careful walking and carrying, Hope talked to the young child in her arms. "Since the beginning of time in this world, there have been some who would deny the gentle beauty which is our essence. The existence of these people cannot be explained. At each opportunity they breathe fire and deliver horror and with the puffing of chests and the sneering of lips declare themselves to be all powerful. During the moments of terror, there were those who had come to believe this was true. In their shivering they feared the wickedness before them and, because this lived in human form, they came to be afraid of themselves. If such an evil existed, would it also reside in them? Was it buried deep within their own being? With this thinking they lost all ability to smile.

As I tenderly carry you, I will seek the people with these heavy hearts and talk to them and you will hear me tell of my mother and father and of a gentle loving cousin. I will say the stories of the man whose kindness was without limit and of a doctor who could help both the body and the spirit. I will speak of one who I did not know but who chose to risk everything to save the life of a beautiful child. The many compassions which came to pass in the long and torturous walk will be recounted. I will do this not to tell them about my wonderful memories, but to awaken theirs."

That is the story she was told on her second earthly day as she was carried by her mother who had gone out in search of those who were most in need.

Hope did not wait for the passing of the seasons before naming her child. After the birth, which happened in a house of sticks and plastic, she was called Faith.

ഛഛഛ

James and Mr. Patterson found themselves in a meticulously restored colonial structure. Their rooms had been tastefully appointed with furniture representative of the bygone era. After showering, each lay on his bed looking up at a revolving ceiling fan. This was for effect; air conditioning provided the primary source of relief. They shared the same emotional state and it moved freely between fatigue, confusion, euphoria, and fear. James, having traveled the longest, was the more drained of the two but both could be accurately described as exhausted. In an hour, they would be dining in the fine restaurant adjacent to the lobby. A handful of officials were scheduled to join them. It turned out, including the man with the Queen's English and themselves, six were at the table. A rather tall person spoke first.

"The task has not proven to be easy. We wanted to do this for a considerable time, but one must be careful in the approach. An evil came to the country that is beside ours and though this evil was crushed, some of it scattered and continued to breathe. It did so on the tops of buildings and in the caves of mountains and in the dark corners. Its appetite for blood remained. But in the last years those with these depraved hearts have somehow vanished. There is now the feeling it is safe to return, though things like this are never certain." He smiled and brought a fork that held a large piece of meat to his mouth.

The next to speak did so in his language. The man who had the Queen's English interpreted after each completed thought. "The people in this camp come from many places, and there are some whose lives have only known confined boundaries. Before the sending away can be done, it needs to be understood who belongs where. What village? What neighborhood? A greater difficulty beyond the requirement for this list has also surfaced.

"There are those whose only wish in life is to go home, but others continue to be haunted by the different forms of devastation and are truly afraid to do this returning. These people know that nothing, on which to build a future, exists in the place they live. Though there is not enough food for the stomach and a difficulty in replacing the needed things that wear with the passing of time, they hesitate to do this leaving. But as it is planned, their camp will disappear. We must find ways to get all of them home but this should not be done in the same manner that cattle are moved."

The last one to speak did not require an interpreter. "I am from the country whose wound is healed; the scar, however, is still easily seen. We have been working feverishly in the hope of reducing its brilliance, and one of the ways we are doing this is to prepare for the returning. This required much effort.

"In the villages and by the pathways bombs were buried into the ground and they still wait. They are not just one here and another there; they are hidden in many places. Some who stray from the normal ways of moving are then killed or injured because they came too near. We tried to find these bombs, and have made discoveries, but we fear countless more still hide. Ammunition that did not do what it intended to lingers in the field, hoping for a plow to strike so its purpose can be fulfilled. Some have been found, but it is certain not all. Even in the returning, a piece of the nightmare will be relived.

"We struggled to restore the wells. Their homes are mostly burned, and we only have a part of what they need to do the new building.

"For those who came from the neighborhoods in the cities, we will take them there and give them a bit of money. We will hope they will find their way but realize many will not. Still, it is better to save some than none at all."

The one who spoke first did so again. He had finished his meal. "Now you understand the difficulties in the leaving and the receiving. Nothing in this world, it seems, is done easily." He lifted his glass. "Thank you, Mr. Patterson and Mr. Terrance. Thank you for coming and providing this help." The other three raised their glasses. It seemed to be a genuine toast.

In Search of Sticks

❧❧❧

Home—the word had not been heard for the longest of times. Its retrieval caused enormous pain and as such was buried in the deep crevices of the mind. When first used by those who had escaped, it was done so with the feeling of returning, with the understanding their refuge was temporary and soon they would be going back. That lives, in some way, would be rebuilt. The seasons began to repeat themselves for the second or third instance and the realization that accompanied this, but which had been resisted, could no longer be ignored. To reduce the misery they did not talk of the season of gentle rains or the friendly hills and no mention was made of the remembrances when there had been occasions for celebration. Even the times of tribulation were not spoken about. It was not said, "As difficult as it is here, this does not compare to the year of immense tragedy when the sun's assault proved too great." All barriers which held back the past needed to be respected. Loved ones who had left this earth were spoken of, but with reference to the soul and not in the ways that talked of what was lived in and walked through. This is how it had been with the remembrance of Rose. It was always understood the place of sticks and plastic was a house, but even with the history of births and deaths that occurred within its area, it could never be known as a home. No one spoke of home.

Once the rumors of a returning began to surface, every effort was made to suppress the thoughts which might normally accompany this story. Anticipation followed by disappointment would most certainly lead to the resurrection of heartache.

At the appointed hour, six-thirty a.m., James and Mr. Patterson reappeared in the lobby and minutes later they moved to a small breakfast room and drank bitter coffees. In an effort to disguise the taste, Mr. Patterson loaded his up with spoonful after spoonful of sugar, taking sips after each infusion of sweetness. Still fatigued, few words were exchanged. By eight, breakfast had been ordered and by nine everything consumed. Shortly afterwards, the four arrived. No apology was extended. In this part of the world, two and a half hours between the planned meeting time and the actual arrival is well within the parameters of acceptability. Everyone was on the road by ten-thirty.

It took a while to extricate from the city, and when this happened, it did so abruptly. A barren, rocky, outwardly lifeless landscape stretched beyond sight. Both James and Mr. Patterson swallowed simultaneously. Some fear was in the saliva.

The procession consisted of two cars, a driver and three passengers in each. As well, there were trucks and buses and other vehicles that would prove useful in the repatriation process. Many had already arrived at the camp and waited for final directions. During the two-day trip, lengthy periods of silence separated the times of conversation.

"Mr. Patterson, Mr. Terrance, if you permit me to, I would like to ask a single question." Hearing nothing to the contrary, the man who spoke the Queen's English continued. "As you know, we are grateful for your effort but how is it you have come to do this thing, you who live on the other side of the world?"

Not knowing how to respond, the two looked at each other and then away, locking on to the expanse which lay before them. James broke the silence. "It is difficult to ignore an aching heart, especially if it is understood the hurt is needless. I am doing this to help but also for selfish reasons. Knowing there is less pain in the world should lead to a greater sense of personal happiness. And I have come to fear that we are measured by what we do, as much as by what we do not. So I take this path."

Mr. Patterson stared at James for a long time. "Curse you, James. I was a happy guy until you came along. Accomplished, respected, important—then *you* arrived, complete with a truckload of voting pressures. Still, I managed the fallout and did okay, that is until I started reading your blog. I realized I might actually be able to do something. Since then I have had many sleepless nights." He spoke directly to the man who knew the Queen's English. "I am here to help so I can get some sleep."

They fueled up and bunked down at an outpost. No colonial hotel option existed. The landscape had changed; it was still arid but there was less rock and the soils were deep red.

Well into the drive on the second day, the man who spoke the Queen's English raised his arm and pointed to the distance and said, "If you look closely, over there on what seems to be the edge of the world, you will discover our destination." Mr. Patterson and James sat up as alert animals do and squinted into the sun. Their spit remained acrid. "When we arrive, some officials will be waiting for you. They will want to shake your hands and take you to places so you can see their efforts. With pride they will show you the schools and the hospital and the rows of houses and the locations where water and food are given. Much of this has been accomplished because of their spirits. When the dismantling starts this will be a joyous event, but it will also be mixed with a kind of sadness. It is difficult to build something while praying for its eventual destruction. This is what they have done. It would be good if you could extend your thanks to as many as possible. This should not be achieved with money but with words. We will arrive in less than an hour."

ళళళ

Everything unfolded just as the man who knew the Queen's English had said. One person followed another and gave their thanks. As this was received, it was also given.

Great pride could be heard in the voice of the speaker. "Here, in this building provided by the generous people of this world, is where the weak receive some of that which is needed to assist in the restoration of strength. In this place we look after those who have been unlucky. We help with the cuts and bruises and shattered bones. We take care of the people who suffer from fevers and uncontrolled trembling and from painful and demanding dysentery. Others make appearances and they are also helped. These include some who choose not to eat all that is presented so a child or grandchild can have more and become strong and stay well."

James and Mr. Patterson moved down the line, thanking each for their contributions and their caring. This was done in the respectful way of true acknowledgment.

They absorbed the details. The different technologies and many of the things associated with diagnosis and cure were nowhere to be found. Both struggled with the definition of generosity.

Wishing to distance himself from this thinking, James asked, "And who is over there, the one who quietly sings?"

Someone whose hand had just been shaken did the answering. "She often comes and gives that which, even with our training and your magnificent gifts we cannot. The life she is comforting drifts between two worlds and will soon leave this one forever. Her song tells of this sick person's inner beauty and how such a wonderful soul will be openly received."

Both Mr. Patterson and James looked away in a desperate effort to avoid the collision. It was too late. When pieces of a planet collide there is no way to quantifiably measure the impact. However, it can accurately be described as immensely powerful. It was amazingly hot; neither of them noticed.

The day was spent moving from place to place and saying the things which should be said. In the process, they walked by the houses made of sticks and plastic and that did not rise to the height of a man; they entered crowded schools where there were few books and no desks. They stood by those who lined up for water and they smelled the stale dirt that had been trodden by thousands upon thousands of feet, the dust of which settled on any perspiring pore exposed to the air.

While doing this, the two began to understand something of the rhythm of this new world and instead of saying, "Thank you for the hard work in making sure everyone has access to food and water," they said, "Thank you for dedicating a piece of your life so others may live." "Thank you for teaching" became "Thank you for keeping the mind vibrant and the threads of distant hope strong."

As they visited the different places, people were passed; some appeared to be aimlessly moving while others walked with purpose. Many, seeing the newcomers, starred at James and Mr. Patterson who, in turn, did not avoid this contact. Rather, in their search for meaning, they looked closely to discover the stories. These were found in the eyes and in the way in which people held their bodies and in the scars and other forms of injury. For James, all faces were familiar. They had been woven into the fabric of the Flag of Truth.

"There she is!" James could hardly contain himself.

"There's who?" Mr. Patterson was startled by the intensity.

"Over there, the one who sang the song to the person who lay dying." The unexplained excitement in his voice did not diminish.

Sometimes in life there are things that defy explanation yet somehow are still understood. To James, this was not a chance meeting; it was a sign. Despite all efforts by his entourage to encourage continuous movement—"We are expected in another place," "There are others to thank," "A meal waits for you,"—he could not be dissuaded.

Faith was safely cradled in the folds of cloth which kept her close to her mother's body. Hope gently held the arm of a young woman whose sight had been cruelly stolen. Disease had done its damage. People walked by and with this came the distractions of noise and smells, but for this moment in time Hope only knew of the struggling life beside her and as with all mothers, the gentle breathing of her child.

James moved to Hope, and when she looked up it was part of a natural sequence. The man who spoke the Queen's English stayed with Mr. Patterson and James. Almost unconsciously the three began to walk with Hope, Faith, and this young woman who would no longer see.

"I do not understand why I have had this thinking but this visit was expected. Your presence has long been anticipated. Still, the time of the arrival was not clear." Hope said this in a matter-of-fact manner. Though they had never met, she knew of their existence much in the same way they were aware of hers.

"I am Hope; the child who I carry closely is Faith. And this lovely gentle person who sees in different ways is called Violet."

The man who spoke the Queen's English gave his name: the others, with the help of his interpreting, provided theirs "This is James Terrance and mine is Edward Patterson but many call me Ned."

After some fumbling questions, Hope said, "We will go to the house and after the welcoming drink I will tell you the things about the living and the dying that you wish to know." James and Mr. Patterson and the man who spoke the Queen's English followed Hope, Faith, and the lovely woman without sight.

While doing the sitting Hope told the story of a happy child and her gentle and caring cousin whose spirit moved in ways that few understand but all are grateful for. She described the wonderful village and the families where love knew no limits. This was spoken of in the way which brings forth the kind of smile that lies deep within. She spent a special time talking about the tall and the thin man who had visited for only the smallest of moments. She spoke of his essence which was beyond the use of adjectives.

Not all of her remembrances were the welcoming kind. She recounted Rose's struggles and told the story of her new sister. In the giving of the details of the coming and the staying of the great evil she spoke of deaths without blood, of the people with fire, and the girl who chose kerosene. The time of the dying of the strong young man killed in the circle where all things commonly important were discussed was also spoken of. She described these occurrences much in the same way one would say what part of the day it is after discovering the place the sun takes in the sky.

When Hope spoke of the different kinds of suffering during the long walk her voice became quiet and the man who knew the Queen's English and who needed to do the translating had to strain to hear. He struggled to find the right English words and he cried. Tears also ran down the cheeks of James and Mr. Patterson. Try as they might, these flows could not be quickly stemmed.

She then explained what was happening to bodies and spirits in the camp where she now lived. While looking at the distant travelers, she said, "In the times ahead when I share my memories, I will add to the stories and speak of two who came from the other side of the world, and the words I use will be the ones reserved for those who are the most cherished. Thank you for guiding us back to our homes." She looked into their being and in the process captured them in her heart and mind.

James and Mr. Patterson stumbled while shaping a reply and when it came, it arrived in the form of a protest. "They did not deserve to be mentioned in the same breath as Rose or the good doctor or the tall and the thin man who was also named Ned or the one who rescued a young girl whose name is the same as the mother of the great prophet or, indeed, of any soul who suffered through the times of the great evil and the heartbreaking exodus. But the stories they tell in the years to come will most certainly speak about all of these people. The remembrance of a young mother's spirit whose love and strength knows no equal would guide each of their sentences."

In the early evening, James and Mr. Patterson gave more thanks and shook the hands that had been extended. The depth of their expression was deeply heartfelt and any suggestions of their own heroism were summarily dismissed.

Randy Kaneen

HOME

    The myth of the phoenix is well known and the legend is often used to reference the different kinds of reemergence that happen in this world. As difficult as physical reconstruction can be, the spiritual form is the most complex. This is not rebuilding a house or reclaiming a field. The rebirth of this phoenix would not be easy.

    On the day of the returning those who had been close to Rose visited her gravesite. She was introduced to new lives and there was a begging of forgiveness for not doing the visiting. People did what they could to restore a look of caring.

    In the late afternoon of the second day Hope, carrying her child Faith, found some moments to be alone with her dear cousin. And in the telling of her stories the tears that she had not permitted for so long came forth and they presented themselves as great rivers.

HOME

In a few days, James was scheduled to find himself back behind a desk. As before, work demands would require him to access personal expertise in efforts to create critical water flow efficiencies.

Melanie and he were on the deck chairs soaking in the sun's rays. She read while his eyelids slowly closed. James found himself sitting with Hope and he felt the emotions that come to those who help and he basked in this warmth. But his mind drifted. He knew there were many more camps, and he remembered the stories he had been told about other desperate lives.

As James moved between the world of "what is" and "what could be", the predictable late afternoon breeze arrived. The Flag of Truth, which had been at rest, once again began to unfurl.

Randy Kaneen